The Yearning Heart

SYLVIA BROADY

Allison & Busby Limited
11 Wardour Mews
London W1F 8AN
allisonandbusby.com

First published in 2011.
This paperback edition published by Allison & Busby in 2018.

A CIP catalogue record for this book is available from
the British Library.

10 9 8 7 6 5 4 3 2 1

ISBN 978-0-7490-2369-0

Typeset in 10.5/15.5 pt Adobe Garamond Pro by
Allison & Busby Ltd.

The paper used for this Allison & Busby publication
has been produced from trees that have been legally sourced
from well-managed and credibly certified forests.

Printed and bound by
CPI Group (UK) Ltd, Croydon, CR0 4YY

Dedicated in memory of my beloved husband
Barry James Broady
29.11.1935–08.03.2005
who always believed in me

Chapter One

Burton Banks, East Yorkshire, Summer 1941

Fran Bewholme fled along the river bank avoiding the lane, not wanting to meet anyone, not wanting to explain. Ignoring the aching stitch in her side, she ran on, brushing past tall reeds and wild grasses, startling moorhens bedded for the night. She felt the thin material of her new blue dress flap and cling around her bare legs. The pain in her chest pulled tighter, causing her breath to come out in short, staccato pants. She gulped for air, succeeding only in taking in the humid stillness of the night.

At last she reached the back of the house. Silhouetted against the night sky, it looked eerie in the pale moonlight. She darted through the timber yard to the back door. Letting herself into the empty house, she dashed up the two flights of stairs to her attic sanctuary. She flung herself on the bed, buried her face in the pillow and only then did she allow herself to cry. Heartbroken, confused, her body heaved as she sobbed. Caught up in her unhappiness, she didn't hear the footfalls creaking on the stairs.

'Well, my lovely, what ails you?' The sarcastic voice broke into her distress.

Startled, she turned over on the bed to see Victor Renton, her sister's husband, in his army uniform. His swarthy, powerfully built physique, filling the door frame of her bedroom, swayed unsteadily. Shame coloured her tear-stained face that she should be seen in such a state.

'Where is everyone?' he demanded.

Trying to control her sobs, Fran gulped, 'At the pictures.'

'Isabel should be here,' he grunted. 'I need her.' He stumbled as he turned to go, and then changed his mind. Glancing over his shoulder, he smiled slyly at her. As if he had come to quick decision, he spun round, and in three long strides, he was by her bedside. Dropping down to her level, he put a finger under her chin and asked, 'Why the tears?'

Startled by his nearness, she remained silent.

'Go on, you can tell me,' he coaxed.

She was surprised by his attention because he usually ignored her. Was he being kind to her, treating her like a grown-up? Suddenly, she had this overwhelming urge to unburden herself, so she blurted out the sorry story.

'Charlie Moxon took me to the barrack dance and said I looked sweet in my new dress. Then Dora Parker, dressed like Betty Grable, came and dragged him onto the dance floor. They smooched in a way that Charlie never did with me and then they sneaked off.' A loud sob escaped and she hiccupped.

Victor leant closer. 'Go on,' he said. His breath, smelling of beer, wafted across her face.

She shrank back, not liking his nearness, but at least he wanted to listen to her. She gulped, bit her lip and continued. 'I found them in the bar, kissing. I shouted at him to come with me. He told me I was just a kid and too young for him. A crowd gathered, some of them were girls from my last year at school, and they all laughed at me.' She closed her eyes, but couldn't stop the hurtful scene replaying. They made her feel such a fool. How could she stay after such a public humiliation? Hugging her arms tight around her trembling body, she thought of the tender kisses she had once shared with Charlie. 'I thought he loved me,' she whispered.

Victor's eyes narrowed, 'Frances Bewholme, what do you know about love?'

She shrugged, affronted, and not wanting to show her ignorance, adopted an exaggerated tone. 'Of course I know about love. I'm sixteen. I'm a woman.'

He laughed, hoarsely. 'And that you are, my lovely,' Lightly, he ran his hand down the smooth skin of her exposed leg. Hastily, she pulled down her rumpled dress and lowered her eyes from his gaze.

Unsteadily, he rose to his feet. 'I've got the very thing to soothe you. Back in a minute.'

She laid her head on the pillow, thankful to be alone once more, and closed her eyes. When she heard Victor returning, she sat up and swung her legs over the side of the bed.

'You're very kind,' she whispered shyly as he pressed the tall tumbler of clear liquid into her outstretched hand. Lemonade, she thought. But it didn't taste like any lemonade she had drunk before. She took a deep swallow and coughed as it burnt down her throat. It was great of her brother-in-law to treat her like a grown-up. He sat down next to her on the bed. He had taken off his jacket and rolled up his shirt sleeves, showing off the strength of his muscular arms. The heat of his body touched hers and she felt comforted. She sipped more of the drink, savouring the sensation of the liquid fire running down her throat and into her belly, making her feel good.

She drained her glass and giggled. 'That was nice.'

He took the empty glass from her hands and placed it on the floor. 'Now, what shall we talk about?' He slipped an arm casually about her shoulder, drawing her nearer to him. She didn't resist. Victor was unexpectedly nice, brotherly.

'How would you like a proper boyfriend, one who can show you real love?'

Her deep blue eyes widened and she giggled again, feeling so light-headed and deliciously warm and tingly, and so grown-up. 'Yes, please.'

'Let me show you.' He leant across her, one hand cupping her budding breast. This wasn't the way brothers were supposed to act, she thought, though she felt powerless to stop him.

Suddenly, his lips were crushing hers, taking her breath away. He forced her mouth open with his tongue. Surprised, she clung to him, overwhelmed by the rippling sensation cascading through her as his tongue explored her mouth. Excitement gripped her. Abruptly, without warning, he pushed her back onto the bed, pushing up her dress to reveal slender, white thighs.

'Take your dress off,' he ordered, hoarsely.

Obeying in a trance, she watched in awe as he dropped his trousers and pulled off his shirt. She gasped in amazement, stopping what she was doing. She'd never seen a man naked before. Impatiently, he forced her dress over her head and ripped off her undergarments. She was surprised that she felt no inhibitions at letting a man see her without a stitch of clothing on.

'God, you're beautiful,' he moaned, his eyes glazing over.

She felt so light-headed and dreamy as, smiling at him, she held out her arms. The next moment he was on top of her, his hot body melted into hers. At first it hurt, making her back arch, which seemed to excite him more. But soon, she was lost in a rapturous frenzy that went on for ever and ever.

She must have drifted into sleep, for when she woke he was on top of her again, kissing her breasts, curling his tongue round her firm nipples. But this time she was sober. Fear gripped her and, panicking, she tried to push him away, but that only succeeded in rousing his passion higher.

When he was spent, he gripped her hands in a vice above her head. She felt his breath on her face, thick, rancid with tobacco and drink. 'Well, my lovely. That's proper love. You can have it anytime from me.'

Thoughts of her sister came into her mind. Shame and guilt overcame her. What had she done? As if he had read her mind, he said. 'This is our secret. You tell no one. Do you understand?'

Frightened, she whispered, 'Yes.'

His dark eyes mocked her as she struggled beneath him to free herself. 'You want it again?'

Terror seized her. What if her parents and her sister found her like this? What would they say? What would they do? He laughed callously at her stricken face.

Just then, there was the sound of a door opening and voices. She froze in horror. They were home. He clasped a rough hand across her mouth. 'Don't you forget, this is our secret. You tell no one. Understand?'

He released his hand, and, hardly daring to breathe, she nodded in reply. Noiselessly, he went from her bed and from her room. She lay rigid with shock, unable to move, unable to think. From below, she heard voices and her name mentioned, and then Victor's loud voice carried up to her.

'She's got a headache and gone to bed.'

Frightened that her mother would come up, Fran scrambled into bed and pulled the covers up to her chin. She would have loved a bath, to cleanse her body in an attempt to banish all traces of his lingering smell, of sweat, tobacco, drink and . . . she couldn't bring herself to think of that.

Restless in bed, feeling sore and bruised, Fran could not sleep. Remorse set in and her mind ran wild. Dear Lord, she had committed a sin, an unforgivable sin, and with her sister's husband. What if Isabel found out, or her mother? Agnes would surely slay her, for she didn't think twice about hitting her youngest daughter. Guilt saturated every part of her body, and of her mind. And she knew that she must never tell anyone of this dreadful secret.

A few days later, Victor Renton went back to join his unit and Fran breathed a sigh of relief. She pushed him and the incident to the back of her mind and vowed it would never happen again.

For a time, except for the night sky flashes and sounds of the distant air raids on the city of Hull, life at High Bank House seemed to carry on as normal. Though they had food rationing, her mother always seemed to provide food for the table. They never went hungry. Fran had given up sugar, and didn't miss it, but she longed for a bar of chocolate.

It was about six weeks later. Fran had just rinsed her face in cold water and, raising her head, stared at her reflection in the bathroom mirror. Her face was stark white, and her blue eyes were dark in their sockets. She looked a complete mess. The ravages of the morning sickness had been with her for over a week now and she had missed her period. Her stomach retched again and she collapsed once more over the lavatory pan. Finally, she couldn't be sick any more and, wearily, she rested her head on the wooden seat, wanting nothing more than to climb back upstairs and into her bed. But, to avoid arousing her mother's suspicions, she had to go to work as usual. She worked as a junior assistant in the office of a small seed manufacturer in Beverley and Miss Barker, her superior, would not tolerate lateness.

Downstairs, in the kitchen, Fran could hear her mother preparing breakfast. The very smell of food made her want to retch again, but she forced herself back to her bedroom. She tugged on her serviceable navy skirt, which fitted her now that she'd moved the button, though her neat blouse was tight across her swelling breasts – but her cardigan hid this fact. She let her blonde hair hang loose, Veronica Lake style, to hide her pale face and dark eyes. Treading lightly, she made her way downstairs to the kitchen, wondering if she could escape without her mother seeing her.

Agnes Bewholme stood at the range, busily stirring a pan of porridge and keeping her eye on the bacon sizzling in the pan. As Fran entered she said, 'Give your dad a shout for breakfast.'

Quickly, Fran pulled on her coat and went to call to her father. Then, she grabbed her bicycle from the shed and peddled fast down the lane. With any luck, by tonight, her mother would have forgotten that she'd left without any breakfast.

For a whole week, Fran worked at avoiding her mother. In her naivety, she thought if no one knew of her condition, it would go away, it wouldn't happen. Once she got over the early morning sickness, she felt all right for the rest of the day and was her usual self.

Her sister, Isabel, worked in a newspaper and tobacco shop in Beverley and was always up at dawn to see to the morning deliveries, so Fran never saw her in the mornings.

One morning, after a restless night's sleep, Fran missed the alarm and overslept. She sprang out of bed and instantly wished she hadn't as the nausea swept over her. Rushing down the stairs to the bathroom, she almost collided with her mother on the landing.

'Whoa, my girl,' said Agnes catching hold of Fran's arm. 'What's up with you?'

Fran could feel the retch in her throat and, pulling her arm free, dashed to be sick. Cold sweat wrung her body as she heaved and heaved until she could only taste the bitter bile. She rested her head on the lavatory seat, waiting until the swimming in her head stopped. But suddenly she was yanked to her feet, her body swaying unsteadily.

'You're pregnant!' Her mother's voice hissed in her ear.

Fran felt relief now that her mother knew of her condition and she would not have to bear the burden alone. 'Oh, Mam, I'm sorry,' she cried, falling against Agnes's wiry frame. But she was unprepared for her mother's aggressive outburst.

'You bitch!' Agnes yelled, pushing her daughter back down to the floor.

Fran banged her shoulder hard against the lavatory pan, sending a rack of pain through her body. She let out a sharp moan and caught her breath. Stunned, she looked up into Agnes's faded green eyes, which flashed with disbelief and anger.

'A daughter of mine expecting and not married. You slut!' she shouted. Her mouth working in anger, Agnes raised her hand.

Instinctively, Fran pressed her body against the cold bathroom wall, but Agnes's aim didn't miss. Fran felt the blow to her cheekbone, which sent her head reeling, hitting it against the wall. She screamed with pain and fright. But still, her mother rained blows to her body.

As she did so, Agnes shrieked, 'A bastard child! I won't have it!'

Tears streamed down Fran's cheeks as she sobbed and gulped, 'I'm sorry, Mam, I'm sorry.'

'You will be.' With that, Agnes hauled Fran back up to her feet. 'Now, miss, get yourself downstairs and see what your father has to say.' In her confusion, Fran thought of her dear father and how much she loved him. What would he think? She stumbled downstairs with Agnes in pursuit.

In the kitchen, Will was at the sink washing his hands. He half turned as his daughter and wife burst in, saying, 'What's all the shouting about?'

'You might well ask,' Agnes said, throwing a fiery glance at him. 'I'll let your blue-eyed girl tell you.' She stood with her hands on her hips, her eyes blazing at Fran. 'Tell your father.'

Will looked from his wife to his daughter. 'You're crying, lass,' he reached out to touch Fran. She wanted so much to seek the comfort of his arms, but, instead, she shrank back. Her father looked puzzled. 'Come on, nowt can be that bad.'

Fresh sobs choked in Fran's throat as she tried to get her words out. 'I'm . . .' But Agnes cut in, her voice unforgiving. 'She's expecting a bastard child.'

Will's ruddy face paled, his blue eyes darkened, his voice unusually sharp. 'What do you mean, Agnes?' He turned on his wife.

Agnes, hands still on hips, retorted, 'It's plain enough. She's unwed and pregnant.'

Slowly, Will turned to look at his youngest daughter. 'Say it's not true, lass.' His eyes pleaded.

Fran felt her heart quiver with shame, her legs about to buckle. Gripping the back of a chair for support, she forced herself to meet Will's eyes. 'I'm sorry, Dad,' was all she could whisper. His huge frame seemed to visibly shrink before her as he looked at her in shock. He stumbled to his chair by the fireside. Agnes, now looking completely devastated, sat in the chair at the other side. A dreadful silence followed. Fran could smell it. It was more terrible than Agnes's fury.

Dear God, she thought, *what will they say or do when they learn who the father is?*

Chapter Two

Fran went to work, leaving her parents in shocked silence. She dare not think what their thoughts might be. She only knew that she had hurt them so terribly. Neither did she want to think about her sister's husband.

The day seemed endless until, finally, she was able to return home. She took a deep breath, pushed open the kitchen door and went in. Her parents were there, waiting for her. Fran closed the door and stood erect, frightened, yet ready. For what, she wasn't certain.

It was her mother who spoke first. 'You'll have to marry him and quick.'

Fran stared at her mother, thinking it wasn't possible to marry her sister's husband. But had her mother somehow made it possible? The very thought of Victor repulsed her.

'I won't,' she blurted defiantly. 'I hate him.'

At those words, Agnes flew across the room and, grabbing hold of Fran by the arms, she shook her, screeching, 'You'll do as I say, my girl.'

Fran felt her body sway, like branches of a tree caught in a storm, as Agnes's rage continued.

Suddenly, her father took control. Pulling Agnes off, he gently led Fran to a chair. She sank onto it and, burying her face in her hands, she sobbed.

Agnes made to say something, but Will interjected, 'Let her be, woman.'

At last her sobs ceased, but she still kept her hands covering her face. No one spoke. Then Will touched her arm. 'Cup of tea, luv.'

She felt grateful for her father's compassion, but how could it last? As she sipped the hot liquid, Fran glanced at Agnes who was seated across the kitchen table from her. She looked calmer now, but Fran knew she was itching to say something, so she held her gaze and waited.

'I'll go and see Bertha Moxon first thing in the morning and tell her what her Charlie has done to my innocent daughter. We'll see what she has to say.' Agnes's green eyes flashed with the knowledge that no one got the better of her.

Will nodded in agreement. 'Now are going to have owt to eat?'

Fran felt herself go feverishly hot, and then a chill ran through her body. She had to tell them. They thought Charlie was to blame. She forced her body to the edge of the chair and opened her mouth. But no sound came out. She coughed, clearing her throat. 'It's not,' she whispered.

Agnes looked at her sharply. 'What are you blathering about?'

Fran felt physically sick and her stomach heaved. She made a dash for the outside lavatory. She stayed outside as long as possible, wanting only to crawl into bed and sleep, and forget.

She heard the back door open. 'Frances! Get in here, now,' her mother commanded.

Wearily, Fran pulled herself to her feet and went indoors. She had to tell them before Isabel came home from work. Taking a deep breath, she said. 'It's not Charlie.' Her parents looked at her simultaneously. 'It's Victor. He's the father.'

'Victor?' questioned Agnes. Then, her eyes filled with realisation. 'Not our Isabel's Victor?'

'Yes.' And, with that, Fran fled from the room.

In the sanctuary of her attic bedroom, Fran flung herself onto her bed. She didn't cry, not any more. What was the use? She half expected her mother to come charging up the stairs, but she didn't. After a while, Fran turned over on her back and stared at up the ceiling, wondering about her future and that of her unborn child. What would become of them? She drifted into a fitful sleep until she was woken by raised voices coming from downstairs. She could hear her mother's high-pitched shouting and the mention of her name. Fran shuddered. Then, the most pitiful crying seemed to fill the whole house. Isabel.

Fran could smell her own fear as she drew up her knees and hugged them close to her trembling body. She could imagine the whole scene downstairs and the pain on Isabel's face. At that precise moment, Fran wished she were dead. She remained in the same position for what seemed hours, or was it minutes? She wasn't sure. The back door banged and she heard the heavy footsteps of her father on the gravel path outside. Eventually, the cramp of her legs made her move. Her head was clearer now and her heart beat faster as she realised the terrible nature of her situation. She was pregnant, unmarried and the man responsible was her sister's husband. He had taken advantage of her vulnerability and now she was in disgrace. Her thoughts raced. Would her mother send Isabel away to make a home of her own for herself and Victor? For it was impossible for them to live under the same roof. Surely, her mother would see that.

Her thoughts in turmoil, not able to think of anything logical, Fran lay awake for a long time until she drifted into fitful sleep. She tossed and turned, waking up in a cold sweat and a feeling of rising panic. The room felt airless, crowding in on her. She flung back the bedclothes and went over to open the window, pulling up the lower sash frame. She leant out to breathe in the night air, pungent with the tangy smells of the river. The moon, high in the dark sky, sent its silvery beam down to catch the ripples on the slow-moving water. The distant sound of an owl, seeking its prey, broke the silence of the night. She stared out of the window for a long time until the grey dawn appeared. A new day. And she wondered what it would bring.

She crept downstairs and into the empty kitchen. She raked the fire, threw on a log from the basket on the hearth and curled up on her father's big, leather armchair, wondering what Agnes would decide to do about her younger daughter becoming pregnant by her elder daughter's husband. It felt strange, as if it was someone else who was in this dreadful predicament.

Stretching and yawning, she felt different this morning: she didn't feel sick. She sighed with relief. She didn't know much about babies, only odd snippets gleaned from overheard conversations. Babies were a subject not talked about in the Bewholme family. Isabel, it seemed, was unable to conceive. Fran was lost in thoughts when her mother came into the kitchen.

'What are you doing up?' Agnes demanded.

Fran scrambled from the chair, saying, 'I couldn't sleep.' She turned to leave the room.

'Where are you going?'

'I'm going to get ready for work.'

Agnes sprang forward. 'Oh no you're not, my girl!'

Recoiling from her mother's anger, Fran stepped back a pace. 'I feel all right.'

'*You* feel all right. What about the rest of us?' Agnes shouted. 'You stay in your room until our Isabel has gone to work. And then I'll deal with you.'

Now that she had all the energy and vitality of her sixteen years back, Fran didn't want to spend time shut away in her bedroom. She spent three whole days confined to her room and was only allowed down when Isabel was not home. She wondered what had happened about her absence from work, but a tight-lipped Agnes only said, when asked, that it was now none of Fran's concern. She'd much sooner be at work. If she was earning, at least she could pay for her keep. She fretted that she had added another burden to her parents. When Agnes was calmer, Fran would try and persuade her mother to let her return to work.

On the fourth morning, Agnes came up to Fran's room and instructed, 'Pack your case.'

Fran's mind raced. Were they going away on holiday? 'Where are we going?'

'You'll find out soon enough.' With that, Agnes closed the door behind her.

Fran stared at the closed door and her heart began thudding, not with excitement like when she was a child going away on holiday, but with trepidation and fear. She stood up and put her hands over the slight swell of her belly and thought of the baby growing inside her. She did not want to think of the unknown ahead, but her thoughts persisted and they frightened her. Never again would she be that innocent girl of sixteen, but a woman and a mother. What kind of future would she have without a husband to provide and care for her? Her father had business worries of his own, especially with all the uncertainties of the war. Although she was never her mother's favourite daughter, and less so now, Agnes was her only support. For that Fran was grateful.

As the train rattled and chugged along, Agnes closed her eyes. How could history repeat itself? It was a question she asked herself repeatedly. She thought back to her own miserable childhood and how she had suffered for being illegitimate. It made her even more determined that a grandchild of hers would not endure the stigma. Her head ached with trying to come up with a workable solution. And Isabel: she had threatened to divorce Victor. What a scandal that would cause. He had got off lightly, escaping back to his unit, facing no shame, leaving behind a heartbroken wife and a trail of destruction. Could she repair the damage?

After the long wait on a windblown station at Doncaster, they boarded the connecting train. Fran had been glad of the warmth of the crowded compartment. But now, the heat of stale bodies, smelly feet, tobacco smoke, mixed with the strong cheese and pickle being devoured by the big woman opposite, made her feel nauseated and uncomfortable. She wasn't complaining, because they were lucky to have a seat. In the corridor outside the compartment, people, mostly men in uniforms with blank faces, were jostled and squashed, cigarettes dangling from their mouths, blowing smoke into what bit of air was free. At last, the train pulled into a station with no visible name. Agnes reached for her overnight bag and nudged Fran to get her case. 'Where are we?' she asked her mother.

'We're not there yet,' was her terse reply.

As they trudged along the platform, Fran felt the despair seeping into her body and into her heart. She'd been trying to think of the journey as an adventure, something thrilling as a sixteen-year-old girl might. But with her mother's stony silence, Fran knew she was deluding herself.

They caught a slow country bus which stopped at every village. She listened to two women sitting behind her, grumbling about the bus service being cut. 'Shortage of petrol, they say, but how are we supposed to shop and feed our families? Tell me that.'

The other woman replied, 'It'll be a man that's made the rule. They don't have much sense.'

A glimmer of a smile flicked across Fran's face as she agreed with the last sentence. She was never going to trust a man again. If Charlie Moxon hadn't ditched her so cruelly, she wouldn't have gone home early from the dance and encountered Victor Renton, who used her vulnerability for his own gratification. She wouldn't be in this predicament. She slipped a hand across the slight swell of her stomach as she had done countless times over the last few weeks, always with the naive hope that there wasn't a baby growing inside her. She let out a low sigh. Poor baby, she thought, it wasn't its fault what had happened. Suddenly, she felt her heart tug, sending a warm, protective feeling through her whole body. She closed her eyes and made a vow to love and cherish her baby, and to do right by it, whatever it would take. She sat back in her seat, the warmth still glowing. It was her first positive decision.

The last leg of the journey found them walking down a muddy, rutted lane. 'I thought they could at least have met us off the bus,' Agnes muttered angrily.

At last, out of the greyness of the long, tedious day, a rambling farmhouse came in sight, built of red brick and two storeys high. They went round to the backyard where a chained dog howled at their arrival. A barn door flapped in the wind and chickens pecked around the yard, but no one came out of the house to greet them. Agnes knocked on the brown-painted wooden door, long past its prime. There was no answer, so she turned the knob and pushed open the door. 'Anyone at home?' she called as she peered inside the empty kitchen. 'They must be out working; we might as well go in. Wipe your feet.'

Fran wondered who *they* were. She stepped down the two steps into the kitchen, where a cat was curled up on a chair. On top of the stove was a big iron kettle, black with soot. Everything in the kitchen seemed to be of various shades of brown. It was dark and gloomy and it took a few seconds for Fran to accustom her eyes.

Mother and daughter sat in silence, Agnes, with her eyes closed. Fran, looking at her mother, noticed her lovely auburn hair, usually so neatly curled, was hanging lank and dull, and flecked with grey. Her shoulders sagged, as did her whole posture. It was as if the fire had gone out of her. Guilt assailed Fran and she turned away to stare out of the window on the flat landscape, wondering why she and her mother were here in this house. At the bottom of her heart, she knew the reason, but she didn't want to voice it out loud, not wanting it to be true.

It was about an hour later when there was the sound of voices in the yard outside and the barking of the dog. The cat on the chair stirred for the first time, flipped up one ear, leisurely stretched and then slid off the chair and went under the table out of the way.

Edna Gembling, larger than life, burst into the kitchen. Fran stared at her. She'd never before seen a woman with a sack tied round her shoulder, only the coalman back home. 'Made yerself at home, I see,' Edna boomed. She turned to Fran. 'Jump to it then, girl, make a pot of tea.'

Startled, Fran glanced at Agnes. 'You heard Mrs Gembling. You're here to work.'

Her fears had been spoken out loud. In a trance, Fran set about the task. The woman had taken off the sacking and was now sitting on the chair vacated by the cat, toasting her smelly, woolly socked feet on the hearth of the kitchen range, a big cast iron stove, with two hotplates on the top, an oven to the side and a fuel burning compartment at the other side.

'Put a log on,' said Mrs Gembling, motioning to a huge basket of logs in the dark recess next to the stove. 'Mr Gembling keeps the basket full, but it'll be your job to keep the stove going.'

That night, after a meal of greasy mutton stew, which lay heavy in Fran's stomach, she tried not to toss about in the bed she was sharing with Agnes, who was deep in sleep. But her mind kept going over what had been decided by her mother and the Gemblings. She was to stay here until the baby was born and work her passage as housekeeper. Mrs Gembling would be working on the farm with her husband, as their two sons were away fighting for king and country.

Morning came, and Agnes was preparing to leave. Mr Gembling was going into the village and was giving her a lift to catch the bus. By now, Fran was in a state of panic. She was hot and trembling inside and yet on the outside she felt like ice. She wiped her clammy hands down the sides of her skirt, her mouth dry. She blurted, 'Mam, when will I see you again?' looking pleadingly into Agnes's cold, green eyes. For a moment, she thought her mother was going to show her some compassion.

'There's a war on, in case you've forgot, and I've our Isabel to think about. You have only yourself to blame for getting into this mess. Be thankful the Gemblings have agreed to have you in your state.' She buttoned up her best brown coat, straightened her felt hat and pulled on her gloves, all the time avoiding Fran's eye.

'But, the baby, what will I do?' Her voice broke.

Agnes turned and took her daughter by the shoulders and looked her full in the face. 'I'll make all the necessary arrangements. When the time comes, Mrs Gembling will get in touch with me and I'll come.'

'Thank you,' Fran mouthed. She watched her mother climb into the cab of the battered old pickup and raised her hand to wave, but Agnes never looked back.

Fran went back into the kitchen, empty save for the cat on the chair. She wanted to cry, but felt too stunned to do so.

Chapter Three

Cut off from all contact with her family, the next months on Gemblings' farm were long and tedious for Fran. Although she wrote to her mother regularly, Agnes never replied. The Gemblings were hard-working folk, dedicated to their land and animals. From what Fran could grasp from their sparse conversation in the evenings, theirs was a mixed farm. She knew there were cows, and a few hens and geese waddled and pecked about the yard because it was one of her many tasks to feed them, and Mr Gembling talked about his potatoes and turnips, and mentioned ploughing fields, and sowing oats and barley. The one bright spark to enter Fran's life in those dark, lonely days was Maisie.

One day, as she fed the hens and geese, Fran chattered to them, speaking her thoughts out loud in despair of having no one to talk to about her condition. 'The baby's kicking like a footballer today. I hope it's all right.' She put the pail down and ran her hand over her growing belly.

'First sign of madness when yer talk to yerself.' Startled by the voice, Fran nearly fall over the pail. A strong hand steadied her. 'Sorry, I didn't mean to fear yer.'

Fran stared into the soft, pearl-grey eyes of a round-faced young woman whose mass of light brown, curling hair tumbled onto the collar of her dark green coat. Having never met anyone but the Gemblings, and now being confronted by a stranger, Fran was conscious of the shame of being unmarried and pregnant. Against the stranger, she was aware of her own shabby appearance: her skirt held together by elastic, of the buttons of her blouse straining across her swelling breasts and of her humiliation of being wrapped up like an ungainly, bulky parcel in Mrs Gembling's outsized, faded cotton pinny. Fran bit on her lip and lowered her eyes, and it was then she saw the battered attaché case resting at the young woman's feet. Before she could speak, the other girl spoke again.

'I'm Maisie Thomas. I'm a Land Army Girl,' she said, her voice full of pride. 'I'm billeted here.' She waved a hand in the direction of the farmhouse.

At last Fran found her voice. 'I'm Fran Bewholme. I'm the maid of all work.' There was a bitter edge to her voice, but if Maisie detected it she didn't comment.

'When's bairn due?'

Fran was shocked by Maisie's directness, but answered, 'March.' Wearily, she bent to pick up the empty pail. 'I expect you could do with a cup of tea.'

Inside the kitchen, Maisie took charge. 'You put yer feet up. I'll mash up.'

The two girls chatted with ease. Maisie was to share Fran's bedroom and the other two land army girls were billeted in the village. Town girls, they wanted excitement on an evening and the local pub was full most nights with the RAF crews from the nearby aerodrome.

In the evenings after supper, when the table was cleared and the pots washed up, Fran and Maisie escaped up to their room. Here, they would drink cocoa and talk about the day's happenings and on these dark cold nights, Fran slipped on the thick woolly bed-socks which Maisie's mother had knitted for them for Christmas. This evening, Maisie led the way upstairs with the candle and Fran, now heavy and in the last month of her pregnancy, followed slowly. She was glad to undress and crawl into bed. On and off, all day, she'd had this terrible back ache. When she mentioned it to Mrs Gembling, she replied, 'Backache! If you had ter work yon fields, you'd soon knew about backache.'

'I thought it might be the baby coming,' Fran persisted.

Mrs Gembling sniffed, then replied, 'According to yer mother, you've got another two weeks ter go.' With that statement, she turned away.

Fran confided in Maisie. 'Do you think it's the baby coming?'

Maisie thought for a moment, her mother had had ten children, then said, 'Mam always had 'em quick. When we got up in the morning, the bairn was there.'

Fran watched Maisie fiddle with the battery wireless. Restlessly, she tried to move into a more comfortable position. She sat up to drink her cocoa, but still the ache persisted. Suddenly, she let out a loud moan.

Maisie looked up from the wireless and, seeing her friend's distress, quickly offered, 'I'll run down and fill yer a hot water bottle.'

The heat from the bottle soothed Fran and, to the strain of Victor Sylvester's orchestra playing on the wireless, she drifted off to sleep, only to be woken up a couple of hours later with an agonising pain, low in her expanded belly. She jerked up with a start.

'What's up?' asked a sleepy Maisie.

'It's a boxing match.' Fran gasped as another pain gripped her.

Maisie, now alert, swung from her bed and, lighting the candle, held it close to Fran's face. 'You look a funny colour.'

'It's the baby coming. I'm sure.' She let out a low moan and ran a hand across her brow, wiping away the beads of sweat, but they kept coming back. 'It's coming, I tell you!'

'Don't fret, first bairns always tek their time,' Maisie said reassuringly. 'I'll go and wake up Mr Gembling to tek yer to hospital.'

'And let my mother know so she can come.'

In the delivery room in the nursing home, the huge overhead electric light dazzled Fran's eyes as the pain intensified, ripping through her belly. She couldn't stop the scream. Sweat poured from her brow into her eyes.

The midwife wiped them clean, saying, 'Be brave, Mrs Renton.' She turned aside to Agnes. 'I'll have to call the doctor to perform a Caesarean section.' Then, turning back to her patient, she said soothingly, belying her anxiety, 'I won't be long, Mrs Renton. Your mother's here.'

Fran clutched at her mother's arm and, through a short respite of pain, she asked. 'Why does the midwife keep calling me by our Isabel's name?'

'Shut up, you fool. Haven't you caused us all enough trouble and shame? I've booked you in under Isabel's name to save face. Do you want the whole world to know about your bastard?'

Fran didn't answer. It was her sin, so she must pay. She wondered how Victor Renton was paying for his sin. Suddenly, a bolt of fire whipped through her body and she was lost in the most terrible, gut-wrenching pain. Then, darkness invaded her.

Later, when she came to, it was to a soft whimper. Fran opened her eyes, taking a moment to focus in the dim room. A young nurse was attending to the crib at the foot of the bed. 'Nurse,' she called feebly.

The nurse came to her side. 'Mrs Renton, it's lovely to see you awake. I'm Nurse Meredith, but you can call me Betty when Matron's not around.'

Fran smiled weakly. 'Can I see my baby, please?'

'Babies, Mrs Renton. You have twins, a boy and a girl.'

Taken aback, Fran asked, 'Are you sure?'

'I was at their birth.'

Tears welled up in Fran's eyes at such a miracle. She tried to sit up, but found she didn't have the strength. Gently, the nurse tucked pillows either side of Fran for extra support. 'I'll place the babies in the nest of pillows so you can see them.'

'They are so tiny,' Fran murmured, her heart overflowing with tenderness and love. Then, she was surprised by her fierce feeling of protectiveness towards her babies, something that she had never experienced before. She gazed at them: their fragile beauty so perfect, her son with dark tufts of hair and her daughter with fair wisps of hair. Slowly, because she found it such an effort, she slid her hands to her babies, grasping their tiny fists with her little fingers. 'Oh,' she sighed with pure pleasure and wonderment as all three bonded together.

Later, Betty said, 'I can borrow my brother's camera to take the babies' pictures and then you can send them on to your husband.'

'My husband,' Fran stuttered, bewildered. Then she realised her mother's subterfuge. 'Yes, it's kind of you.' Fran had been upset when Agnes returned home straight after the births, but, now as she thought about it, perhaps her mother was busy making arrangements for Fran and the babies' homecoming.

The next day, Betty took the pictures: one of Fran with the twins and a separate one of each baby. 'He'll develop them in his dark room this evening and I'll bring them in tomorrow.'

'I'm very grateful,' Fran said.

'It's a favour to me,' Betty said. 'He's based on the aerodrome three miles away. His work is important though he can't talk about it. When the war's over he's going into freelance photography,' Betty added, with pride.

The pictures were a treasure. Fran gazed at them in delight. 'I've no money to pay your brother, but if you let me have his address then I can send some money on to him,' she said, apologetically. She collected no wages for working for the Gemblings, only her lodgings and food, and she had come to expect nothing from her mother. She didn't even receive a Christmas present. She dashed away the hurt. It didn't matter now she had her babies. They would be her world and she would always take care of her son and daughter.

'Don't worry about the money,' Betty said. 'Now, what names have you decided on?'

Fran's face lit up with joy. She announced, 'Michael for my son and Christine for my daughter.'

After a week, Fran was wondering how soon she could go home and asked the ward sister.

'Mrs Renton, you have had two difficult births, with an emergency Caesarean section. You will be here for another week, and then you must have plenty of rest, at least two months.'

Fran closed her eyes, trying to think what would be the best routine for her babies, when Betty entered the room.

'Sorry to disturb you, Mrs Renton.'

Fran hated being called Mrs Renton, but not as much as she would have hated being called Isabel. She loathed this subterfuge her mother had forced on her and longed to tell Betty to call her Fran, but she daren't upset her mother any more than necessary.

'I've come to prepare to move you into the main ward,' Betty said.

'Whatever for?' Fran was dismayed. Here in this small room on her own with her babies, she did not have to answer any awkward questions.

'Sister has just informed all staff that next week we are changing over from maternity to nursing the injured armed forces, and the single rooms are to be made ready first.'

In the main ward, Betty was busy attending to other new mothers. Fran noticed that one of the women was crying and Betty was comforting her.

Later, when Betty came to put Michael back in the crib, she brought Christine to her. Fran glanced in the woman's direction, at her empty arms and whispered, 'Where's her baby?'

Betty put a finger on her lip and whispered back, 'It was stillborn.' Fran's eyes welled up. She was so blessed with two babies.

The week soon passed and Fran and the woman who lost her baby were the last to leave. They sat in the dayroom waiting to be collected. The woman came across to stand and stare at the twins and Fran had whispered, 'I'm sorry.' The woman didn't speak and moved back to her chair.

Fran turned her attention to practical matters and wondered how she would manage in her attic bedroom with two babies to care for. Then an idea came to her.

'Are you ready then?' were Agnes's first words to Fran. 'The taxi's waiting.'

'Yes,' she replied, looking with loving pride at the twins snug in their makeshift crib by her side. Eagerly, she began, 'Mam, I was thinking. I won't be able to manage the stairs at home, can I have the front room for me and my babies until I'm well enough?'

'Your babies!' Agnes sneered through tight lips. 'How can you care for babies when you are not fit to care for yourself?'

Fran gripped the arm of the chair, determined not to let her mother upset her. 'When I'm well, I—'

Agnes cut off her words. 'Don't think I'm having you in my house after the trouble you caused our Isabel.' She hissed with disgust. 'You're a trollop. You're going back to the farm and I'll take charge of the bairns.'

The woman, whose child had been stillborn, stared with open curiosity and interest at this exchange between mother and daughter.

Fran struggled to get to her feet, but she was still weak and her legs buckled beneath her.

'See what I mean,' Agnes said, wagging a finger in Fran's face. 'Now, my girl, you'll go back to the farm and make no fuss, and be grateful to the Gemblings for being willing to take you back. Our Isabel was born to be a mother; she's going to help me with the bairns.'

'Isabel, why?' Fran couldn't think why Isabel would want to help look after her children.

'Why?' Agnes said with such vehement. 'They're half hers. Didn't you commit an unforgivable sin with her husband? You have no rights, girl.'

Fran put her hand to her head to stop the whirling. Her mouth felt like cardboard, dry and rough. She banged her thigh against the chair side as she slumped, suddenly drained of all energy to fight her mother.

'Anything wrong?' It was Betty.

Agnes became all sweetness and smiles. 'She's tired and upset at having to leave so soon.'

Betty bent down to Fran's level and kissed her forehead. 'You take care.' Fran strived to find words to tell Betty of her plight, but none came.

The woman, who had lost her baby, slipped a piece of paper into Agnes's hand. 'If I can help.'

At the farm, Fran struggled down the stairs to the kitchen. Maisie was kind: she brought her a cup of tea each morning before setting off to work. But, during the day, Fran had to fend for herself. As Mrs Gembling was fond of telling her, 'Don't expect us to fetch and carry for you.'

She leant against the kitchen sink to get her breath back. Glancing out of the window, she saw only miles of nothing and hated it. How she longed to go home, to hold her babies again. She ached to feel their warm bodies next to hers, to inhale their sweet baby smell. Tears threatened. Angry with herself, she dashed them away. She must stay positive and concentrate on getting well, back to her full strength. Then, she would go home and she would take care of her babies. Nothing else mattered to her.

The ringing of the farm telephone broke into her thoughts. For a moment it startled her because it rarely rang when the Gemblings were out. It must be something urgent. With slow and painful steps she made her way into the front parlour used as the farm office.

Her hands trembled as she picked up the receiver. 'Gemblings Farm.'

'It's me,' said the terse voice.

'Mam!' Fran exclaimed with surprise. Then she realised it must be important for Agnes to telephone.

'Bad news.' The statement was stark.

Fran leant heavily against the desk, her insides knotting. Was one of her darling babies ill?

But nothing prepared her for what Agnes said. 'It's Christine, she's dead.' Her words were blunt, shattering and heartbreaking.

Chapter Four

York, 1958

Fran Meredith walked down the Shambles of York on her way home from the bookshop where she worked. On reaching High Petergate, she pulled up her coat collar against the frosty air of the January evening and stopped briefly as she did most evenings. She glanced to her right, catching her breath at the sight of the magnificent York Minster silhouetted against the darkening sky. The view always gave her heart a lift, helping to take away the loneliness of going home to her empty basement flat.

She turned into the narrow street where she lived, her thoughts of Michael, her son. He would be sixteen in March. Agnes's cruel action had thwarted Fran at every turn when she made desperate attempts to see Michael or contact him. So, gradually, over the years, and against her natural maternal instincts, Fran came to accept the rules which Agnes had laid down. It hadn't been an easy decision to make. Her arms aching to hold her son, to hear him call her *Mam*, to laugh with him and soothe him when he was ill. An involuntary sigh escaped her lips as the chill wind caught her cheeks. Her paramount concern was Michael's welfare and education. Reluctantly, she had given in to this agreement thrust on her by Agnes for her son to live with Isabel until his sixteenth birthday. Then he would be told the truth. She said the words aloud. '*Michael, I am your mother.*' Her heart filled with love for her son whom she had not seen since Agnes snatched him so heartlessly from her all those years ago. Now Agnes was dead so now there was no reason to stop Fran from rightfully claiming her son. And Isabel must accept this fact.

The wind gusted and, hugging her coat closer, she hurried on down the street. Over the years she had saved hard, going without the luxuries of fashionable clothes. She lived quite frugally. Her only extravagance was an annual holiday when she would take the train to Scarborough. Here, she would delight in walking by the sea, planning and dreaming of the future she would share with Michael.

Inside the flat, she switched on the light of into her small but comfortable sitting room, switched on the standard lamp and glanced round, pleased with her effort to make the room cosy on a tight budget. She had re-covered the old sofa in a colourful chintz pattern and added scatter cushions stitched from remnants of material. In front of the sofa stood a low occasional table, and a writing bureau and chair placed near to the window to catch the light. She'd painted the walls a pale primrose to give her the sense of basking in sunshine. She bent down and lit the gasfire, looking up at the delightful painting on the wall above of children frolicking by the sea. She pretended that the little boy building a sandcastle resembled her son. This was her home: suitable only for one person. But when Michael came to her, they would choose a home together. It would be such joy.

She made herself a simple meal of beans on toast and, carrying it on a tray into the sitting room, she switched on the wireless. 'In Town Tonight' was on and she liked the sound of voices, they helped to take away the emptiness. A tiny pang of regret filled her that the marriage to Peter, brother of Betty, the nurse at her babies' birth, didn't last. He was a charmer, but fickle.

Peter was the freelance photographer who had developed the pictures of her twins when they were born. Quite by chance, after the war, she met up with Betty when shopping in the nearby town of Sleaford. Betty invited Fran to her wedding, to be held in the local church, and there Fran met Peter. He was taking the photographs, and afterwards she found herself sitting next to him at the reception and enjoyed his charming company.

'There's a good flick on at the Majestic, Fred Astaire and Rita Hayworth in *You Were Never Lovelier*, fancy coming?' Peter said, giving her a dazzling smile, his dark eyes twinkling.

Her heart missed a beat. 'Yes,' she answered shyly. 'Oh, I'd love to come.'

Peter had an ancient Ford car and picked her up at the farm, and they rattled into town. Inside the cinema, they sat in the back row, like other courting couples. She experienced a thrill of delight when he slipped an arm around her and drew her close to him.

Afterwards, they found a coffee bar and talked about the film, discussing the magical dancing of Fred and Rita. 'Hollywood is where all the best people are, the women are so glamorous,' said Peter with passion.

Wide-eyed, Fran said, 'Their dresses were so beautiful.' She sighed, looking down at her well-washed dirndl skirt.

'One day, I'll take you to America,' said Peter, in earnest. 'It's my dream to go there.'

Fran thought of her dream, her yearning to be reunited with her son. From her handbag, she drew out the little leather wallet and opened it, showing Peter the pictures of her two precious babies. 'Remember this?'

Peter looked closely, saying, 'Of course I do. Where are your children now?'

Fran took a deep breath before speaking. 'My little girl died.' Tears pricked her eyes as she remembered her tiny, fragile daughter, taken from her. 'And my son is with my sister and my mother. And I want him back.' The tears pooled her eyes and her throat choked with emotion.

Peter slid along the bench seat nearer to Fran and slipped a comforting arm about her shoulders. Taking a handkerchief from the breast pocket of his jacket, he tenderly wiped away her tears. When he finished, he gazed into her eyes and she into his. 'Now, tell me why your son does not live with you.'

So, Fran told him the whole story. When she'd finished, she felt drained.

Peter sat back, deep in concentration, and then he spoke. 'Will you be my girlfriend?'

Taken aback by the surprise of his words after such a short acquaintance, she answered, 'Do you really like me?'

'Yes! We would make a great team.' He glanced at his watch. 'Time to drive you back to the farm. Can you get away tomorrow? I'll take you out for a spin and we can talk some more.'

Delighted, and warm and bubbly inside, Fran replied, 'I finish at one on a Sunday.'

On Sunday, they talked and talked, Peter, of his ambition to become a top photographer and Fran, of her yearning to bring up her son and for them to be together for ever.

After that Sunday, they saw each other at every available opportunity. One day, Peter came with some exciting news. 'I've been offered a job in London.'

'How wonderful for you,' responded Fran. 'But I won't be able to see you.' She would miss his attentiveness, his humour and his passionate kisses. A hot blush spread across her cheeks.

'As I said before,' Peter said, taking hold of her hands. 'We make a good team. Frances Bewholme, will you marry me?'

She experienced a wonderful floating sensation. Marriage? She never dreamt or expected it to become a reality. She would be able make a home and Michael would come to live with them. 'Oh, Peter, yes, I will marry you.'

Everything happened in a whirlwind. The banns were read at the village church, she wore Betty's wedding dress. Maisie was her bridesmaid and Betty's husband, Alan, gave her away. She really wanted to have her father to walk her down the aisle, but Agnes said it was too short notice to attend.

They had a small reception in the village pub where they spent their wedding night. And, the next morning, they were on the train to London. At last, she'd escaped from Gembling Farm.

They found rooms in an old house near to Green Park. 'Only temporary,' said Peter, 'until I am established.' She smiled with happiness. The future looked good and Michael would soon be with them.

She found work in an insurance office. It was dull and routine, but she didn't mind as she would be able to save for them to rent a bigger flat, and soon, Michael would come to live with them. Each day, this dream drove her on. But Peter's dream of being a top photographer was proving difficult.

'I know I'm good,' stormed Peter one night. 'But they want me to start at the bottom, taking photographs of boring dignitaries and I'm destined for greater heights.' So, he left that job and found another, equally unfitting for him so he left that one too.

One night, he announced that he was going freelance. Uncertain, Fran asked, 'What does that mean?' Peter lit a cigarette, blowing out a halo of smoke. Fran didn't like him smoking, but it seemed to calm his nerves.

'It means, my darling wife, we will have to rely on your wages until I get established.'

'I don't mind,' Fran said. She was happy to be of help to her husband.

The dream she nurtured, to rent a larger flat for Michael to live in with her and Peter began to seem as distant as ever. How naive she had been. It took her two years to realise that for Peter she was his meal ticket. While she continued working in a dull routine office job supporting him, he promoted his photographic ambitions. Models were his speciality. They were mostly naked in front of his camera and then in his bed. She endured his philandering for five years and filed for divorce. Her only sadness was they didn't have children. She moved to York to be nearer Beverley and Michael.

The divorce added fuel to Agnes's ruthless determination that Michael would stay with Isabel until he was sixteen. No matter what plans Fran put forward, they were refused. One day, so angry and frustrated with Agnes, Fran caught a train to Beverley. Michael was eleven by now and she guessed which school he would be attending, for Agnes would have chosen the best one. It was afternoon when she arrived. As she passed a baker's shop, her stomach rumbled with hunger pangs, but she didn't have time for food, she needed to see her son. She hurried down the busy street, thronged with shoppers, people on bicycles and a man pushing a handcart. She kept her head down, not wanting to see anyone from her past, not wanting to explain her presence. Breathlessly, she came to the school gate. The playground was empty. Her stomach knotted. Was she too late? A sudden wave of desolation swept over her as she clutched the cold, iron railings for support. The sound of singing reached her ears. Pure and clear, she listened and her heart sang in tune. *Michael, I am here, Michael, I am your mother.*

The first rush of boys tumbled out of school into the playground. Eagerly, Fran scanned their faces, looking for her son. More boys came out. One dropped a satchel and others fell over him, their laughter filled her ears and her heart became full of mother love. Smiling, she turned back to look for Michael. She would take him to the little teashop next to the bakers and treat him to the biggest cream bun. Now, only a small trickle of boys came out of school. And then there was none. Had he been kept behind for misbehaving? She was about to enter the building, when a woman came from the side of the school wheeling a bicycle.

'Good afternoon,' the woman said. 'Can I help you?'

'I'm looking for Michael Renton. Has he been kept back?'

The woman seemed surprised. 'No, Michael was one of the first pupils out of school.'

Fran felt the knot of unease in her stomach. 'Are you sure?'

'Most certainly, I'm his teacher. May I ask who you are?'

Fran wanted to say, *I'm Michael's mother*, but instead she said, 'I'm a family member.'

'Well, no doubt you will find Michael at home.'

Fran nodded and turned away, sensing the teacher watching her go. Desolation returned two-fold to swamp her. She loathed herself and anger stirred within her at not being able to recognise her own son. She should have known him instinctively. Tears blinded her eyes as she hurried away from the empty playground, her insides leaden. Michael was so precious to her, and yet she had failed him. Did he wonder why his mother had abandoned him? So many questions left unanswered. She had written to him many times, trying to explain about the situation of his birth and the reason why she couldn't care for him when he was first born. She had never received a reply and, in truth, she didn't expect to because Agnes would have destroyed the letters. The hard fact was Michael was unaware that she was his mother. She never missed sending him a birthday card. Once, after a quarrel when Michael was tiny, when she signed her card *Mam,* Agnes had threatened to accept no more cards. So she had resigned herself to simply, *Fran.* She wrote to her mother, asking for a photograph of Michael but, as usual, Agnes ignored her request.

All that happened such a long time ago. Now, Fran's eyes strayed to her handbag where she kept the photograph of Michael, the one taken of him as a baby, a photograph so precious to her. Outside her tiny flat, the wind howled, she sighed. She had procrastinated long enough. Now it was time to write the letter. It was the most important letter of her life. She felt quite light-headed and her heart began to sing.

A loud knock on the flat door startled her. She didn't move to answer, but waited, hoping whoever it was would go away.

'Fran,' called a female voice through the letter box. 'It's me, Laura.'

Laura lived in the flat above Fran. Reluctantly, she rose from her chair, wondering what she wanted. She opened the door to a young woman in her early twenties with short, curly, black hair, wearing a pair of fashionable trews and a tight sweater. The cold air blasted and Laura was shivering on the step. 'Anything wrong?' Fran enquired, politely.

'Been stood up again and on a Saturday night. Do you fancy sharing a Babycham with me?' She held two small bottles high, her brown eyes wide with anticipation. Fran hesitated, not speaking. The letter, she must write it. Laura ventured cheerfully, 'Or you're welcome to come up to my flat.'

Fran thought of Laura's untidy flat and her one uncomfortable chair, or the alternative, the cushion on the floor. 'Come in,' she said, opening the door wide.

'Bottles have been out on the windowsill, so they're nice and cool,' Laura bubbled.

Fran's heart sank at the young woman's jollity.

Laura followed Fran into the kitchenette. 'I haven't brought any glasses.'

Fran brought out two tumblers from the cupboard and a packet of nuts and raisins left over from Christmas, opened them and tipped them into a dish. Laura followed into the sitting room.

'You've got it nice.' Laura glanced around appreciatively. It was the first time she'd been in Fran's flat. 'It puts mine to shame, but I'm never in it much to do anything.'

Fran glanced in the direction of the bureau and the virgin sheet of writing paper. Sighing inwardly, she turned her wilting attention back to Laura and asked, politely, 'Have you any close family?'

'They emigrated from England a couple of years ago to Australia,' she replied, helping herself to some nuts.

Fran ventured, 'Why didn't you go with them?'

'A big hunk of a rugby player said he loved me. The bloody cad ditched me. End of story.' She reached for a bottle and topped up their glasses.

Fran watched the white bubbles swirling around the glass. For a fleeting moment she was reminded of when she was a girl, sitting on the river bank with nothing more to do on a hot summer's day than to gaze at the fish darting in the clear water.

As they sipped, nibbled and chatted, some of Laura's zest for life began to rub off on Fran. To her amazement, she was quite enjoying the younger woman's company. She sat back on the sofa and curled her legs beneath her, feeling more happy and relaxed than she had done in ages. Laura sat on a cushion on the floor. Fran found herself talking about her divorce from Peter.

'So, you've no kids?' asked Laura, draining the last of the drink into their glasses.

'Not with Peter.'

Laura looked at her quizzically. 'So you've got a dozen somewhere else?'

Before Fran could stop herself, she answered, 'I have a son.'

Laura glanced round the room, expectantly. 'Where is he?'

'He lives with my sister.' Fran avoided Laura's wide, brown eyes.

'Say if I'm being too nosy, but why doesn't he live with you?'

Tears sprang into Fran's eyes, and she felt angry and sad at the same time. 'It's complicated.'

'Sorry, Fran, I am being too nosy.'

Fran swallowed hard, fighting her emotion. She jumped up, muttering, 'Excuse me.'

She crossed over to the kitchen, willing herself not to cry. Her hands were shaking as she filled two tumblers with orange juice. She heard Laura searching for a programme of music on the wireless. Now calmer, though feeling a little foolish, she wondered what Laura must think of her.

She returned to the sitting room with the orange juice, and Fran was surprised to see Laura waltzing to the dance music on the wireless. They both laughed and the tension eased.

They sipped their drinks in silence for a while. Laura coughed and, raising one pencil-slim eyebrow, she asked, 'Have you a photo of your son?'

Fran reached for her handbag and drew out a worn leather compact. She pressed a catch and it sprung open to reveal two sides. She passed it to Laura. Her voice shook a little as she said, 'This is Michael.'

Laura studied it. 'He's quite a cutie. Who's this pretty one?'

Even after all these years, she still had to steel herself. She swallowed hard before replying. 'That was Christine, Michael's twin. She died as a baby.'

Laura's voice was a whisper. 'How sad, it must have been heart-breaking for you.' Her brow furrowed. 'How old is Michael now?'

Suddenly, into her mind leapt the agonising painful moment and the callous way Agnes had delivered the news of the death of Christine. The shock caused her health to suffer even more. If it hadn't been for Maisie's care in looking after her, she wouldn't have survived.

'Fran.'

She blinked. 'Sorry, miles away. Sixteen in March.'

'You must have had him young.'

'I was.' Fran realised that she must have been Michael's age when she became pregnant and was cast adrift from her home and family.

Laura handed the compact back to Fran. 'Will you see him on his birthday?'

Fran stared longingly at the faded photograph. She could almost smell the scent of the newly bathed body of her beloved son and the touch of his warm, tender skin against hers filled her mind. 'Yes,' she replied, her voice soft but firm.

Later, when Laura had gone up to her flat, Fran wrote the letter to Isabel. The letter she had waited sixteen long years to write. Soon, her yearning would be over.

Chapter Five

Burton Banks, 1958

Isabel Renton shook with anger as she read the letter again. She was in the privacy of her bedroom at High Bank House and she let her fury erupt. 'How dare Frances? How dare she?' Isabel shouted at the faded green walls. Then, just as quickly, her anger evaporated to be replaced with gut-wrenching fear. She flopped down on the bed, her energy deserting her. Her head throbbed as the words reverberated in her head . . .

. . . *I am coming to see Michael, as agreed by mother, on his sixteenth birthday. It is time he learnt the truth about his birth, that he is my son and that I intend him to live with me.*

What truth? How could she tell Michael that his father committed adultery with her sister? This would be her worst nightmare come true.

She lay on the bed with her eyes closed. The letter had come in the morning post and, recognising Frances's handwriting, she slipped it into her cardigan pocket to read later. Somewhere in the recesses of her mind, she had been expecting, even dreading, Frances would make some sort of move towards Michael. Now, she had. And Isabel wasn't sure how to tackle it. Her first instinct was to hide him away and forbid Frances to come and see him. But he wasn't a small boy now, and she didn't want to arouse his suspicions and have him asking awkward questions. So far, he viewed Frances as a distant aunt.

With an effort, she lifted herself from the bed. She was trapped with her father. Ever since her mother's death, Will's health had deteriorated, he became more demanding. It was only Michael who kept her going. Her heart ached with a tight emotion and she put her hand there to steady it. Life without him wouldn't be worth living.

She wasn't sure how she would survive the day at work. She worked part time as a receptionist at a doctor's surgery in Beverley, the late afternoon shift, when Michael would be home from school to keep Will company. Grandfather and grandson had a special relationship. Not quite father and son, because Will wasn't active, but they talked a lot together. Isabel was grateful for Will's interest in Michael because he never knew his father. Victor had been killed during the war, and the only feeling Isabel experienced when she received the news was one of relief. Yet again, her sister wanted to create havoc in her life.

That afternoon at work, Isabel was busy, with no time to dwell on the letter. The telephone rang constantly and some patients still mixed up the new appointment system. Her patience was stretched and she was tired when into the surgery strode a tall, silver-haired man.

'G'day,' he said pleasantly in an Australian accent.

She was just about to retort what was good about it when he disarmed her with a most charming smile. Despite her weariness, Isabel found she was returning his smile. She even fitted him in to see the doctor. He introduced himself as 'John Stanway' and explained that the manager of the hotel where he was staying had recommended this surgery.

At the end of the session, when she was tidying up, John, having seen the doctor, made a point of coming to see her in reception. He glanced at her name badge and said softly. 'Isabel, that's a pretty name.' She blushed and he said, 'Mr Renton's a lucky man.'

'I'm a widow,' she replied.

'I'm sorry,' he said. 'I'm a widower, and life is lonely at times.' He glanced into her eyes.

She responded, 'I suppose so.' She was never lonely with Michael to love and care for, though sometimes she missed the company of a man, someone to care for her.

John was speaking again. 'I appreciate your kindness in fitting me in at such short notice. Would you care to have dinner with me one evening?'

She stared at him. It was as if he'd read her mind.

'I'm sorry, perhaps that was too bold of me.'

She shuffled some leaflets on the desk, her hands trembling. 'No, it's just that well it's been a long time since anyone asked me.' She swallowed hard. He must think her a foolish woman.

His tanned face creased into a ripple of smiles. 'It's a long time since I've taken a lady out. I guess I'm a little rusty, but I would be honoured.'

She found herself accepting, graciously.

Over the following weeks, Isabel and John shared many a meal together at his hotel, and she invited him to Sunday lunch to meet Michael and Will. They both took to John, liking his open, friendly ways. John was a generous man, both with his time and his money. She learnt a lot about his life and family. With his son, he ran a winery on the outskirts of Melbourne and he was in Britain on business, combining it with looking up distant cousins in Yorkshire. Now he was leaving for home, and soon he would be disappearing from their lives.

As she dressed for a final meal with John, before he returned home, Isabel realised how much she was going to miss this dear man. In his company, she was able to push to the back of her mind the letter from Frances. She just wanted to ignore it, disregard its contents. But soon she would have to reply, but what to say? She certainly wasn't going to give up Michael.

John had chosen to take her to a country inn with a renowned restaurant. They were shown to a table in a secluded corner where the silver shone resplendently on the white linen cloth. The room, with low oak beams, was warm and cosy, obliterating the bleak, February night outside. From where they were sitting, Isabel watched one of the waiters put another log on the fire and, within seconds, the gentle flames blazed. She contemplated the uncertainty in her life. It had always been there in the background, never a threat, until now. Michael was her life and she would fight for him, whatever it would take.

'You're very quiet.' John's voice broke into her thoughts.

She glanced across at him. 'I'm going to miss you,' she answered truthfully.

'Not for too long, I hope.'

She held her breath, wondering what he meant. He leant across the table towards her, catching her full attention. 'I meant to say this to you later, but I can't wait.' She could almost feel him taking a deep breath. 'Isabel, would you consider marrying me?' His Australian accent rolled softly.

Stunned, her eyes widened in amazement as she held his

intense gaze, her heart give a little lurch and her body tingle with undiluted pleasure. A proposal of marriage was the last thing she expected. Furtively, she glanced about the dining room, as if she imagined everyone to be listening. She swallowed hard. He'd taken her completely by surprise. Though she was aware of their friendship, nothing intimate had passed between them except a kiss on the cheek, a touch of hands.

John reached across the table. His strong, capable hands reached for hers and she felt his tension. He spoke quickly. 'I realise it's sudden and we've only known each other a short time, but it's been a long time since I've enjoyed a woman's company as much as yours and you are a beautiful woman. I am ten years older than you, but you make me feel as if I'm still in my forties. Isabel will you marry me and live in Australia with me?'

The warm tender touch of his hand on hers sent her heart spinning as if she was a young girl once more. Australia! Her mind catapulted into overdrive and to Frances's letter. Was this the answer to her problem? The ideal solution, a possibility she never dreamt of. Yes, she would cross to the other side of the world to keep Michael close by her side. She felt giddy with happiness.

'Isabel?' He held her gaze.

She found her voice. 'You took me by surprise. Only three weeks, quite a whirlwind courtship.' His face faltered. She added softly, 'I'd love to marry you John, but my son?'

Without hesitation, he replied, 'Michael comes as well.'

'Oh, John,' she said, tears filling her eyes.

John refilled their glasses and raised his to hers. 'To our future.'

Hopefully, she thought, Michael will see Australia as an adventure. The obstacle would be her father.

Later that night, in the privacy of her bedroom, Isabel stood before the Edwardian wardrobe mirror. Naked, she studied her body, something she hadn't done for years. John had said she was beautiful. She couldn't ever recall anyone else telling her so. Her hands smoothed over the generous curve of her stomach and she sighed. Perhaps if she cut out cakes and peddled faster on her bicycle, her shape might improve. Then it occurred to her, would their relationship be physical? A faint tinge of excitement touched her inner core.

She slipped a nightgown over her nakedness and dropped into bed, drawing the eiderdown up to her chin and shut her eyes. But she couldn't sleep. Her mind kept on replaying the action of the evening, of John's marriage proposal and of Frances's letter. Now she would reply, but the contents of the letter wouldn't be what Frances was expecting.

After a fitful night's sleep, Isabel awoke very early in the morning. She lay for a moment trying to sort out her jumbled thoughts. She needed to talk to someone and try to make sense of it all. She glanced at the bedside clock and groaned. It was only just after six.

As soon as politely possible, Isabel rang her friend and confidant, Deirdre Baker.

'Can we meet? There's something I need to talk over with you.'

'Sounds intriguing. About eleven at Miss Martha's. What's it about?'

'I'll tell you later. Bye.'

Isabel entered the kitchen, where Will was sitting by the fireside. 'Where's my breakfast?' he grumbled.

'Here you are, Dad,' she said, absently, placing a tray of tea and toast on his side table. Will didn't answer. His expression bleak, he continued to stare out of the kitchen window, which looked out onto his dilapidated joinery workshop and yard.

'Dad, don't let it get cold.' She hesitated a moment, then said, 'I have to go out.'

'You're always out,' he moaned. 'And Michael spends too much time playing that record player. I don't know why I bother to keep on living.'

'And neither do I,' she muttered under her breath.

Not wanting to antagonise Will further, she said, 'On my way home, I'll buy you a nice piece of smoked haddock for your dinner.'

He turned and glowered at her, suspiciously. 'You're up to something, aren't you?'

'Chance would be a fine thing,' she replied, sharply, as she slipped into the hall. She put on her navy wool coat, tied on her headscarf and picked up her handbag. 'See you later,' she called. Will didn't answer. She sighed; her father was never easy. She set off on her bicycle.

Deirdre was already seated at a table in an alcove as Isabel entered the teashop. She sat in the seat opposite. Deirdre was dainty, with light brown, neatly permed hair, kind, tawny-coloured eyes and dressed in a pink twin-set with a row of pearls – the very opposite of Isabel, who was tall, with dark hair and eyes with a sullen temperament. But, today, a soft glow surrounded Isabel.

Deirdre waited until the waitress finished taking their order, then spoke. 'You look absolutely blooming. So what's so urgent it couldn't wait?' She grinned, a mischievous twinkle in her eyes.

Isabel told her of John's proposal of marriage.

'Congratulations! You're a dark horse. You never gave a hint you were serious about him.'

'It was a surprise to me, too,' Isabel replied with a laugh.

'What does Michael say?'

'I'll tell him when he comes home from school, but I don't see a problem with him. It's my father I'm not looking forward to telling. What am I going to do with him?'

'Take him with you,' was Deirdre's matter-of-fact response.

'But would he come?'

'Try asking him.'

Isabel marvelled at her friend's common-sense approach. Perhaps that was why they'd remained friends all these years. They had met first as young mothers at the baby clinic, Isabel with Michael and Deirdre with her daughter, Shirley. Deirdre was easy to talk to and a good listener and so, over the years, they had remained good friends.

'Have you told John about Michael's adoption?' Deirdre asked.

Isabel's eyes clouded. 'John and I have a lot of things to discuss,' she replied, brusquely.

Deirdre reached out to touch her friend's clenched hands. 'I don't want you to make things difficult for yourself. And, there's Michael.'

'What about Michael?'

Deirdre sighed deeply. 'Will you now tell Michael that he is adopted? We've discussed this before and you've always said when he's old enough. And now . . .'

Isabel snatched her hands away from Deirdre's touch. Thank goodness she had never told Deirdre or anyone else who Michael's birth mother was. 'When we settle in Australia,' she snapped. But in her heart she knew she would never tell him because he would ask questions. How could she tell him that his father had raped her sister? However much her mother had chosen to disguise and hide the fact, it was the truth.

Later, when Isabel told Michael her good news, he cheered, surprising Isabel by his spontaneous reaction. 'Are we really going to live in Australia with John, Mam?' Michael asked again. They were both upstairs in his bedroom and out of Will's earshot.

His eagerness shone in his face and eyes, echoing his voice.

'You don't mind?' Isabel asked.

'You try to stop me going. What an adventure! Just wait until I tell my pals.' He vaulted over his bed and pulled an atlas from his bookshelf. As he studied the map of the state of Victoria, he traced his finger from Melbourne to the mountain and hill ranges of Dandenong. Isabel, looking over his shoulder, could sense his enthusiasm and it whet her appetite for more knowledge of this country that would become their home. Yet, it seemed unreal, frightening almost. Could it happen? More than anything in the world, she didn't want to lose her son. To keep him by her side, she was prepared to cross oceans to the other side of the world. No sacrifice was too great. She was fortunate, John was a kind, caring man and they got on well together. She sat on the edge of the bed, watching Michael. It was a great relief to her that he had so readily accepted this blind leap into an unknown future. But she was dreading telling her father.

Michael suddenly looked across at her and asked, 'Is Grandad excited?'

She bit on her lower lip. She now saw her father as a burden, and one she no longer wanted to bare. Lord knows, since her mother's death, she'd done her best for him, but it never seemed enough. 'I wanted to tell you first.' She omitted to mention her talk with Deirdre. 'I'll speak to him after we've eaten. Are you going out?'

'I was, but I'll stop in.' His boyish face became serious.

She rose from the bed and patted his shoulder. 'It would be better if you weren't here. You can speak to Grandad about it later.'

That evening, after supper, while Isabel washed up the pots, Michael regaled his grandfather with what he'd been doing at school. 'What yer going ter do when you leave?' asked Will.

Michael shot his mother a quick glance before answering. 'I'm not sure.'

'You youngsters have it cushy. I started work at eleven. Up at five sharp and six days a week.'

Michael had heard this tale many times, but he replied politely, 'Did you, Grandad?'

Will lapsed into deep concentration as if remembering his youth and Michael made his excuses.

Isabel made a pot of tea and set the tray on the table next to Will's chair. She drew up a chair on the other side and poured out the tea. 'Dad.' He inclined his head slightly in her direction. She handed him his cup and she let him have a sip first, then, taking a deep breath, her heart thudding, she began. 'I've something to tell you.'

'I knew it. You're up to summat!' Will spluttered, tea spraying the front of his checked shirt.

She forced herself to take a drink of her tea, then revealed, 'John and I are getting married.'

A log on the fire spurted and hissed. Will's face turned as red as the flames, his words came out with coughs and gasps. 'Married? You mean you and that foreigner?'

Indignantly, Isabel retorted, 'John's not a foreigner, he's an Australian. And yes, we are getting married.'

Looking puzzled, Will said, 'But you hardly know him. And why do yer want to?'

'Because he's asked me. And I've been a widow long enough.' She moved her chair back, away from the heat of the fire.

'Well, I'll be blowed. I didn't imagine another man would tek you on.'

'Why not?' she demanded, angrily.

'You'd have enough to do, looking after Michael and me and . . .' His rheumy eyes narrowed. 'This is still my house.' He pulled himself up in the chair, his back ramrod straight, wincing with pain as he did so. 'And I'm still boss. So mark my words before yer do owt daft.'

Isabel laughed a nervous pitched laugh as she drew out her trump card. 'You've got it wrong. I'm going to live with John in Australia, and so is Michael.'

Will's ruddy face turned grey and the cup in his hand rattled, tea spilling into the saucer.

Isabel jumped up, hoping he was about to have another stroke. 'Dad, do try to stay calm.' She peered anxiously at him and hurried over to the pine dresser. She poured out a measure of brandy and hurried back to him. 'Drink this – it'll make you feel better.' She held the glass to his thin, blue, dry lips. After a few sips, the colour began to return to his face.

He drank all the brandy and then spoke. 'I'm right shocked. It's the last thing I expected.'

Going back to the dresser, she poured herself a brandy then returned and sat down to face Will. 'You are shocked that someone cares enough about me to want to marry me.' She couldn't keep the note of bitterness from her voice.

'Aye, mebbe, but you don't have ter go away. This house is

big enough for us all. I've a bit of money put by – we can do the place up.'

Isabel was surprised at Will's admission of savings; he'd always professed to have only enough money for his funeral. Wearily, she rose to her feet, picked up the empty glasses and refilled them. It was going to be a long night. She let Will ramble on until he became short of breath. Then she spoke. 'John's in the wine industry, his business is in Melbourne, so he can't live here. I am going to marry him, and Michael and I will live with him in Australia. Dad . . .' She leant forward in her chair and drew a deep breath. 'You can come with us. We can still live as a family.' Her eyes pleaded. Experiencing guilt at leaving him behind.

Will turned away from her and stared deep into the smouldering fire. Outside, from the river bank near the inn, came the sound of happy voices. Inside, the tension of silence hung. It was Will who broke the uneasy quiet. His face set in granite, he rasped, 'I'm staying here. This is my home.'

A wave of relief swept Isabel at his decision not to come with them, but, then he posed another problem. 'I suppose you could go—'

He cut her off with his rising voice. 'I'm not going to be shoved into the workhouse.'

'Dad, they don't have them any more. They have nice residential homes now.'

'Same difference. I'm still not going.'

'But, how will you manage on your own?'

Will's reply was razor-sharp. 'You can send for our Frances. She can look after me. And she can settle in before you go.' And just as quickly his mood changed to one of sorrow, his voice full of emotion he said, 'I shall miss our Michael.'

'Michael!' Isabel threw up her hands in despair. 'Oh my God, she can't come here.'

'Why not? He's—'

Isabel covered her ears, not wanting to hear what her father was saying.

Chapter Six

Stillingham, Lincolnshire, 1958

Tina Newton, still in shock, went home to an empty house. She slumped on a chair in the chilled sitting room, her damp coat clinging to her petite frame. Numb with grief, she stared into space, unable to believe. How could it be? Her lovely, caring mother Maggie – dead!

Over and over, Tina replayed Maggie's final hours. It started with the telephone call earlier that morning. She had been surprised to receive the call at the department store where she worked – no one ever rang her there. *Heart attack.* The words resounded still in her head.

Panting from running so fast, she caught the bus to the cottage hospital on the edge of town. The journey was a blur. In a draughty anteroom, she waited to go into the ward to see Maggie.

'The doctor's with her,' said the nurse in a quiet voice. 'I'll take you through in a moment.'

Tina twisted her short, red hair into corkscrews, thinking that when she left for work earlier that morning, her mother looked fine. Maggie didn't leave for her job in a factory canteen until eleven.

'Bye, Mam,' she'd called. Maggie, who was on her second cup of tea, smoking her first cigarette of the day and reading her library book, propped up against the sugar bowl, replied 'Bye, love.' Just a normal morning, so what made her ill?

The nurse reappeared. 'Tina, I'll take you to your mother now.'

Along a quiet corridor, Tina walked in a trance, her mind and body tense. Entering the ward, Tina gasped with shock, her insides contracting violently. She was unprepared for the sight of Maggie wired up to monitoring equipment. She looked so frail and pale. Only her hair, dark against the stark white of the pillow, bore any resemblance of the mother she loved. Her senses numbed, Tina sat by Maggie's side. She felt unable to comprehend the magnitude of Maggie's illness. It was like a bad dream, only she was awake. Tina squeezed Maggie's limp hand, but no response, no sign that she knew her daughter was here.

Then, suddenly, the rhythm of the monitoring equipment turned erratic. Tina stared at it for a full second and then at Maggie. 'Mam!' she cried fearfully.

A nurse appeared and quickly checked the monitor. 'She's arresting.' Within seconds, a doctor appeared and ushered a trembling Tina from the room.

Outside, alone in the corridor, Tina leant against the cold, hard wall. She wanted to shut her eyes, erase all traces of her mother's illness and will her back to how she was that morning. But her eyes refused to close. She wondered what they were doing to Maggie, or if it was the machinery which had gone faulty and they were putting it right.

Eventually, the door opened and the doctor came out. 'Can I see her now? I want to . . .' Her voice faded as she saw the doctor's weary face. Her insides wrenched and she began to tremble.

His touch was gentle on her shoulder. 'She hasn't much time left.'

The panic was evident on Tina's open face. 'What can I do?' she whispered, not quite taking in the doctor's words.

'Talk to her.'

In a daze of unreality, she sat by her mother's side. Maggie was no longer connected to any machinery. She lay serenely quite still. Tina's heart contracted painfully as she was gripped by a frightening terror at the quickness of Maggie's deterioration. Her skin had turned a translucent bluey white and her breathing was so shallow. She stroked the limp hand and then held it in hers. Fighting back tears, her voice breaking, she began talking to her mother. At first her words came out in a jumble and then she began to recall snippets from her childhood, things which they, mother and daughter, enjoyed doing together. Like shopping on a Saturday morning, looking for bargains. 'Do you remember, Mam, when you sent me into Hamilton's to buy a penny duck? I thought they would throw me out of the shop because where would you buy a duck for a penny. It turned out to be a savoury slice, which was made popular when meat was on rations, and the holiday we had in Scarborough, paddling in the sea, running from the waves. Do you remember, Mam?' Looking earnestly into her mother's motionless face, Tina saw a slight twitch of her lips and Maggie gave a deep, shuddering sigh. Then there was silence.

They were very kind to her and gave her a cup of tea while the necessary documents were dealt with. But, all the time, Tina was expecting to wake up from this terrible nightmare.

Now, she was at home, alone, unable to believe her mother was dead. It seemed so unreal. But it was true. And yet, how could it be? She couldn't understand it.

All night, she sat in a chair in the cold sitting room, going over in her mind Maggie's last hours, trying to see what she should have done to prevent this tragedy. If only she had taken more notice of Maggie that morning to see if she was ill, but she seemed her usual self. Then the thought occurred to her – had Maggie been poorly for a while and not mentioned it? She pondered a moment, but surely Maggie would have said. She often complained about indigestion and asked Tina to bring home a packet of strong mints. But nothing else. Tina sat on, her mind and body numb with sorrow. As the night passed, her body chilled and she felt as though she'd become an icicle.

Then a strange thing happened; she heard Maggie's voice, her lovely soft tones seemed to drift around her saying, '*Put the kettle on, love. We'll have a nice cup of tea. It'll do us good.*' The flood of hot tears stung her cold cheeks. '*Come on, love, stop dilly-dallying.*'

Picking up on the slang left behind by the Yanks, Tina replied out loud, 'Okay, ma'am,' and without hesitation she jumped to her feet and hurried into the kitchen and filling the kettle.

She was about to pour the tea, when she a loud rapping sounded on the front door. She sighed deeply; it would be one of the neighbours. The street door opened onto the sitting room and, opening it, she was surprised to see a man standing there. He was of medium height, stocky build, with a round face, his grey eyes held a look of compassion, and his sparse wisps of thin brown hair were windblown.

'Miss Newton, I'm Reverend Fairweather.'

For some unfathomable reason, she wanted to giggle. But the giggle threatened to revert to tears. She let out a huge convulse gulp.

'I'm very sorry. I've just heard of the passing of dear Mrs Newton.'

Tina knew he was the vicar of Saint Peter's Church where Maggie had worshipped most Sundays. Tina never went to church, except at special times like Easter and Christmas.

She gestured him in and he followed her through to the tiny kitchen where he hovered awkwardly in the doorway. 'Sit down,' she offered. He sat on one of the narrow chairs. In a trance, she poured out two cups of tea and placed them on the Formica tabletop. Wearily, she sank down on the chair opposite the vicar, her eyes downcast.

After a few silent moments, he pushed the brimming cup towards her. 'Drink up, my dear.'

She clasped the cup in both hands, drawing comfort from its warmth, and sipped the hot liquid. Suddenly, her stomach rumbled with hunger and guilt filled her. How could she think of eating at a time like this?

The vicar cleared his throat. 'Miss Newton.'

She glanced at him, some of her old spirit rising. 'Call me Tina, I ain't that ancient.'

He nodded and said, 'Tina, I know Maggie was a widow. Have you any other relatives?'

She considered for a moment. 'There was once an aunt or a cousin who came to visit, but that was years ago.' Tina recalled the woman dressed in a smart coat and hat. She asked Maggie lots of questions and even wanted to inspect Tina's bedroom. Tina hadn't liked the woman and wasn't sorry that she never came to visit again.

'Well, my dear, if you will permit me, I will help you with the funeral arrangements.'

'Funeral . . .' Tears welled up and the ache in her body came shuddering back. She bit on her lip, her voice barely audible. Frightened at what lay ahead, she asked, 'What do I have to do?'

The bleak January wind sliced through the graveyard of Saint Peter's Church as Margaret Mary Newton was laid to rest. The damp earth and the fragrance of delicate snowdrops mingled in tribute. From the graveside, a small group of mourners followed Tina Newton. She wore her best grey coat and a black hat. Her mother had a thing about hats, she loved to wear one for special occasions, like now. Tina's heart wrenched with sadness and the wind tore at her cheeks, bringing more tears, which fell unheeded. Her forlorn figure moved slowly along the gravel path.

Inside the church hall, the high wall heater threw out little warmth and Tina couldn't stop shivering. She stood just inside the doorway, uncertain what to do, not sure what was expected of her. How she longed for Maggie to be by her side, to guide her as she had always done. Tina didn't remember much about her father – he had died when she was young. Her lasting memory was of him sitting by the fireside, smoking and coughing. He'd been injured in the war and Maggie made excuses for him saying. *'He wasn't always bad-tempered, he was a lovely man before the war.'*

'Tina, come and sit down.' She felt a light touch on her elbow and the Reverend Fairweather guiding her. Around her the sound of hushed voices. More tears threatened. She sank onto a wooden chair. The table before her was covered with a green checked cloth, laid with tea plates, cups and saucers. The Women's Guild, to which Maggie had belonged, had all clubbed together to provide the funeral tea. Two of the ladies were now quietly coming round, serving cups of tea, and plates of ham sandwiches and Victoria sponge cakes.

Although the ladies never voiced so in words, Tina got the distinct impression that they disapproved of her. Her mother had been a good, kind woman and Tina felt guilty for taking her so much for granted. Perhaps, if she had helped around the house more instead of going out dancing and to the pictures, Maggie would still be alive. A lump rose in her throat, choking her and tears welled in her eyes. Under the table, she kicked her ankle hard, making herself sit up sharply and reminding herself why she was here.

Neighbours came to pay their respects: Mrs Johnson from the corner shop, Mrs Booth from next door and her sister Dora, both of whom had gone to school with Maggie, and other friends and neighbours from down the street, reminiscing. This was Maggie's day.

Someone pushed close in the chair next to her, Annie from work. 'Sorry, I couldn't get away earlier, but we've been so busy.' Annie surveyed the room full of mourners. 'You've done your mam proud and given her a good send off.'

Tina was glad of her friend's comforting presence. Annie tried to press her to go to the pictures to see *Miracle in the Rain*, starring Van Johnson and Jane Wyman. 'Come with me and Bert.'

Tina shook her head. 'I'm tired. I'll have an early night.'

Later, at home, Tina sat curled up on Maggie's chair, wearing Maggie's old brown dressing gown. She nestled her face into the floppy collar of the gown, smelling the faint perfume of Lily of the Valley and the warm, comforting smell of Maggie herself. She would have stayed snuggled up all evening, but she mustn't put off sorting out the tin box which held all of Maggie's official bits and pieces. The Reverend Fairweather had said she needed to deal with the insurance policy and to claim towards the funeral fees.

'Could you do it?' she had asked him. It troubled her, prying in Maggie's box.

He thought for a second and then said, 'Maggie would wish her daughter to sort out her documents, but I will help if there is anything you don't understand.'

Tina brought her mind back to the present. She uncurled and stretched out her bare toes to catch the warmth from the fire. It was the first time she'd raked out the cold ash from the grate and relaid the fire, and now it blazed, sending out dancing flames. With a deep sigh, she rose to her feet and went over to the mahogany sideboard and opened the drawer. She traced the lid of the tin box with its raised pattern of roses and leaves. It had been Maggie's mother's box and Tina had never been allowed to touch it, let alone see its contents.

Gently, she lifted up the tin, surprised that it felt heavier than she imagined. She settled back onto the chair and, for a moment, she stared absently into the fire. She was an intruder even to be handling the tin, never mind delving into its contents, which were so private to Maggie, but it was a task she must now do. Maggie was always strict about paying things on time and everything being in order, so now it was up to Tina to make sure Maggie's affairs were all in order. The tin box balanced on her knees, she steeled herself to open the lid. It was stiff – she supposed it hadn't been open for some time. She gave it a huge jerk and the lid sprang open. Inside, on the top, rested old photographs. Were these the last things Maggie had looked at?

'Oh, Mam,' she cried. Grief overcame her and huge tears slid down her cheeks. 'Why did you have to go and leave me?' Through wet lashes, Tina gazed down upon a photo of Maggie and her taken at Scarborough. She recalled the feel of the golden sand, soft and warm as she sifted it through her toes, and Maggie laughing as Tina frolicked in the sea, her knitted swimsuit stretching down to her knees with the weight of the water. A recollection stirred: it was the posh lady, the aunt or cousin, who had given Maggie the money for this holiday.

As she went through the box, Tina thought, for the first time, that it would have been nice for her to have had a brother or sister, someone to share her grief with, to hold her hand. But she had no one. She was completely alone. While Maggie had been alive, giving Tina her full attention and unconditional love, Tina would have resented another sibling, but not now. Tears came again and she sobbed uncontrollably.

She dried her eyes on one of Maggie's big, white handkerchiefs. What use were tears and feeling sorry? But she did need something to steady her nerves. She rose from her chair and went to the fireside cupboard where Maggie kept her medical supplies and found the small bottle of whisky. She poured a small measure and swallowed it in one gulp, shuddering as the fiery liquid rushed down her throat. Surprisingly, its warm glow in the pit of her stomach helped to calm her; soon, she began to feel more in control of her emotions.

Back to the box, Tina waded through the pile of receipts Maggie had kept, going back years. Fancy, she thought, paying ten shillings for a hat and nine pence for trimmings. She found the insurance policy Reverend Fairweather had mentioned – it had a contact address. She hated writing letters, but it had to be done.

She found letters to Maggie going way back, and from people Tina didn't know. At the very bottom of the tin sat a document folded in quarters. Carefully, she opened it out. It looked very formal. Her birth certificate. Fancy going to all that fuss to record her birth. Still, she mused, it showed who you were. She peered closer. She wasn't aware of being born near Gainsborough, she'd always assumed Stillingham. She supposed it was because it had been wartime.

As she scanned the certificate further, a chill gripped her heart. Her mouth dropped open in surprise and shock. She wanted to shout something, but words failed her. Her eyes misted so that the lettering on the certificate became blurred, merging into a mass. In an angry swipe with the sleeve of the dressing gown, she wiped her eyes dry and focused on the faded handwriting.

Mother, Isabel Renton. Father, Victor Renton.

Who were these strangers? Not her parents. And she was definitely not Christine Renton. She was Tina Newton. There must be some mistake. She gulped and swallowed hard, her emotions over flowing. This was not her birth certificate. Then whose? And where was hers?

Chapter Seven

Armed with a bulging paper carrier, Tina Newton sat in a back pew, enduring the Sunday service at St Peter's. She was waiting for a chance to speak to the Reverend Fairweather. The singing of hymns and the sermon were lost to her as she went over and over in her mind what she had found in Maggie's private box. The strange birth certificate with her date of birth, but with neither her name nor Maggie's on it. Then there were the letters from a Mrs Agnes Bewholme to Maggie, but with no address on them. Tina gave an involuntarily shudder as she recalled in frustration how she had scattered the contents of the box all over the floor and found a letter inside another envelope. It was an official looking, judging by the letter heading. On closer inspection, it seemed to concern her. But, why would anyone want to send money to Maggie for her? It was baffling.

She sat for ages, wondering what to do with the documents and who to turn to for advice. She thought about asking her friend Annie, but she had a fancy for gossip and Tina didn't want everyone knowing about her business. Besides, Maggie would not have approved. Her only hope of help would be from the Reverend Fairweather.

The service came to an end and, clutching the carrier, she edged forward to wait until most of the congregation had departed before she joined the line to shake the vicar's hand.

'Miss Newton, Tina,' the vicar exclaimed in surprised. 'It is a pleasure to see you at church.'

Suddenly, Tina felt physically sick with fear and hunger. She couldn't remember when last she had last eaten. 'I need your help, Vicar,' she said and then, remembering her manners, uttered, 'Please.' She delved into the paper carrier and showed him a wad of documents.

Alarm registered in his eyes, but he recovered quickly and she could almost see his brain selecting the right words to say to her. Her heart sank: she expected he would be too busy.

'Tina, would you care to join me for dinner? My housekeeper has left me a casserole in the oven and there is plenty.' It usually did for his Monday dinner as well, but that was no matter.

Surprised by his invitation, her face lit up. 'That's kind, Vicar, thanks.'

They made an odd couple as they walked side by side through the churchyard to the vicarage. She was petite with bright red hair and he, stockily built and balding, not quite the father figure. The vicarage was an old Victorian house of genteel dilapidation, rambling and built to house a family and servants, not a bachelor.

The vicar swung open the heavy, half glass-panelled door and ushered Tina inside. Rising above the musty smell of old books was the delicious aroma of the casserole. She felt and heard her stomach rumble. 'Excuse me,' she said lowering her eyes in embarrassment. He led her through into the dining room and she was pleased to see a fire glowing in the hearth. The table was set with a white linen cloth and with silver laid out for one.

'There is cutlery in the sideboard and I'll see to dinner.' He bustled off.

For a few moments, Tina stood inside the door not moving. She'd never been inside a room like this before. It was so spacious. Her living room and kitchen would fit into this room. She crossed the faded carpet to the sideboard and ran her hand over the well-polished top. She guessed it must be ancient. Maggie had liked the new utility furniture. She felt like an intruder as she opened the drawer to take out the cutlery, although the Vicar had given her permission. It flashed through her mind: would Maggie have approved? The thought of her mother brought a lump to her throat. How she missed her mother, her gentle, caring manner, her love. The silver fell with a clink back into the drawer as Tina's hands flew up to her face. Overcome with grief, her body was racked with uncontrollable sobs.

She didn't hear the vicar enter the room until he spoke. 'My dear child, come and sit down.'

He led her to the dining table, drew out a chair for her and poured out a glass of water from the jug on the table. 'Drink this. You'll feel much better.'

The vicar passed her a big, white handkerchief. She hid behind it until more composed. He left the room and returned minutes later, carrying two steaming plates. He placed one before her and the other in his place, then he fetched the cutlery.

She looked at the huge plateful, not sure if she would eat it all. The vicar began to eat and, in between mouthfuls, he spoke about what Maggie's involvement in the church had been. 'She was a staunch member, always ready to help. She was on the flower arranging rota, refreshments at various functions, always willing to lend a hand with the polishing of the brasses.' He gave a deep sigh, as if remembering something.

Tina sat quietly, thinking what a good person her mother had been. Tina's most vivid recollection was of the church Christmas parties Maggie used to organise. The lip-smacking jelly and custard, fairy buns, angel's wings, and the games: pass the parcel, musical chairs and many others. She spoke her thoughts out loud. 'Mam was always there for me, ever patient when I was naughty and sometimes rebellious. I don't understand.' She pointed to the carrier bag propped against the wall near to the door where she had left it. 'What's that about?'

The vicar dabbed his mouth with his napkin and rose to his feet to remove his empty plate and, surprisingly, Tina's empty one. He placed them on the sideboard and, picking up the carrier, put it on the table in front of Tina. He moved his chair to her side and sat down. 'Now, my dear, you tell me what the problem is and I'll do my best to help you.' He smiled kindly at her.

Tina gulped, feeling bewildered and totally bereft by Maggie's sudden death. She withdrew the sheaf of letters and documents from the carrier and her hands trembled as she passed them to him. 'Vicar, I'm not sure what to do with these or if they're anything to do with me.' She said, her body shivering with cold and uncertainty.

He glanced at her forlorn expression and said, 'Sit nearer the fire while I study these.'

She sank into an old leather armchair and stretched out her legs so that her toes caught the warmth from the fire. She glanced at the garden through the long window, seeing a patch of green lawn edged with huge trees, oak or sycamore. She wasn't sure what they were in their winter skeletal form. Nature was never her strongest subject and Maggie's garden was a window box in the backyard.

The vicar coughed and, startled, she jerked her head and glanced his way. He rose from the table and came to her. 'It seems, Tina, that you may have been fostered as a baby. The documents seem to indicate this. With your permission, may I ask my solicitor to check out the known facts and verify them for you?'

She couldn't believe what she heard and just stared blankly at him. Patiently, he repeated his words.

Her voice was shaking as she whispered, 'Maggie isn't my real mother? How can that be?'

'Didn't she tell you of your origins?'

'Never!' She exclaimed as if it was a sin. Then her eyes filled with tears.

He brushed away a single strand of hair from his furrowed brow. 'Tina, you must take comfort that Maggie was a good Christian woman who loved you dearly and, in every sense of the word, she was a wonderful mother to you. Nothing can ever alter that fact. Always remember that, my dear.'

Her mind in a whirl, not able fully to comprehend the situation, she stammered, 'If Maggie wasn't my real mother . . .' She gulped, feeling a choking sensation in her throat. When she spoke, her voice barely audible. She asked, 'Then, who is my mother?'

He glanced again at the birth certificate, which he still held in his hand, but he could not lessen the blow. 'It would appear to be a woman named Isabel Renton.'

Chapter Eight

York

The letter from Isabel finally arrived. Fran had almost given up hope. She had decided to give Isabel until the end of the week and, if an answer to her letter hadn't arrived by then, she would go to catch the train to Beverley and confront Isabel.

Coming in from work, Fran went into the kitchenette and dumped the string-bag of shopping on the Formica table. Not waiting to take off her coat, she tore open the envelope.

The words were stark black written on cold, white paper. No salutation, no sign of forgiveness. But none of this touched Fran, only the bluntness of the words. That one sentence shattered her most cherished dream. She read it again, but the words and the meaning remained the same.

I am to be married again and Michael and I are going to live in Australia.

Fran stood rigid for what seemed hours. All she could think of was that Australia was on the other side of the world.

'Oh God,' she cried so plaintively. 'How much longer have I to be punished? To be kept apart from my son?' There was no answering reply.

Her limbs stiff and numb, she pulled a stool from under the table and sank on to it. Resting her elbows on the table, she cupped her hands to her chin and made herself think. She must plan what her next step would be. One thing was sure: she wasn't going to give up without a fight.

Isabel had made no mention of telling Michael the truth about his birth. Could she legally do that, whisk Michael off to the other side of the world? Shouldn't Isabel be consulting her, after all she was Michael's rightful mother?

But Agnes had been cunning. In the nursing home where Fran had been confined with her babies, Agnes had booked her in under the name of Isabel Renton. She said to save face, Fran being an unmarried mother and so the babies wouldn't have the stigma of illegitimacy. Fran dearly hoped Michael had never suffered that burden. But, later, with hindsight, over the years, she came to realise her mother's subterfuge was double-edged.

She could consult a solicitor, but to do so she would need proof of facts. Maisie knew the truth of Michael's birth. But Maisie had married the elder son of the Gemblings and they had four children. Mr Gembling had died and Mrs Gembling, now an invalid, was looked after by Maisie. Would it be fair to drag Maisie to the courts on her behalf? No, she decided, Maisie had her own problems, though Fran knew she would help if she could.

Before Fran married Peter Meredith, she had told him of her son and she had also told his sister, Betty. Betty, the nurse who cared for Fran after the twins' birth, had been very upset. 'You should have told me.' Fran sighed. Betty had long gone out of her life, married and living abroad. The last she heard of Peter, he was in America, following his dream. Of course, there was Will, her father. But Fran wasn't sure how much he knew about the situation of Michael's birth or if he would say anything in her defence.

It would take weeks to travel to Australia and, judging by the letters Laura received from her mother, conditions sounded very grim. They lived in a hostel, no better than a Nissen hut. She wasn't going to have Michael subjected to those conditions. Let Isabel go off to Australia, but not with Michael.

That was it. She jumped up and thumped the table so hard the shopping from the string bag tumbled out, spilling onto the linoleum floor. The blue bag of sugar burst open, drenching rashers of bacon. But Fran ignored the mess. She was determined to see Michael this very weekend and she would confront Isabel.

On Friday morning, Fran was met by a scene of disaster at the bookshop where she worked. Mr Spencer, the owner, clutched a bucket and cloth in his hands and looked around despairingly. 'In all my fifty-nine years, I've never had to cope with anything like this.' He pushed his spectacles further back on his head, tangling with his thinning, brown hair. 'Mrs Meredith, so glad you are here. We had a burst pipe and there's water everywhere. My precious books,' he lamented, flinging his arms about, the bucket swinging precariously.

Shocked at seeing her usually calm employer in such a state, Fran quickly looked around. The electricity had been switched off and, as her eyes became accustomed to the gloom, she saw the devastation and gasped in horror. At the back wall of the shop, water still trickled down onto the shelves of books. Some shelves were now empty, but not all. Throwing off her coat and rolling up the sleeves of her blouse, Fran said, 'I'd better make a start in clearing those shelves.'

The shop closed for business, they set about clearing up the mess. The plumber arrived in the afternoon to repair the damaged pipe and replace parts. 'Needs lagging, guv,' he said to Mr Spencer, 'or it's gonna happen again. Mark my words. Surprised it ain't burst before now, what with this freezing weather.'

Mr Spencer stood, ringing his hands. 'Is it costly?'

The plumber pushed back his flat cap and eyed Mr Spencer thoughtfully. 'If yer don't, I'll be coming back again in a couple of weeks, and you'll have another mess to clean up.'

Mr Spencer turned to Fran to ask, 'What do you think, Mrs Meredith?'

Fran knew the bookshop was his pride and joy, and that his life revolved around it. 'The plumber's right.' Then, trying to sound enthusiastic, she said, 'Once we are straight again and open for business, perhaps we might have a selling drive to make up for our losses.'

He looked unconvinced. 'But our customers like to come in to browse and take their time.'

'All we need is a quiet corner, a few comfy chairs and to organise a different promotion every week. We could start off with York's history, then maybe a lighter vein, romance.'

'That sounds exciting,' said Miss Blanchard, the other assistant, as she came in from the shop next door carrying four cups of tea.

The plumber, taking a break, chipped in. 'I think the ladies have out done yer, guv.'

By late afternoon, the light had faded and the shop had become cold. 'We'll leave the rest until tomorrow,' said Mr Spencer.

Fran, tired and in need of a hot bath, reached for her coat, still lying on the back of a chair where she'd thrown it earlier. It was then that Mr Spencer's words struck her and she spun round. 'Mr Spencer, have you forgotten, I'm away tomorrow?'

His brow creased. 'I had Mrs Meredith, but in the

circumstances, I would be most obliged if you rearranged your day off.'

Fran stared at him for a full second, realising she had no option; she couldn't let him down, not after such devastation. He was such a good and fair employer, and she enjoyed working here. She'd still catch the train to Burton Banks on Sunday. She heard Miss Blanchard saying. 'I can come in on Sunday, Mr Spencer.' They were both looking at Fran.

'I'll be here tomorrow,' she said, too brightly, not wanting to let her employer down. But she wanted so much to see Michael. She sighed, regretfully. Now it would have to be the next weekend.

But the next weekend the shop was far too busy, books needed to be reshelved. Much to her acute disappointment, it was necessary for her to help, again, on Sunday with new stock.

Michael was so near, yet so far away, but hopefully not for much longer. She managed to pin Mr Spencer down into letting her have time off in March for Michael's birthday. She had to be satisfied with adding the Monday to the Sunday, because Saturdays proved far too busy.

She had written to Isabel again, making known her strong objections to Isabel taking Michael to Australia. She had suggested that Isabel wed her man and she, Fran, would take care of Michael. He would come and live with her in York. After all, he was her son. Waiting for a reply sent her emotions into a seesaw mode.

Isabel answered by return post. Surprised, Fran ripped open the envelope and read in disbelief.

. . . Michael is very happy and looking forward to our new life in Australia together. Neither you, nor York, holds any competition. On the other hand, Father wishes you to come home and care for him as he considers it is your duty to do so . . .

Fran felt as though her heart and soul had been squeezed from her. Stunned, she stared at the letter. Unbelievable that Isabel could be so cruel. Over the years, Fran had accepted the rules Agnes had set down: not to interrupt Michael's growing up and his well-being, but to wait until he was older. So, with great difficulty, acting in her son's best interest, she stayed away. But now she yearned for the love and the recognition of her son. She was his mother. She had given birth to him, not Isabel. She leant against the cold, painted wall and buried her head in her hands, as her emotions overflowed and her body was racked with painful sobs. She wasn't sure if she could carry on living like this. Her whole life was focused on Michael.

'Fran, what on earth is the matter?' Fran raised her tear-stained face to see Laura standing in the doorway. 'I did knock. The door was open,' Laura said with uncertainty.

'Come in.' Fran sniffed, fishing in her coat pocket for a hanky. She dried her eyes, feeling rather foolish, a grown woman crying. Pathetic.

She busied herself making a pot of tea, her back to the silent Laura. By the time she had the tea tray set, she felt more in control of her feelings. She forced a smile as she turned round, placing the tray on the table. 'Sit down.' She gestured to Laura to pull up a stool.

Laura sat down, saying, 'I didn't mean to intrude, but I heard you crying as I passed by.'

Still with her coat on, Fran poured the tea. 'Actually, your timing was just right.'

'It was?' asked a troubled Laura.

'Yes, feeling sorry for oneself is not good. Can you bear to listen to my woes?' Looking puzzled, Laura just nodded. So, Fran told Laura about Isabel's plans to remarry and take Michael to Australia, and of her thwarted plans to go and see him. Laura listened in silence. When she'd finished, Fran asked, 'What do you think?'

Laura spent moments deep in concentration. Then she said, 'Isabel might be bluffing. Why not go along with her, humour her? See how things really are.'

'It's a possibility, but come what may, I am going to see Michael on his birthday.'

Excitedly, Laura said, 'How about if you arrange a party for Michael's birthday. Make a big thing of it. Splash out.'

Fran smiled. 'For one so young, you have great perception. On Michael's sixteenth birthday, I was always going to make myself known to him, but I didn't want anything too formal. A party, now that's a great idea.'

This time, Fran didn't waste time writing to Isabel. She gauged a time when Michael would be at school and her father would be dozing, mid-morning, and she knew the telephone was situated in the hall. She had asked Mr Spencer's permission to use the office telephone.

Now, as she dialled High Bank House's number, her heart and mind did double somersaults. But she hung on, listening to the burr of the ring, and then Isabel's receptionist voice answered.

'Isabel, it's me, Frances.'

There was a gasp and Isabel replied sharply, 'What are you doing, ringing this house?'

Fran stood tall, not that Isabel could see her, but it gave her confidence. 'To inform you that I am coming to see Michael for his birthday.'

'No!' the word was a screech.

Fran held the telephone slightly away from her ear. 'Isabel, nothing you say will make any difference. I am coming.'

'We're going to Australia.'

'Are you really? Michael is my son.'

'You forfeited all rights to him. I am his mother.'

'It was our mother who betrayed me.' Her voice faltered to almost a whisper. 'I would have never given up my child, the son I gave birth to.'

'It is my name on Michael's birth certificate.'

'But you and I know that is false.'

Silence followed, and then Isabel spoke, her voice strained. 'If you come to see Michael, promise me you won't tell him. Think what it would do to him.'

'He is old enough to be told the truth.'

'I shall take him away and you will never see him,' Isabel's voice rose hysterically.

Fran flinched at her words, but said quietly, 'I shall be coming to see Michael for his birthday.'

'You are not going to tell him?'

She didn't answer directly, but replied, 'I am planning a birthday meal for Michael on Sunday at the Burton Hotel and I intend to see my son.' Fran said firmly.

'I suppose I must agree,' Isabel replied grudgingly.

Quickly, before Isabel ended the conversation, she said, 'I will be staying at the Burton Hotel and I will organise everything. Will you ask Michael to invite his friends or shall I ask him?'

'No. I will,' Isabel shouted down the line.

When Fran replaced the handset on its cradle, her hands shook.

Now, at last, she was going to see Michael and to talk to him. This would give her the chance to establish his true feelings about going to Australia. She leant against the cool office wall, her heart and mind racing. She felt jubilant. The yearning to be reunited with her son would soon be a reality. There was so much she wanted to know about him. She winced at the futility of all those lost years. They had so much to make up. And she wanted to tell him that she had never stopped loving him. He was her child.

Chapter Nine

Towards the end of February, the Reverend Maurice Fairweather collected Tina Newton to drive her in his black Austin, to New Holland to catch the ferry to Kingston upon Hull. She felt quite vulnerable as she sat next to the vicar, clutching her handbag tightly. Inside was her week's wages plus her holiday pay and a small amount of money left over from Maggie's life policy, after the funeral expenses had been paid. Also, it contained her birth certificate, which the vicar's solicitor had checked for its authenticity. She found it hard to believe that those people named were her parents. Parents don't just give you away.

'Tina, it's not too late to change your mind,' the vicar broke into her thoughts.

She glanced at him, her voice was barely a whisper. 'Now Maggie's gone, I want to belong to someone. Find my real mother.' She wasn't too bothered about a father. 'And I might have brothers and sisters, a whole new family,' she added wistfully.

The vicar sighed inwardly and said gently, 'Tina, try not to expect too much.'

She replied, her voice harsher than she meant, 'I know what you think, why would she want me now when she had already given me away.' She turned away so he couldn't see her hot, angry tears.

At the ferry-boarding stage, the vicar extended his hand, saying, 'God be with you, Tina. I do hope you find what you are looking for.'

On impulse, ignoring his hand, she dropped her case to her feet and flung her arms around his neck and kissed his cheek. Then, standing back, she picked up her case and said, 'Thanks, Vicar, for being my friend.' His care and help had touched her heart and she would miss him.

His face reddened, but his eyes shone. 'That's the nicest thing anyone has ever said to me.'

Boarding the ferry, she stood by the rail and waved to him. She stayed there until she could no longer see his figure. She gripped the rail tightly, trying to prevent the tears which threatened as the awful sensation of loneliness swamped her. Around her, she could hear the happy voices of passengers. Abruptly, she swung away and made her way down the stairs to sit below.

Huddled on a corner bench, she contemplated her future or the lack of it. She realised now that she had been too headstrong in not heeding the vicar's advice. He had suggested trying to trace Isabel Renton and then writing to her, to build up the relationship. She could hear his voice now. '*Tina, this may be painful, but have you given any thought to the fact that Isabel Renton might not want to have contact with you?*' But Tina was too impatient. She was determined to find this woman and demand to know the reason why she abandoned her own daughter.

She wasn't sure what connection Mrs Agnes Bewholme, if any,

had with Isabel. The vicar had been in touch with the solicitors mentioned in the documents, but they had moved offices and the file of Mrs Agnes Bewholme was presumed lost in a fire or in transition, and no one could recall a woman of that name and the letters Maggie had kept from Agnes didn't have an address.

Tina was relieved when the ferry docked at the pier and she stepped on terra firma. She hung on to her beret as the wind whipped hard, raw to the touch on her cheeks. She was glad to be wearing her winter coat, her sensible shoes and warm stockings.

Her pace was quick as she walked through Market Place, past Posterngate to Whitefriargate, marvelling at the lovely shops, but she had no time to stop and admire. At last she reached the station and caught the train to Beverley, each stage of the journey taking her nearer to Isabel Renton. She must have dozed because the next thing she heard was the porter calling out the name of the station. She stumbled to her feet and reached for her case from the overhead rack. She alighted onto the station platform and followed the scurrying passengers out into the rain drenched town. She sheltered in the lea of a wall, withdrew from her pocket a piece of paper the Vicar had given her and studied the address written on it. She wasn't sure of the direction and looked around to ask someone, but the passengers had all gone and the porter was nowhere to be seen. She spied a shop across the road and she stepped off the pavement.

Suddenly, there was a screeching of brakes and the scraping of tyres as the motorcycle skidded on the wet, greasy road surface. The rider, swerving to avoid hitting Tina and missing her by inches, caught her case, wrenching it from her hand. Shaken, she gasped in dismay as she saw her case hit the road with a crack and burst open, scattering her belongings across the wet, dirty road.

She screamed at the young man and his pillion passenger, both of whom were struggling to right the machine.

'It was your stupid fault, stepping out in front of me,' retorted the driver angrily. Then he turned to his pillion passenger. 'Are you all right, mate?'

With the sleeve of his jacket, the youth brushed away the blood from his cut lip. 'I'll live.' He glanced at Tina who was now sitting on the edge of the pavement, trembling.

Seeing his friend now had control of the bike, he swung off to come and crouch down by Tina's side. 'Are you OK?'

Fighting back her tears, she fumed, 'Of course I'm not!' Her lips quivered and her upturned gaze faltered under the intense blue of his eyes. Suddenly, the tears began to flow. She wanted her mother, Maggie, to hold her, sooth her, but she was dead, gone.

'She's in shock,' said a woman's voice. 'She needs a strong cup of tea.'

Looking through her tears, Tina gulped. 'My clothes . . .' Her best green skirt and matching blouse lay in a murky puddle of water with all her other clothes.

The woman took charge, and said to the youth, 'Take her into that cafe and I'll pick up her things.'

He spun round and called to the motorcycle driver, 'You coming, Joe?'

'You go on. I wanna see if me bike's all right.' They found an empty table in a corner of the noisy cafe. There was an awkward silence between them. Tina kept her gaze averted and looked down at her torn stockings, her only good pair. Her skirt and knickers, wet from sitting on the pavement edge, clung cold and uncomfortable to her shivering body.

'There you are.' It was the woman. Relief flooded through Tina.

'I've ordered tea,' she said, slipping Tina's case beside her chair. 'I'm Nancy Davis. What's your name, love?'

'Tina Newton.'

'I'm Mike,' said the youth.

Just then, the waitress brought the tray of tea and biscuits. Nancy poured, adding a liberal spoonful of sugar to Tina's cup. As she gulped down the hot liquid, it reminded her of sickly syrup, but it worked, helping to steady her nerves and she began to be more like her perky self.

Joe sauntered into the cafe and slid into the seat next to Mike and nodded to Nancy, but ignored Tina. This immediately raised her hackles and she snapped at him. 'Found a scratch on your precious motorbike?'

Joe rose to the bait. 'Lucky for you, it's okay or it would have cost yer.' He pulled off his old ex-RAF flying helmet to reveal ginger hair and a pale, freckled face. Mike was tall, with thick dark hair, while Joe was shorter, but wiry looking. They seemed an odd group, Tina petite, with her beret and red hair both bedraggled by the rain, and Nancy round and motherly.

Tina's foot touched her case. 'Thanks for picking up my clothes.'

'That's all right, love, but most of them are wet and a bit dirty.' Tina's smile dropped from her face. 'I'll tell you what, I'll take them home and wash them. You can collect them tomorrow.'

Tina gazed at Nancy's honest face, which reminded her of Maggie. 'Are you sure?'

'There's only me and Cyril and he's a long-distance lorry driver and won't be home until tomorrow night, so I've plenty of time on my hands.' Her broad smile took in all three.

Tina glanced at the two youths, who both looked bored.

'Are you one of them new-fangled tourists?' asked Joe,

indicating the case. She gave him a withering look. 'What are you here for then?' he questioned.

She straightened her back, tossed back her head and replied, tersely, 'None of your business.'

Quick to stop the situation from becoming too heated, Nancy turned to Tina, saying, 'Shouldn't you be going now, love?'

'I suppose so.' She put her hand in her pocket and scrambled for the slip of paper with the address written on it, but it wasn't there. She bent down to search the floor. 'It's gone the address where I'm meant to be going. I had it before you knocked me down.' She glared at Joe.

Mike pulled a mangled piece of paper from his jacket pocket and held it up. 'This it?'

Tina snatched it, smoothed it out on the tabletop and stared at the nearly illegible writing. Tears pricked her eyes and she sniffed to try to disguise them, blinking them away. 'It's where I'm meant to be staying,' she mumbled. 'But I don't know where it is.'

Joe squinted at the address. 'It's not far from the garage where I work. I can give you a lift.'

'On a motorbike?'

'Not scared, are you?' His eyes mocked.

'Course not.' But she was. She'd never been on one before.

Nancy wrote her address for Tina. 'I live down by the beck, so you can't get lost.'

Tina stood up and gave her an affectionate hug, saying, 'Thanks, Nancy.'

'I'm meeting Shirley so I've got to go,' said Mike.

Lucky Shirley, thought Tina, as she watched his athletic stride as he disappeared from view. Outside the rain had stopped. Tina wiped dry the pillion seat with the sleeve of her coat before hitching herself up on to it. As they went round corners, she closed her eyes as she leant her body the same way as Joe's. The late afternoon air caught at her cheeks and she felt revitalised, right down to the soles of her damp shoes. When Joe brought the bike to a halt, much to her surprise, a pang of regret caught at her and she found herself saying, 'That was great.'

'You can have a spin anytime.' He grinned, showing his two crooked front teeth.

On impulse, as she swung off the bike, she asked, 'Has Mike got a motorbike?'

'No chance, he's not an earner like me.'

She shrugged and turned to the house. Darkness had crept across the sky and there was no light on at 3 Fordham Street. She felt a twinge of uneasiness seep through her cold, damp body. She knocked on the door, but there was no reply. She knocked again. Quickly, she turned to Joe who was about to kick off, panic rising, she said, 'Mrs Dixon was expecting me.'

'I'll wait,' he replied.

This time, she banged hard on the door. Suddenly, a sash window shot up in the house next door, and a man poked his head out and shouted. 'Mrs Dixon's in hospital. She's had a fall.'

'But I'm supposed to be lodging with her,' said Tina, not quite taking in the situation.

'Sorry, can't help.' The window was closed.

Anxiety mounting, she turned to Joe. 'What am I going to do?' She was in a strange town with nowhere to go. Her first thought was to go home and forget Isabel Renton. On the vicar's advice, she had paid a month's rent on the house. 'A bolthole if you need to come back,' he said.

She sighed deeply. She was a failure before she'd even started.

'You can come home with me,' Joe offered.

'You what?' she said, colouring up. 'Are you trying to pick me up?'

He glared at her. 'Don't be daft. I can have the pick of any girl I choose and I certainly wouldn't pick you. You're like our moggie that fell in beck.' He began to kick start the bike. She made a snap decision.

'I'll come,' she said, 'but no funny business.'

Sensing her uneasiness, he replied, 'You can have me sister's bed. She's staying at a friend's.'

'What about your parents?'

'There's only Dad and he's working a late shift.'

She hitched herself back on the bike and they sped off to Joe's house on the other side of town.

She was surprised how modern it was. 'Nice, ain't it?' he said, grinning. Opening the front door, he led the way into the kitchen. She sat at the yellow Formica-topped table, watching as he heated up a tin of tomato soup, whistling as he did so. He seemed in control of his life. Hers was a total disaster. Tears prick her eyes and she hastily dashed them away as Joe turned round.

Tina devoured the meal quickly, surprised how hungry she had been. Her clothes were stuck to her body and she would love to take them off, have a good wash and go to bed, but how could she say that without it being misinterpreted?

Joe broke into her thoughts. 'We got a television,' he announced proudly. 'Want to watch it?'

A yawn escaped her lips and she felt very drowsy. 'Sorry, I'm tired. I could sleep for ages.'

Thinking it sounded as though she was ungrateful, she said, 'But if you want me to, I will.'

He grinned. 'No, that's all right. Not often I get to watch what I want.'

She got to her feet. 'Is there anywhere I can get a wash?'

'Bathroom's upstairs, top of the landing.' He grinned, adding, 'Posh, ain't we?'

She laughed. Feeling more confident, she asked. 'Could I borrow some pyjamas?'

'I'll get you something.'

Pink satin pyjamas, his sister Maureen's, Tina guessed. She had left her damp clothes on a clothes horse in the kitchen, hoping they would be dried by morning.

Maureen's room was pretty, in co-ordinating shades of green and very tidy. Tina snuggled down in the comfy bed, closed her eyes, the pull of sleep immediate. So, it came as a shock to be rudely awakened, an hour or so later, by someone yelling at her.

'What the devil are you doing in my bed?'

Startled, Tina wondered where she was, as she stared up at the angry-faced young woman with Titian-coloured hair, who had whipped back the blankets. Tina remembered. 'Joe's sister.'

'Right. And who are you?'

Woken by the commotion, Joe, clad in striped pyjama bottoms, strutted into the bedroom.

'Oh, it's you, Sis. I thought you weren't coming home.'

'Get rid of her, out of my bed. Now,' Maureen shouted, flouncing from the room.

Tina glared at Joe. 'Right mess, this is,' she said, swinging her legs onto the floor. She shivered as she left the warmth of the bed. 'Now what am I going to do?'

Joe tugged at his tufts of ruffled hair, and said, his voice full of sleep. 'You can have my bed.'

'You're joking.' She had visions of him sneaking in with her during the night. She was halfway across the room when he barred her way.

'Look, it ain't my fault. I didn't know she was coming home.'

'Well, I'm going.'

'Don't be daft. Where do you think you'll go?'

Seeing the futility of the situation, Tina burst into tears. She wanted her mother, Maggie, to feel her soothing arms about her. How she wished . . .

'Come on,' said Joe, putting a comforting arm round her shoulders. 'There's the settee.'

For a long time, Tina lay awake on the lumpy settee, with a blanket firmly tucked around her, wondering what on earth possessed her to come to this awful town. Why hadn't she taken the vicar's advice to find out about Isabel Renton first? The woman had abandoned her so why would she want to see Tina again? Tomorrow, Tina vowed, she was going home.

Chapter Ten

Next morning, Tina was up washed and dressed. No one else was awake and the house was silent. It was too early to go round to Nancy's house to collect her clothes, so she went into the kitchen. Her stomach rumbled, and her glance strayed to the loaf of bread and the dish of butter left out on the table top. She felt sure Joe wouldn't begrudge her a slice of toast. The smell of newly toasted bread was comforting, but gave her a touch of home sickness, a longing for her home and she missed her mother with an ache she hadn't believed possible.

Was she being a coward, going home at the first sign of a setback? It made more sense to do as the vicar suggested in the first place and to discover more about Isabel Renton. She could write to her, if only she had an address. Agnes Bewholme, named in the letter to Maggie, had used a solicitor's address in Beverley. But, when the vicar had contacted them, they had no knowledge of a Mrs Bewholme. It was possible that her file was destroyed in a fire and since then, they had moved to new premises and no one working in the offices recalled an Agnes Bewholme. The hospital where Tina was born was now derelict. It was as if she didn't exist.

'Blimey, you're up early,' Joe said, as he ambled into the kitchen. 'Fancy a cuppa?'

Shaking herself out of her reverie, she nodded. She didn't look at him as he moved noisily about the tiny kitchen. He plonked a mug in front of her and pulled up a chair and sat opposite her, but didn't speak until he'd drained his mug. Then, he said, 'I've got an idea. Wanna hear it?'

She glanced at him, thinking he was handsome in a rugged way. He grinned at her as if reading her thoughts and she quickly looked down and shrugged her shoulders.

'I could take you to Nancy's. You've got her address.'

After she had collected her clothes, she could then go home.

'It's a good idea of mine, don't you think. You could offer Nancy the same money.'

Slightly confused by his last sentence, and completely misunderstanding him, she replied, 'How much do you think for cleaning my clothes?'

He looked baffled. 'How the 'eck do I know? It's the lodging money I'm talking about.'

Then it hit her. 'You mean for me to stay at Nancy's?'

'You've got it.'

'Joe, you are a wonder.' And, in a moment of spontaneity, she hugged him, liking the warmth she felt from the touch of his naked upper body.

'Gerroff, woman,' he huffed, but rather pleased.

Two weeks had passed and Tina stood looking out of the sitting room bay window of Nancy Davis' house. It was a cosy house with two bedrooms and a box room for Nancy's sewing, a tiny bathroom, a sitting room, a kitchen with a veranda built on leading to a tiny garden where Cyril, Nancy's husband, grew vegetables. Nancy welcomed Tina into the bosom of her home while Cyril tolerated her. He was a long-distance lorry driver, so Nancy was glad of Tina's company and told her not to worry about money. But Nancy worked, cleaning for her ladies and Maggie had brought Tina up to pay her way. So she had applied for jobs and, within a week, she had found employment at a department store in town. She had the relevant work experience. Later on, she would train for something more ambitious. Proudly, she had hand Nancy two weeks board and lodgings of three pounds. 'I don't need all this,' exclaimed Nancy.

'It's what I gave my mam.'

Now, Tina turned absently from the window and glanced around Nancy's living room, with its soft, comfortable furniture and modern tiled fireplace, where a fire burnt brightly each evening. There was a bowl of apples on the top of the fancy metal tea-trolley, and a jar of boiled sweets on the shelf beneath. It was a reassuring room. It gave her a sense of security, something she desperately needed at the moment. Fleetingly, she wondered what kind of house Isabel Renton lived in. She shook her head, not wanting to think about the woman and turned back to looking out of the window. Her face lit up and her insides gave a little flutter as she saw Joe's motorbike swerved to a halt outside the house. He was taking her for a spin to the coast.

Over the few weeks she'd been in Beverley, they had become quite friendly. Tina had told Joe snippets of her life, just enough to satisfy his curiosity: of her mother's untimely death and how, having no other relatives, she had decided on a fresh start. A good friend had recommended Beverley. True, up to a point, but she didn't feel ready to reveal her real reason for coming – not yet. The knowledge that Maggie was her foster mother still hurt and the fact that the woman who gave birth to her had abandoned her was too painful to talk about.

Tina smiled and waved a welcome to Joe, locking the front door behind with her brand-new key, which Nancy had had especially cut for her.

She climbed up behind him, smelling a faint odour of grease and oil. She pulled her coat tight so the wind wouldn't whistle through it. 'Here, grab this.'

She took the dark blue woollen object. 'What is it?'

'A balaclava. Pull it over your head. Keep you warm.'

She did so, grumbling, 'I bet I look a bonny penny.' Joe's reply was lost in the revving up of the engine. As they sped the open country roads, she was glad of the warmth of the encasing hat. She loved the freedom of the bike, a totally new experience for her. It helped to blow away her doubts and fears. As Joe increased the speed, she felt the wind whizz passed her, caressing her, sending her senses into total exhilaration. She clasped her arms tighter around Joe's waist, loving the nearness of his body. She felt truly happy for the first time since Maggie's death.

They travelled on, passing fields showing new shoots of crops, slowing down as they approached sleepy villages, waving to old men sitting on benches on the green. At last they reached the salt blown sands of the coast of East Yorkshire. Parking on the cliff top, they stood close together, looking out to sea. The area was wild and rugged, and nothing like the seaside trip Tina had taken with Maggie to a bustling Scarborough. Here was just the wide expanse of the North Sea, the low cliffs tufted with grass, the unblemished sands, and the distant horizon shimmering with the unknown. The pure magnificence of nature took Tina's breath away. She whipped off the Balaclava, the breeze lifting up the ruffles of her hair and her nostrils filled with the tangy smell of sea and fresh air. 'Joe, it's magic! What is this place?' She turned to him, eyes shining.

He laughed at her joy. 'Turmarr. My secret place. Not even Mike knows about it.'

'I'm honoured, sir.' She gave a mocking curtsey. 'Race you.' Then she was away, half slipping half running down the soft clay cliff face. At the bottom, she tumbled and Joe was there to haul her to her feet and they sat on a boulder. 'I'm going to take off my stockings and shoes.' He watched as she kicked off her shoes and slowly, tantalising, undid her suspenders and rolled down her stockings, placing them carefully inside her shoes. Before he could move, she was off again, racing along the sands. She loved the feel of her bare feet on damp sand and the tiny grains which stuck to her skin. Joe soon caught up with her, his own feet bare, long and narrow in contrast to hers. Hand in hand they made for the shore line; here they frolicked, braving the cold sea water, loving the surf of the waves. Their energies were tireless as they moved further along the coast, their enjoyment brimming as they laughed and called to one another.

Suddenly, Tina stopped and turned to look back along the beach, her eyes skimming the cliff top. 'Joe, I can't see the bike.' She shaded her eyes from the glare of the brilliant sky.

'Don't worry. I know every inch of this coast.' He took hold of her hand, saying, 'We'll go back now. It's getting colder.' They rubbed their feet dry on the grass and she was glad to don her stockings and shoes. Next time, she would bring a towel.

As they prepared to mount the bike, impulsively, Tina flung her arms about Joe and hugged him. 'Thanks for such a magical time.' Next moment, his lips were on hers, soft and warm, melting into hers.

Gently, he drew away from her, his brown eyes glinting, holding hers. 'Anytime,' he whispered, 'Just say the word.'

When they arrived back to Nancy's house, the night was already drawing in and lights were on. Tina slid off the bike, saying. 'Thanks for a great time. It was special.' She wanted to kiss him. But he might think her too forward. She half turned and he caught hold of her, drawing her to him. He looked into her eyes, as if reading her thoughts, his lips touched hers and she clung to him, feeling their passion and tenderness – a feeling that she had never experienced before.

Breathlessly, they drew apart, both looking deep into each other's eyes. Joe whispered, 'Does this mean you're my girl?'

She replied simply, 'Yes, Joe.' She watched him go and then let herself into the house.

There was a lovely aroma to greet Tina as she went through into the kitchen where Nancy was preparing the evening meal. Nancy smiled a welcome and Tina felt her heart, so full of Joe and this motherly woman, over spill with love.

'Hello, love.' Nancy greeted her. 'My, you've got plenty of colours in your cheeks. Different from that pasty-looking girl I first met.' She bustled around, bending down to take a tray from the gas oven. 'Hot cakes to go with ham and eggs, and apple pie and custard for afters.'

'You spoil me.'

'I think you need a bit of pampering after what you've gone through.'

Tina felt a lump rising in her throat, she didn't want to cry because she was so happy, but she couldn't stop the tears from falling.

'Oh, love!' Nancy said, enveloping Tina into the bosom of her arms, stroking the tangle of hair. And, when Tina was quiet, she said, 'Now, dry your eyes and let's eat. And, afterwards, you and I are going to have a serious talk.' After the meal, they settled comfortably by the fire, Nancy and said, 'Tina, love, you can tell me to mind my own business. I know you've recently lost your mother, but there's something more.'

Then it came spilling out. How, after Maggie died, Tina found out that she was only fostered, that she was really someone else's daughter and that she didn't know why she had been abandoned. Tina went up to her room and brought down her birth certificate to show Nancy.

Nancy studied the document carefully as if she was looking for clues to a crossword puzzle. 'Isabel and Victor Renton are your real parents. But where are they? And who is this Agnes Bewholme who registered your birth? The only address on the here is the hospital where you were born.' Nancy looked across at Tina. 'Have you checked there?'

Tina explained about her friend Reverend Fairweather. 'He checked for me. Just after I was born, it was turned into a hospital for wounded troops and now it's derelict.'

'What about the solicitors, don't they know anything?' Tina told her about the lost files. 'It seems to me there've been a lot of shoddy workers, not keeping proper records.' Aware of Tina's misery, she added, 'But, it was wartime and things happened.' They both lapsed into silence.

Tina was feeling so mixed up, one minute wanting to find her real mother and the next minute feeling the fear of rejection, and then grieving for Maggie. She gulped back more threatening tears.

The next day, she sent a postcard to her friend.

Dear Reverend, just to let you know I've got a job in a department store and also to give you my new address: 27 Churchill Close. Mrs Nancy Davis is a lovely woman and I'm living as one of the family, she's so kind. I heard that Mrs Dixon is home from hospital and staying with her daughter. I haven't found Isabel Renton yet . . .

Tina bit on her pen. She couldn't think of anything else to say.

Chapter Eleven

From the kitchen window of High Bank House, Isabel watched Michael climb onto the motorbike behind Joe Miller. She wished that Joe hadn't deferred his National Service. She supposed it was because of his apprenticeship. He was two years older than Michael and only worked in a garage. They had both taken part in a school concert when attending junior school and it surprised her why Michael should remain friends with Joe, despite her opposition. She had ambitions for Michael to go on to higher education, not waste his time with Joe or Shirley, though she supposed Shirley was better than that girl Joe had teamed up with. She was so common looking, with her dyed red hair, and the skirts she wore were quite indecent, especially when riding on the motorbike. Only the other day they had been in the post office queue in front of her and Joe, still as cheeky as ever, had shouted, 'Morning, Mrs Bell,' the name he obstinately called her. It had arisen when she'd insisted he called her 'Mrs' and not 'Aunty'. At first he called her 'Mrs Isabel', and then he shortened it to 'Mrs Bell'.

Rain began to spot the window and Isabel's thoughts turned

to Australia. It promised a warm sunny climate, new home, new husband, but most important was the security for her and Michael. Living in Australia would provide the greatest possible distance from Frances. She winced at the recollection of Frances always trying on some pretence or other to win Michael back. Agnes had put a stop to all that nonsense, but now she was gone. So, it was up to her, Isabel, to thwart any scheme which Frances might be planning. Like now, with Michael's sixteenth birthday looming and Frances insisting that the silly agreement, which Agnes had concocted all those years ago, still held good. Isabel's eyes hardened. Not as far as she was concerned. That is why the meeting with Frances on Sunday must run smoothly. As far as Michael was concerned, she was coming through to Beverley to discuss looking after Will. Which was true, but this could have easily have been discussed by letter. It was the unsaid, which bothered her. Would Frances make a fuss and instigate a claim on Michael through the courts? Though Isabel was named as Michael's mother on the birth certificate, the record was falsified and this worried her. A shiver ran through her body, but she quickly shook it off.

She turned her thoughts to the better things, of the day when she had first held Michael in her arms. From that day, her love for him was unconditional, her reason for living. He was her son in every sense of the word. When he'd cried with teething troubles it was she who soothed him, nursed him through chickenpox and kissed away the tears on his first day at school. No one was going to take him from her. Vehemently, she cried out loud, 'No one, not even Frances.'

'What's that?' Will, roused from his catnap, stared blearily at Isabel. She ignored him.

Later on, Isabel was upstairs in her bedroom, surveying the

contents of her wardrobe. She was looking for something fitting to wear for the lunch on Sunday. She wanted to create the right impression, to boost her confidence. Pulling out garments at random, she held a favourite of hers, a navy-blue dress with a white Peter-Pan collar, which she had often worn when out with John, but it wasn't quite right. Michael called it 'nunty'. She would have liked something new, a dress to make an impression. But she was saving up to buy material to have dresses made to take to Australia with her, as well as accessories. Michael also would need new clothes, he was growing so fast. She sighed and turned back to rummage once more in the wardrobe. Most of her clothes were ancient and from time to time she remodelled them, adding collars, trimmings and occasionally changing a worn dress into a blouse. She supposed the thriftiness came from the war years of make do and mend and it was hard to break the habit, though she was determined to do so once she was established as John's wife in Australia. She thought of Deirdre's warning to make sure John wasn't out to deceive her. But she, Isabel, had no money so that wasn't the reason for him wanting to marry her. No, Isabel knew in her heart, and as sure as she could be, that John cared for her and he was genuine in his desire to make a home for her and Michael.

She had almost reached the end of the rail and pulled out an old brown coat, which had been intended to be cut up to make a rag rug and had been forgotten about. As she swished it along the rail, a garment hidden beneath the coat slipped off the hanger and she saw a flash of yellow material as it curled on the bottom of the wardrobe. She bent down to pick up the garment, feeling the soft cotton, now limp with age. As she shook it and held it up for inspection, a choking gasp escaped as she recognised the dress. She flung it across the bedroom as if it had bitten her. A hot sweat gripped her and she trembled. She collapsed on the bed and stared up at the ceiling. And there on the white-grey expanse, like a picture screen, flickered that terrible day. A memory for ever etched in her subconscious, coming to the fore when she least expected it.

Images flashed through her mind, recalling how that day, back in 1941, had started happily. She sighed deeply, wanting to erase the memory, but try as she might, she couldn't. She had been so naive, wanting to believe she was the only woman in her husband's life. But disillusionment of his faithlessness left a hard core in her heart.

In 1941, she had been helping to organise a dance to raise money for the war effort and she had bought a new dress to wear for the occasion. She had seen the dress some weeks ago and had been paying money weekly to the shopkeeper and now the dress was paid for and hers. She wanted Victor to be proud of his wife. This was his embarkation leave. She dreamt that at the dance, heads would turn when they saw her on the arm of her handsome, soldier husband, just like at the pictures and the thought thrilled her. She would show them that he was hers. Then it happened. Her world was blown apart . . .

. . . 'I'm home,' Isabel called, merrily. She was eager to show her parents and Victor her beautiful, yellow cotton dress, a colour which would catch everyone's eyes. She glowed with pleasure over her choice and Victor would love it, she felt sure. The colour showed off her dark brown hair and cream skin to perfection. Going through into the heart of the house, to the big kitchen, she was surprised to find both her parents slumped in their chairs on either side of the fireplace, staring into space. This pulled her up sharp and she frowned, saying, 'Have you received bad news?' But they didn't speak. Her mother didn't have any living relatives. Was it Aunt Maud, her father's sister?

Suddenly, Agnes broke the silence, saying in a strained voice, 'It's our Frances.'

Isabel stared at her mother, a cold, sinking feeling filled her. 'Has there been an accident?'

'She's pregnant.' Agnes's voice hit the air.

'Pregnant!' Isabel repeated, not sure if she'd heard correctly. 'Is it true?'

'Yes,' Agnes snapped.

Then, for the first time in her life, Isabel witnessed a look of terror on her mother's face. This frightened her. She forced out the question. 'There's something else?' Her body abruptly sagged and she sat down on the nearest kitchen chair.

Agnes looked to Will, but he didn't speak, just lowered his head as if in shame. Visibly, she braced herself. 'The father . . .' She faltered, pulling the handkerchief from her apron pocket, and wiping the tiny beads of sweat from her brow.

Isabel stated, 'It's Charlie Moxon.'

'No.'

Feeling puzzled by this reply, she shifted uncomfortably in her seat, her mother's uncharacteristic behaviour frightened her. 'Who then?' she blurted.

Agnes buried her face in her hands and when she did look up; her face was as white as a sheet. Her voice was little more than a whisper. 'It's Victor.'

Stupidly, the name didn't register as Isabel stared at Agnes. 'Victor who?'

Agnes buried her face again and couldn't speak. It was Will who answered. 'Your husband.'

Isabel felt her whole body stilled, held in motion and then it exploded and she screamed. 'No, it's not true! Not Victor?' She jumped up, knocking over the chair, rushing to her mother's side. 'Say it's not true,' she pleaded.

Agnes tried to hold her sorrowing daughter close, but Isabel would not be consoled, pushing her mother away. Agnes murmuring repeatedly, 'I'm sorry, so sorry.'

Not listening, she stumbled upstairs to find Victor, but their bedroom was empty. Her sobs echoing, she ran outside. She found him in the joinery office, alone, sitting at the desk, smoking a cigarette and reading a newspaper.

'Isabel.' His dark eyes narrowing, he asked, 'What's up?'

Rage fired her. 'You might well ask, Victor Renton. How could you?' Her face puckered, distorting, ugly, as she fought to control her tears. Never before had she confronted him. Her voice quavered, her finger wagged. 'I've put up with your philandering ways away from home, but my own sister?' Humiliation, hurt, betrayal, self-pity mixing with anger, she lost her reasoning. She flew at him, her sharp, long nails clawing at his face, drawing blood.

He caught her wrists, imprisoning her. 'What's that vixen been telling you?'

'She's pregnant! My little sister is pregnant by you. You bastard!'

Victor paled, releasing his wife. 'Never. It was only the once,' he lied. 'A mistake, believe me.'

She gawked at him, lips quivering. 'You don't deny it?'

'Why should I?' He gave a harsh chuckle. 'It proves I'm a man. I can father a child. I'm not cold and barren like you,' he taunted.

Wrenching her hands from his grasp, she backed away from him, his cruel remark adding to her devastation. She caught her body against a protruding corner of the metal filing cabinet. She didn't feel a thing, so great was the pain which struck at her heart. She fled from the office and stumbling through the yard, she fell against a wood stack where she was violently sick.

After that fateful day, she had thought of ending her life, but Agnes had cajoled her, bullied her, forcing her to stay married to Victor, promising to make everything all right. Agnes started by sending Frances away to stay on a farm in deepest Lincolnshire with distant relatives.

Then, two things happened which changed her life. Victor was killed in action. And then, when Agnes placed the baby, Michael, in her arms, she began to live again.

Now, Isabel sat up and swung off the bed. She picked up the yellow dress and, with a vengeance, she ripped the thin material to shreds, now more determined than ever to keep Michael, her son, close by.

'Mam, are you there?' The sound of Michael's voice bought Isabel up sharp. Feeling emotionally drained, she replied as calmly as she could, 'Yes, Michael, I'm coming.' She went from the bedroom onto the landing and looked over the banister at her son in the hallway below.

He looked up at her, saying, 'I've promised to go into school to help shift some scenery. Any chance of an early tea, Mam?'

'Of course, love. I'll be down in a tick.' She went into the bathroom and splashed her face with cold water and then rubbed it vigorously on a rough towel, wanting to remove all thoughts of the infidelity between her sister and Victor.

After tea, she walked down the garden path with Michael and watched as he strode down the lane. Just as he reached the bend, he waved. She blew him a kiss. This was one of their little rituals that began on his first day at school. Now it was only done in private and mostly in a joking fashion. A doting mother she maybe, but she wouldn't think of embarrassing him.

She went into the front room, so rarely used these days, to hunt the shelves of the bookcase to see if there was a book on Australia. Suddenly, there was a crash from the kitchen. Closing the glass doors of the bookcase, she went into the kitchen to investigate what her father had knocked over this time. It was his small table and the contents of a mug of tea swam on the floor.

'You never got me baccy,' he accused.

Ever since she had made it quite clear to him that she and Michael were definitely going to live in Australia, he had become clumsier. He was doing it out of spite, trying to make her feel guilty. Never once did he consider her happiness. Since her mother's death, he had grown into a crusty old man. Bitterly, she thought of her wasted years spent in this house. First, by a cheating husband; second, by a dominating mother; and now, her father who didn't appreciate the sacrifice she made to care for him. Well, let Frances have a taste of it now and look after Will.

She eased Will back into his chair, wiped up the spilt tea and fetched his baccy from the dresser drawer. Thinking ahead to the meeting with Frances tomorrow, she didn't want to upset her father so she didn't rebuke him, anxious for him to be in a reasonably co-operative mood.

Will lit his pipe and blew clouds of smoke, drawing on it with pleasure. Isabel hated the foul-smelling smoke and opened a small side window. She looked at him with disdain. His unshaven chin, the dribbles of food down his crumpled shirt front disgusted her. Before she could stop herself, she blurted. 'I hope you're going to smarten yourself up for tomorrow.'

Will inclined his head slightly, just enough to glare at Isabel. 'No!'

'What do you mean, no? You'd better. I'm not having you showing me up. It's the best hotel in Beverley we're going to and Deirdre and her husband will be there,' she snapped, her dark eyes flashing. 'You don't want your wayward daughter to see you looking like a tramp.'

Though cracked lips and pipe jutting from the corner of his mouth, he spat. 'I'm not going. If our Frances wants to see me, she can come here.' And, with that, he reached out and turned the wireless on full blast.

'Dad, will you turn it down,' she yelled. He ignored her. 'Dad, please.' Still, he continued to ignore her. Unable to cope with his mood, she rushed from the room to the sanctuary of her bedroom. She leant against the closed door, her heart pounded so fast she thought it would burst. Then, through clenched teeth, she muttered. 'If I stay here much longer, I swear I'll swing for him.'

Chapter Twelve

Fran hurried through the narrow streets, crowded with visitors and shoppers and, by cutting through snickelways, she reached home in record time. Mr Spencer had taken pity on her by suggesting that she worked her dinner hour and leave at four. Her case was already packed, waiting by the door. She scribbled a hasty note to Laura to let her know she had gone away a day earlier and pushed it through her letter box.

At the station, she dashed along the platform. The guard, whistle poised, give her a frown and waited a few seconds for her to scramble aboard the train bound for Beverley. The whistle shrilled, the engine moved and steam billowed. Getting her breath back, Fran walked along the narrow corridor, glancing in the compartments to see if there was a vacant seat, but they all seemed to be full. Looking for a suitable place to lean against, she spied, in the compartment nearest to her, a man in a corner with his legs sprawled across the width of another seat.

She squeezed her way in. 'Excuse me,' she said politely. His face was turned to the window and he didn't answer her. More loudly she repeated it, but still no response.

An elderly man sitting opposite, lowered his newspaper to say, 'He's asleep.'

Her action was so quick that she surprised herself. She kicked the sleeping man on the shin. Startled, he woke up, staring bleary eyed at Fran. 'Is this seat taken?' she asked sweetly.

Jerking his head, he looked round in bewilderment. 'I'm sorry, I'd no idea the train was full.' In one swift movement, he undraped his long legs and pulled his thin frame into a sitting position. 'Be my guest,' he said, patting the now vacant seat.

'Thanks.' She was just about to put her case on the overhead rack, when he jumped up.

'Let me.' She murmured her thanks again and sank down on the seat.

'I'm Nick Saunders,' he said. The hand he extended was long and thin, but his handshake was firm and solid.

She glanced sideways at the man, seeing his unkempt brown hair, his gaunt face with such dark shadows etched beneath sad eyes. Those sad eyes watched her. Quickly, she averted her glaze. 'Frances Meredith,' she said, withdrawing her hand from his.

She could sense him studying her and, for something to do, she began rummaging in her handbag. In her hurry to get away, she'd forgotten her book. It still lay on the table by her bedside, but her fumbling fingers found a notebook and pencil. So, she decided to make notes of the things she wanted to ask Michael. Favourite sports, books, music and . . . She paused; she had no idea what a sixteen-year-old boy liked.

'Hard to concentrate,' Nick Saunders' voice interjected into her thoughts, indicating her doodling on the notepad.

She looked down to see that she had drawn a row of matchstick men and he was studying the page and what she had written about Michael. She quickly flicked over the page. 'It's private,' she said, irritated by his intrusion

The hint of sparkle which had touched his eyes, evaporated and the sadness returned. 'Sorry,' he muttered and turned away to look out of the steam smeared window. The man sitting opposite lowered his newspaper to look across at them both and then quickly raised it.

Fran stared down at her notes and couldn't think of another thing to write down. Nick Saunders was right, she couldn't concentrate. Was she expecting too much? Michael was her son. He had grown inside her for nine months and she had given birth to him, given him life, but she had not seen him grow up. And yet, that wonderful feeling of the warmth of his tiny body next to hers as he lay in her arms had never left her. She closed her eyes and it was there, so vividly. In her heart, the bond was still strong. But now, Michael was no longer a baby, but a young man. Could he possibly feel anything for her? Would those feelings first nurtured all those years ago survive through time to now? This was the hope which had kept her going all these years. So, it was possible he would he know instantly that she, Fran, was his real mother? She kept her eyes closed and, listening to the rhythm of the train, she hugged those past feelings close, willing them into the future.

She must have dozed, because the next thing she was aware of was Nick Saunders saying to her, 'You've dropped these.'

She opened her eyes to see him holding the notebook and pencil which had slipped from her lap. She reached out to take them. 'Thank you,' she said, feeling slightly guilty about her earlier behaviour. Hastily, she put them back in her bag. Eyes downcast, she peered into the bag, espying an unopened packet of Spangle sweets. As she opened the top of the packet, an impulse gripped her and she proffered one to Nick Saunders.

Surprised, he gave her a grin and accepted. 'Fruity orange, my favourite,' he said. For the rest of the journey they sucked their sweets, not uttering another word.

'Beverley,' the porter called. Fran watched as the train steamed into the station, her heart quickened and her body trembled. Passengers were rising from their seats and still Fran sat there, immobile. She was unaware of Nick Saunders reaching up for her case.

'Are you all right? You're as white as a ghost,' Nick said with concern.

Fran inhaled deeply and got a grip on herself. 'I'm fine.' But she wasn't.

He looked dubiously at her. 'Is anyone meeting you?'

'No. I'm not expected until tomorrow.' Not that Isabel would have met her.

'Family?' he enquired, still concerned.

She bit on her lip. 'Sort of, but I'm staying at a hotel.'

He nodded as in understanding. 'Look, my brother is meeting me. We can offer you a lift.'

She brightened at this, but then said cautiously, 'That's kind of you.'

He must have sensed her wariness, for he said, 'You'll be quite safe with me.'

She glanced into his brown eyes and she felt she could trust him.

He took her arm and carried her case, and she was glad of his strength, for hers seemed to have deserted her, both mentally and physically.

Out on the platform, the cold air hit her and helped to revive her. Feeling the need to say something to this man who had befriended her, she asked. 'You live in Beverley?'

He hesitated before replying, 'I'm planning to live nearby.'

'With your brother?' As soon as the question left her lips she sensed it was wrong. She gave him a fleeting look as they walked out of the station.

His face was expressionless, his voice harsh as he replied, 'No.'

By now, they were outside the station and slow drizzle of rain persisted.

'Over here, Nick,' called a jovial masculine voice. A man with a mane of red hair and sideburns jumped from a mud splattered Land Rover. He strode forward, his hand outstretched. Nick put down Fran's case, and the two men shook hands and affectionately slapped each other on the shoulders. 'Great to see you.' Then, he turned his attention to Fran. 'And who's this little lady then?' He took in her blonde hair under a smart beret, her vivid blue eyes and her slim figure. 'You've picked a good looker.'

Fran blushed, feeling the warm tingle of blood rush to her cheeks and the adrenalin begin to rush round her body. She smile and was grateful to the man.

'Frances, this is my brother, Rufus. Frances and I met on the train.'

Fran extended her hand and Rufus raised it to his lips and kissed it, giving her a wink at the same time. 'Welcome.' She blushed again and feeling a little embarrassed.

Nick picked up her case and Rufus asked, 'Where to?'

'The Burton Hotel, please.'

Soon she was settled on the back seat in the vehicle, next to a friendly golden retriever who wanted to lick her face. She stroked it and then it seemed contented to rest its head on her lap.

Nick and Rufus were talking and Fran turned her attention to gazing out of the window. As they passed people walking on the pavement, she saw a boy of about sixteen, her heart leapt could he be Michael? Her son was born with dark brown hair, but his eyes were the blue eyes of a newly born baby, so she wasn't sure what colour they would be now.

The Land Rover juddered to a halt. 'Burton Hotel,' called Rufus over his shoulder. 'It looks a bit posh, but I dare say you'll be comfortable. Now, if you fancy something with a bit of atmosphere, Nick and I are going to the Old Grey Mare tonight. Log fires, gaslights, good beer and live music – none of that jukebox stuff.'

By now, Rufus was out of the driving seat and opening the passenger door for her. 'Goodbye, she said to Nick. 'Thank you for your help.'

He half turned to her, saying in a quiet voice, 'Glad to help.' She noticed he didn't echo Rufus's offer to join them at the Old Grey Mare.

Rufus handed her case. 'Thank you for the lift,' she said.

He grinned broadly, saying, 'It's not every day I get to see a pretty woman. And, don't forget, tonight at the pub. We can collect you if you wish.'

'I know where it is, but thank you.' He raised an eyebrow and gave her a mock salute.

She turned and walked up the steps of the hotel, her thoughts with Michael, her son.

In her hotel room, Fran soaked in the deep bath for an hour, washing away the grime of the day. As she lay amidst the luxury of frothy bubbles, Fran thought of Michael and wondered how he would receive her tomorrow. Over the years, she'd given a lot of thought to his well-being. It broke her heart, but finally she had agreed to let him grow up uncluttered without any demands from her. She reached out and burst a bubble with her toe. Was her bubble about to burst? The constraints, which her mother had imposed on her, keeping her apart from her son for all these years, had taken their toll. She wasn't a fool but she was in denial. Deep down, she was only too aware that Michael must think of Isabel was his mother. How could he think otherwise if he hadn't been told the truth of his birth? That she, Fran, was his real mother, the young girl who had given him life only for him to be so cruelly wrenched away from her. She thought bitterly of her mother: how could Agnes rest easy in her grave knowing the deceit and the miseries she had caused? Fran would never understand why her mother had acted in such a devious way. She shivered and reached for the warm towel.

After dinner, she sat alone in the lounge, the dead silence of the hotel room promised the night to stretch, long and lonely. She made a quick decision. She knew her way to the Old Grey Mare. In the war years, it had been easy to dress up and wear make-up and so Fran and her friend, Vanessa, would appear older than their fifteen years. Of course, their mothers never knew. Fran sighed, thinking of her lost youth and the lonely years she had spent on the farm in Lincolnshire.

Now, standing outside the Mare, listening to the noise coming from inside, savouring the smell of beer, seeing the shining panels of coloured glass on the wooden door, the intervening years slipped away. She wondered if Vanessa still came and if so, would she recognise her? Would anyone from her past recognise her?

* * *

'What do you think?' Tina held out her hands for Nancy to admire the deep pink nail varnish.

With a pretence of a frown, Nancy studied the deep pink nails and then stood back to admire Tina as a whole. She took in the newly dyed red hair, the smooth, delicate skin of her face, the white see-through lacy blouse, which was all the fashion among the young girls. But Tina's biggest asset was her lovely blue eyes. Gone was their dull sadness. Since her setback at not tracing Isabel Renton through the telephone directory, which they had poured over together, Nancy had encouraged Tina to spend some of her first week's wages on buying clothes and little luxuries, like the nail varnish. 'Do you know what, love, you look just like that film star, Leslie Caron.'

Tina gave a twirl, her full skirt swishing high, showing off her shapely legs.

There was a knock at the front door and Nancy let Joe in. He was dressed in the latest fashion. He wore a Teddy-Boy style jacket with long velvet lapels and drainpipe trousers, and his ginger hair was slicked back with Brylcreem, quiffed and styled into a *DA*. 'Hello, Mrs Dee,' he greeted her.

'Cheeky monkey,' Nancy beamed at him. 'I've said to call me Nancy.'

'My pa always said to be polite to me elders,' he grinned at her.

She shook her head with laughter, her tight curls bobbing. 'Where is it tonight?'

'Surprise,' he said, tapping a finger on the side of his nose.

Now Tina joined in the conversation. 'I hate surprises so you'd better tell me where.'

'Women,' he rolled his eyes. 'Folk Club at Mare's. You can come if you want, Nancy.'

Nancy replied, 'No fear, those gaslights play havoc with my breathing. Besides, I'm off to the club with Mrs Wood. We've got an entertainer on tonight who sings just like Bing Crosby.'

'Your Cyril not home?'

Nancy's smile faded. 'Not while Monday, a rush job on.'

Ah, thought Joe, *we might have the house to ourselves later.*

'Come on, daydreamer, I'm ready,' said Tina, who had been to collect her coat.

'Excuse us, missus, are you going in?'

Fran gave a startled look to the fashionable young couple. He was dressed in the latest Teddy-Boy style and she had the most sparkling blue eyes and ridiculously red hair, but it suited her.

'We'll take you in if you like,' the young man offered.

Suddenly, Fran laughed and said, 'I'm sorry. I used to come here a long time ago, to the folk club, and I was just reminiscing.' She stood to one side, saying, 'I'll follow you in.'

So, the young couple led the way in. Fran followed in a trance along the well-worn stone flagged passage and up the staircase. On the wall, halfway up, she felt sure there was the same well-hacked notice board of her youth. The girl stopped to read it and Fran hung back, listening to her sing-song voice. 'Due to continuous complaints, can all dogs be kept on a lead and off furniture. Thank you.' The couple laughed and Fran joined in. All three entered the room laughing. Heads turned, glum faces smiled. For a moment, panic gripped Fran. What had she let herself in for?

Then, a masculine voice shouted from across the room. 'Frannie, over here.' Relief swept over her as she recognised Rufus. She made her way through the crowded room, dodging wooden tables, benches and sprawled out legs to squeeze on the bench between Rufus and Nick.

'Hello,' she said, feeling a little strange, sitting between the two brothers.

'Nice to see you again, Frannie, and glad that you made it. Isn't that so, Nick?' Rufus's voice boomed over the chatter going on around them.

Nick nodded a half-hearted greeting and Fran got the impression that he didn't welcome her company. She sighed inwardly and was determined to make the best of the evening. Rufus poured out a bottle of pale ale into a glass and pushed it towards her. 'Thank you.' She took a sip, surprised, unaccustomed to drinking beer, she found it quite refreshing.

'I won my bet,' said Rufus.

Puzzled, Fran asked, 'What bet?'

'Nick said it was doubtful if you would come.'

'Oh.' She laughed and glanced at Nick. His lips parted in half a smile.

Taking another sip of ale, she studied Nick over the rim of her glass. His expression was serious and his dark eyes held a troubled sadness. She'd noticed the same air of desolation about him when they had travelled in the train together. But then he'd seemed to pull himself out of it. Feeling a little uneasy, she babbled, 'I used to come here when I was a girl, many years ago.'

'You did? Amazing.' It was Rufus who answered. 'Has the old place changed much?'

She glanced around the room and replied, 'No, it still has the same gaslights, but the atmosphere is livelier.' Suddenly, her eyes rest on a young man sitting at a nearby table and her heart gave a lurch. He was tall, dark with a pleasant looking face and shining blue eyes. She shook herself, wishful thinking.

The folk group begin to tune up. Drinking glasses were quietly placed on tables, cigarettes extinguished and all eyes fixed on the group of three men and a girl. The girl was dressed in a gipsy skirt of shades of red, she wore her raven hair long over her shoulders and her eyes were smouldering, dark as coals. Music filled the room, reaching every corner, through the crowded doorway and beyond to the latecomers standing on the stairs. The girl began to sing. The soft lilt of her Irish voice sent shivers of pure enchantment down Fran's spine as she listened, entranced by the sad story of a woman waiting in vain for her lover to join her, in a country far away from their homeland. As the last note died away ,the cheering was loud and, with a toss of her long hair, the girl bowed low. Then, the tempo changed to an upbeat, catchy tune and, enthusiastically, Fran joined in the clapping of hands and feet stomping, loving it. Even Nick relaxed and joined in.

At the interval, eyes sparkling, Fran asked Rufus, 'Is it like this every Saturday night?'

'No, more is the pity. This is a special event.'

She wanted to ask Rufus more, but someone claimed his attention.

Nick, lounging back on the bench, suddenly swung round to face her. 'Tell me, you must know what is going on in Beverley? Didn't you say to Rufus that you grew up here?'

'I did, but I left when I was sixteen.'

He thought for a moment. 'That must have been the war years. Have you family here?'

'Yes.'

'You keep in touch?'

'Postcards, that sort of thing. The last time I came back was for my mother's funeral. It was not the time for social chit chat,' she replied, sharply. Not that her past was any of his business. She wasn't sure if he was genuinely interested in her or talking for the sake of it.

She hadn't thought about her mother or her funeral for a long time. Her father and Isabel had little to say to her and Michael had been sent away to stay with a friend. The other mourners, not knowing the true situation, cast her as the uncaring daughter.

As if reading her mind, Nick said, 'You're not a close family?'

Unexpected tears pricked her eyes. The music started up, so she didn't have to answer him.

It was after ten when the evening ended. 'Excuse me,' said Rufus, 'I won't be long. Just need to find a telephone.' He ambled off down the stairs.

Nick rose. 'We may as well go down.'

In the downstairs passageway, Rufus was using the payphone. 'Don't worry, Helga. I'll soon be home.' He slammed down the receiver. 'I've got to dash. My wife needs me. See you tomorrow, Nick. Bye, Frannie.' With that, he was gone.

Outside the air was cool and fresh on her cheeks. Fran turned to Nick. 'Thank you for a lovely evening,' she said politely, holding out her hand. Surprisingly, his hand was warm and firm in hers and he held it a fraction longer than was necessary. She turned to walk away and he was suddenly by her side.

'I'll walk you to your hotel.'

It wasn't far, but it was nice to have company. He's a strange man, she thought. He blows hot and cold in the same minute.

After the dim gaslights of the pub, the street lights shone bright, twinkling beneath a jet-black sky. A gentle breeze scented the air with the perfume of almond blossom.

They strolled along in silence. Fran's thoughts were on tomorrow and Michael.

Chapter Thirteen

'Michael!' Isabel shouted up the stairs. 'Are you up yet?' There was no answer. Already the day was off to a bad start. Isabel stomped up the stairs. Hearing a loose floorboard creak, she stopped at the turn of the small landing and his bedroom door opened.

Clad only in his pyjama bottoms, he slouched from his room. The very act of movement made him feel dizzy. He'd celebrated his birthday last night with Joe and his fun girl. That birthday drink Joe had given him was mighty strong, a mix of beer and cider or stout, he wasn't sure which. He wasn't used to alcohol and he shouldn't have drunk so much. His mother would kill him. And now she had this meal thing arranged. A lot of fuss over an aunt he didn't really know. He clung to the banister, his head spinning as he looked down upon Isabel's angry face. 'I'm up.'

'About time. Now get bathed while I'll make you a strong coffee.'

He groaned. He hated that horrible Camp coffee drink.

He felt slightly better after his bath, but his head still thumped. In the kitchen, he found his mother busy making sandwiches for his grandfather's dinner. The thought of a heavy, hot dinner made his insides heave and he wished he could stay at home with Grandad. He didn't want to spend his birthday having to make polite conversation to a boring old aunt in some stuffy hotel.

As he slumped in the nearest chair at the kitchen table, his mother placed a cup of steaming dark brown liquid in front of him. The smell of the coffee nauseated him and his head throbbed even more. 'Mam, have you anything for my headache?'

'That Joe Miller is a bad influence on you, making you drink. You're underage,' she fumed. 'If the police find out and you get a criminal record, they won't let you into Australia.'

He was a fool. He didn't want to jeopardise his going to Australia. It was a dream adventure and he wanted nothing to stop him from going.

'Here.' Isabel thrust two aspirins and a glass of water at Michael, standing over him while he swallowed the pills.

He looked sheepishly at her, saying, 'Sorry, Mam. I won't do it again.'

Her set face relaxed a little. 'Good. Now go and have another bath and this time make it a *cold* one. You have one hour to pull yourself together.'

'Mam, can't I stay at home with Grandad?' he pleaded.

'No,' she yelled at him, but wishing with all her heart he could. But she knew if he didn't put in an appearance at the hotel, Frances would seek him out. And if that happened, she didn't want to think of the consequences, of what Frances would say.

Then Will bellowed, 'Why can't our Frances come here? Save all this ruddy fuss.'

Throwing up her hands in exasperation, Isabel snapped. 'Well, no one's asking you.' She rounded on her son, pointing to the door leading to the staircase. 'Michael.'

'I'm going,' he said, scraping back his chair on the tiled floor. He was glad to escape from his mother, if only for a short time. The only thing that was going to make this meal bearable for him was that Shirley was invited. Maybe they would be able to sneak away early.

Fran checked her appearance in the wardrobe mirror, wanting to look her best. She had saved up for this lovely dress of aquamarine silk with a matching jacket, a pair of sheer nylon stockings and a pair of elegant black suede court shoes. Her blonde hair was fresh and shining in a page-boy style, her make-up light, but her lips bold in rose-pink. She clipped on a pair of pearl earrings. What would Michael think of her? She wanted to create a good impression for her son. No one else mattered. One last look and she was ready to see Michael.

As she walked down the hotel corridor, her heart sang and her whole being burst with happiness. She sat in the front lounge of the hotel, where she had a good view of people entering and she could look through the window to the street outside. She wanted to see Michael before he saw her. Her stomach knotted and tightened, and she held her breath, waiting for this strange sensation to pass. As she did so, Fran considered how she was to greet Michael when he arrived. She wanted to fling her arms around him, hug him close. She flicked her gaze from the doorway to the window and glanced at the passing people, hoping to see Michael. But she only saw a man pushing a woman in a wheelchair. They stopped and the man leant forward to strike a match, holding the flame to the woman's cigarette. She watched as the woman inhaled deeply and the man turned to look across at the hotel. It was Rufus.

Turning her attention back to the lounge door, her heart gave a leap. He was there. Her son. So handsome and smartly dressed in grey trousers, white shirt and a navy blazer. He was taller than Isabel, with dark, thick lustrous hair, warm skin colour and the deepest blue eyes. Her eyes. She felt her insides contract like labour pains. She was on her feet, her arms instinctively began to rise in a gesture to hug him, hold him. *My son, my son*, her inner voice exploded. Did he know who she was? He smiled at her and it was if a great pool of light surrounded them both. Then a dark shadow appeared.

'Michael, this is your Aunt Frances, my sister.' Isabel's voice was polite, but cold. She stood close to Michael, a protective arm about his shoulder.

Mentally shaking herself, Fran extended her hand. Michael's handshake was quick, barely touching hers. Something was missing. This was the moment she had waited for, her reunion with her son. '*I'm your mother*,' her inner voice cried. '*My son, I love you.*' The ache of holding back, the tears threatening to choke her, she felt as though the air was being pumped from her lungs. She fought to control her emotions and her facial muscles pinched and nipped as she tried to smile. She looked searchingly at him, willing him to know who she really was, but his attention was already diverted. Fran followed his gaze, watching his eyes light up and saw a long-legged girl about the same age as him. In that instant, Fran experienced a pang of jealousy for that is how she wanted her son to look at her: with a sign of recognition and affection. She watched the girl swing towards Michael, the skirt of her pretty green floral dress dancing around her in a carefree movement. Her brown eyes were laughing and her shining nut-brown hair hung loose about her shoulders. They greeted with a hug.

Isabel said something. Fran half turned. 'Sorry, what did you say?'

'My friend, Deirdre Baker, and her husband, Henry, are joining us for lunch and their daughter, Shirley.' She indicated the girl with Michael and the couple following behind.

After the formal introductions, they had a pre-luncheon drink in the lounge before moving into the dining room. Fran only half listened to the exchange of conversation between Isabel and Deirdre, her attention centred on Michael, sitting opposite her. He and Shirley chatted about pop songs and she caught the names of Elvis and Cliff and names which didn't mean anything to her. Feeling left out, an outsider, Fran looked down at her napkin lying, snowing white, on her lap. This was not how she envisaged her reunion with her son. This was to be their most precious moment. She did, in fact, feel like an old maiden aunt, taken out for an airing, dusted and then to be put back in the china cabinet. '*Consider this*,' said her inner voice. '*Have you been fantasising about Michael all these years?*' She argued back. '*He is my son.*'

Michael laughed at something Shirley said to him. It was an intimate laugh, which excluded Fran even further. A heated anger welled up inside her and the words began to form, to blurt out the truth of his birth. Then she caught Deirdre's eye. The woman smiled at her and the moment was lost. The waiter came to serve their meal, traditional roast beef and Yorkshire pudding.

'Will you pass me the horseradish sauce, Frances,' said Henry, who wasn't much of a conversationalist. He'd rather be at home reading the Sunday papers and smoking his pipe. But, even those few words, helped her to act normally. Then, everyone chatted about the food, the weather, fashions and football. Isabel fussed over the wine.

'We must have Australian wine,' she told the waiter.

'Are you going to help run the business?' Fran asked, as if she was talking to a relative stranger, as she supposed she was, because

Fran had no sisterly feelings towards Isabel and she knew for a fact that Isabel felt the same towards her.

Isabel turned a frosty gaze on Fran. 'Good heavens, no,' she replied in horror. 'John doesn't expect me to work. He's a man of wealth,' she said, beaming with satisfaction.

Fran just nodded. She could see why Isabel was eager to go to Australia and marry John. But there was no reason why she couldn't leave Michael behind. She leant across the table towards Michael. 'What about you, Michael, have you decided what you want to do?' The words tumbled from her mouth before she had time to stop them.

Michael glanced furtively at Isabel, who was talking to Deirdre, and then he turned his attention back to Fran. His voice was strong, enthusiastic. 'When I get to Australia, I'm going to go to college and then on to university.'

Isabel, who was half listening to the conversation, gasped in astonishment. 'University! You never said anything to me.'

Michael speared a roast potato with his fork. 'I've being thinking about it.'

'Sounds an excellent idea,' Fran heard herself say.

Michael shot an appreciative glance at Fran. 'John thinks it is a good idea.'

'You've discussed it with John?'

'Well, sort of. He asked me what I would like to do once we get to Australia.'

Something flashed across Isabel's face as if she had just remembered something. She put a protective arm about Michael's shoulder, smiled sweetly at him and said, 'If that is what you want, my darling boy, so be it.'

Fran looked in disbelief at her sister. When had she and Isabel ever agreed about anything? For them both to agree, in principle, on Michael's future education was quite something. Fran had to admit that she felt happy about the outcome of her question, although she wished he wasn't so set on Australia. She glanced down at her handbag, resting against the leg of her chair and the white envelope protruding from it.

The waiter came to the table to take their order for pudding. 'Excuse me a moment,' Fran said, rising to her feet. She went through into reception and collected the small parcels she had left there earlier. Returning to the table, she handed them both to Isabel. 'There's tobacco for father and chocolates for you.'

Startle by the gesture, Isabel exclaimed, 'A present for me?'

'They're Terry's best. You are lucky,' Deirdre said admiringly and thought this sister wasn't as bad as Isabel had suggested.

'Thank you,' Isabel managed to say. 'But you shouldn't have bothered.'

Fran sat down feeling slightly giddy. She reached down and extracted the envelope from her handbag. Her heartbeat quickened. She spoke her son's name, 'Michael.'

He stopped talking to Shirley and looked across the table at her. She had his full attention and she smiled at him. 'Michael, this is a gift for your sixteenth birthday. In view of your intention to further your education, I hope you will find it useful.' All the time she spoke, she kept her eyes fixed on his face and he on hers. This was their moment. Taken by surprise, he took the envelope from her outstretched hand and stared at it. 'Open it,' she urged.

He ripped it open and slowly extracted the cheque. He seemed to take for ever studying it, then, 'Wow!' He jumped to his feet and, in his haste, he nearly knocked Shirley off her chair as he came round to Fran's side and kissed her on the cheek. It was a beautiful kiss from a son to his mother. Then he went back to his chair and flopped down. 'Wow!' he uttered again.

Isabel, not believing what had just happened, snatched the cheque from his hands. 'A hundred pounds,' she shrieked, forgetting where she was. Diners nearby looked towards their table.

'Isabel,' said Deirdre, persuasively.

But Isabel was not to be quietened. 'Too much. Far too much,' she snapped.

Fran looked Isabel full in the face and said firmly, 'Under the circumstances, I think the sum is quite in order.' She had intended to give Michael two hundred pounds, but that might have seemed over the top. She could always give him another hundred later.

'What circumstances?' asked Michael, looking puzzled.

Isabel shot Fran a don't-you-dare-tell look of pure hate.

It took all of Fran's self-will not to say, '*Because you are my son.*' But, in her heart, as much as she wanted to say it, she knew now wasn't the right time. Instead, she said in a tone of exaggerated brightness. 'Because I haven't been around for your previous birthdays and this one is very special. The money will help to afford you independence.' She couldn't bring herself to mention Australia. Her hope was that now John was home in his own country, he might be having misgivings about taking on a wife and a sixteen-year-old youth.

Michael smiled, accepting her explanation. 'It's great. I've never had so much money.'

Isabel sat stony-faced. Ignoring her, Fran sat back in her chair to drink in Michael's state of jubilation as he showed the cheque to Shirley. When he flashed big smiles of appreciation at Fran, she experienced a wonderful feeling of euphoria.

As if in a trance, she reached once more into her handbag and drew out a small box camera, bought second-hand from Mr Jones's Emporium in York. 'Michael.' He looked across at her and gave her a most breathtaking smile and she clicked away in fast succession, capturing the wonderful moment.

Chapter Fourteen

Wanting to re-enforce her 'I'm in charge' attitude, Isabel rose swiftly from the table, saying, 'We will have coffee in the lounge.'

'Good idea,' responded Deirdre, a look of relief on her face at this restoration to normal.

Michael interjected, 'Mam, is it all right if Shirley and I skip coffee? We fancy a walk on the Westwood.'

Isabel was just about to tell Michael it was bad manners to leave so early, when it occurred to her that here was a chance to get Michael away from Frances. 'Off you go then,' she said sweetly. 'Michael, say goodbye to your aunt.'

'Bye, Aunt Frances. And thanks.' He patted the breast pocket of his shirt.

'Take care,' she said brightly, wondering when next she would see him. Watching him over dinner had been a weird and yet a wonderful sensation of mixed emotions. All she could think of was when Michael was a babe in her arms and how she loved him so. Now he was tall and strong, no longer a child but on the first step to adulthood, and she was a stranger on the periphery of his life, she who had given birth to him. Much as she wanted to blurt out to him that she was his true mother, she couldn't. She now realised the best way forward was to build up a relationship with him, no matter how tentative. And, she thought wishfully, Australia might not yet materialise. After all, John had returned to his homeland and, who knows, maybe he might reconsider on the wisdom of his proposal of marriage to Isabel. She watched Michael leave with Shirley, two young people happy in each other's company. Would they want to be parted?

She followed the others through into the lounge and, despite the stuffy atmosphere of the room, a chill of unreality swept through her body. Over the years, she'd longed for this reunion with her son, but the years gone could not be ignored. They were his formative years, and she had played no part in them. How foolish and naive she had been to believe Agnes!

Fran sat down next to Henry. Isabel served coffee and Deirdre chatted about people in Beverley, but Fran didn't recognise any of the names. She had been away from her home town far too long. She took a sip of coffee and felt nauseated. She needed fresh air. Making a quick decision, she rose abruptly, addressing Isabel. 'I'm going to see Father.'

Isabel frowned. 'I thought we were going to discuss you coming to care for Father now?' Fran wanted to tell her to go to hell. Instead she kept her lips tightly pressed together.

Deirdre, a born arbitrator, laid a light hand on Isabel's arm. Her voice was firm. 'You can both discuss your father's arrangements later.'

Still peeved, Isabel blustered, 'You surely don't expect Henry to take you in his car?'

Deirdre leant across the table and rattled the newspaper Henry had immersed himself in. 'Darling, will you go to reception and call a taxi for Frances, please?'

'Well,' said Isabel, as Fran gathered her handbag and slipped on her coat. 'You must be prepared for a change in Father. Since mother's death he's become rather withdrawn. Michael's the only one to get any sense from him.'

'Michael,' Fran whispered his name, thinking as always of the baby she once held. Aloud, she said, 'He's grown into a lovely young man.'

Isabel's face softened as she said, 'He's my life.'

Fran stared at Isabel, and then, without a word, she turned and walked away.

Fran alighted from the taxi at the beginning of the lane. She needed a little more time to gather her composure before she saw her father. Her mind and heart were still full of Michael as she recalled every detail of her meeting with him. She wanted to savour every precious second spent in his company, not to forget a single movement, a single word, a single touch. She wanted to remember everything, especially her first sight of her tall, handsome son, the way he moved so easily on his long limbs, the way he laughed, a soft throaty chuckle. She touched her cheek, still feeling his kiss. No kiss had ever been sweeter. Then, a shadow clouded her face. Would she see him again before he sailed away to that distant land? Why couldn't Isabel marry a Frenchman or a Spaniard? Then she could casually have dropped by, on holiday or on business. But, Australia!

Her heart ached and how she longed to tell Michael that she, not Isabel was his mother. Then, common sense told her to think of Michael's future and consider what was best for him, but her heart twisted this way and that, and the turmoil within intensified. She trudged down the lane, thinking of anything to take her mind off her state of unhappiness. The lane seemed narrower than she remembered, hedgerows were overgrown, though they were full of birds as they foraged for food. Her high-heeled court shoes clicked rhythmically on the tarmac surface of the footpath. She stopped to shake a stone from her shoe and, resting her hand on a bar gate, glanced to the field where a crop of rapeseed, raw green, was beginning to sprout.

She reached Bloomsbury's old house, a wispy spiral of smoke curling up from the chimney. Who lived there now? Vanessa had been her classmate and friend, but there had been no contact between the two since Fran had fallen pregnant and was sent away. She suddenly thought of her first love, Charlie Moxon, who had ditched her for another. Sadly, he had been killed in action, as were many others from the area. She walked on, spying in the thicket of hedge a clump of wild primroses their tiny, pale gold faces upturned, shining brightly, their fragrance sweet. The sight of these fragile flowers uplifted her heart. She marvelled at nature's amazing power to produce such beauty amongst wild nettles and scrub land. As if not to be out done, a blackbird perched high in a tree suddenly burst into song. She reached the Anchor Inn and from the open doorway she caught the hub of men's voices, the shuffle of dominos and the smell of tobacco. Nothing much had changed. She remembered her father used to relax here after his Sunday dinner.

She climbed the grass bank and caught her first glimpse of the river. Its sparkling water was awash with silver dancing lights as the sun appeared from behind a cloud. Unexpectedly, her whole body surged with delight. How she'd missed this river. She inhaled its tangy freshness. She slipped under the rail of one of the empty landing stages, the moorings now geared for pleasure crafts, not working barges as she remembered from her childhood. The swish of the river lapped the bank, stirring reeds and grasses, sending a family of ducks skittering further upstream. She felt the pale warmth of the sun on her face as she walked the path along the bank. She rounded the bend in the river and there it was her childhood home! Immediately, she was struck by its isolation. It was reached only by the river or the single-track lane.

High Bank House in the hamlet of Burton Banks was situated on the eastern boundary of Beverley. It was built in 1914 by a local businessman for a son who never returned from the Great War. Since then, it had been in her father's family. Once, the joinery yard had been full of timber, stretching down to the river. Now everything was still, quiet, deserted. The landing stage, once heaving with workers, loading and unloading the barges with timber, now lay broken and partly submerged. She climbed down the bank to the lane leading to the front of the house, which faced away from the river. As she approached, the house seemed to groan with neglect. A broken branch of a willow tree brushed across the red brick facade, paint flaked from the dry sash window frames and the baked, brown front door. Once, it had been a fine house and her mother had cared for it. *More than she cared for me*, Fran thought. But in spite of her past unhappiness, there had been some carefree days of innocent youth spent there: lazy days on the riverbank with Vanessa, picnicking on chunks of homemade bread and blackcurrant jam, washed down by cider they were not supposed to drink, and Fran couldn't resist a smile at this memory. She opened the white picket gate of the front garden and the rusting sneck came away in her hands. She trod her way carefully through the tangled weeds of what, once, was her mother's immaculate flower garden and around to the back of the house.

Quietly, she let herself into the porch and found an old cloth to wipe mud and grass from her shoes. A small window looked through into the kitchen and she saw her father dozing in a chair. She was shocked to see how frail and old he looked. Isabel had given her mild warning, but Fran had given no thought to it, for her heart and mind were so full of Michael. Now, she felt pity for her father, whom she'd always pictured as robust and healthy, and she wondered if he'd suffered another stroke. Bracing herself, she tapped lightly on the door and then entered the kitchen-cum-sitting room.

Will Bewholme stirred in his armchair in front of the fire as the draught from the opening door touched his legs. He twisted awkwardly in his chair, seeing only an outline of a figure or was it two? 'Michael?'

Her heart quickening as he called the name, she hurried to his side. 'It's me, Dad. It's Fran.' She heard his knees creak as he placed swollen knuckled hands on the arms of his chair in an effort to raise himself to look at her.

His face drawn, lips papery, he sneered, 'You took your time coming.'

'Dad!' Stunned for a few seconds, she backed away. His attitude was so unexpected that she didn't know how to respond. Perhaps she had disturbed his sleep and he wasn't properly awake yet. She turned away, saying, 'I could do with a cup of tea, I expect you could as well.' He didn't answer. Enveloped in a strangeness that seemed like a time warp, Fran busied herself. While waiting for the kettle to boil, she looked round the room. Nothing much had changed and it was still her mother's kitchen, with the same green-and-cream-painted walls, the pine dresser and the scrubbed, wooden table. The only thing missing was the old cooking range that only her mother had known how to control. In its place was an electric cooker. She was surprised, though, thinking Isabel, who always had such big ideas, would have modernised the kitchen to her taste. But, for some reason she wasn't sure of, she was glad Isabel hadn't. She found a dusty tray slotted between the dresser and the wall, cleaned it and then set out cups and saucers, a jug of milk, the brown earthenware teapot and a plate of digestive biscuits. She carried the tray over to Will's side table.

She wished she had brought his gift of tobacco with her because it would have given them something to talk about. Pulling up a chair to the other side of the table she sat down and poured out the tea. Handing him a cup, she enquired, 'How are you keeping?'

His big rheumy eyes looked with contempt at her as if to say, 'what a daft question'. And she knew it was. 'Have a biscuit, Dad.' She proffered the plate. He took one and munched. She looked into the fire, fixing her eyes on the bright red glow, which sent out tiny blue flames.

'When are you coming back?' Will ask brusquely.

Resigned to his silence, Fran was surprised to hear his voice and looked up. 'Isabel will be back soon and we are going to discuss the situation.'

'So, I'm a situation, am I?' he flared.

'Of course not, but I live and work in York so it's a big decision to make.' The truth was she hadn't given the care of her father any thought. She didn't want Michael to go to Australia. Then, it struck her, if she came back to care for her father, would Michael stay?

'Well, don't bother about me. I've not long for this world,' Will said, banging his cup down on the saucer. 'You'll be old yourself one day and see then if anyone wants you.'

'Dad! Don't talk like that. You don't have to be old to be on your own and lonely. I've had years of being shut out from this family.'

'That's your own fault for not keeping Michael, then she wouldn't be carting him off to bloody foreign parts.' His eyes filled with tears. 'I love that boy. He's the son I never had.'

Fran knelt by his side. She had never seen her father cry before, not even at her mother's funeral. Shocked, she pleaded, 'Dad, please don't distress yourself. We will work something out. Michael won't stay in Australia for ever.' She wanted to believe that too. 'I'll miss him just as much as you will. While he was here, I knew he was safe. But Australia . . .' Tears welled in her eyes but she forced herself to be cheerful, 'We're a right pair. Let's look on the bright side. It's an opportunity for him not to miss and he will be broadening his horizons, extending his education. He seems happy to be going . . .' Her voice trailed off.

Will sniffed back his tears and reached for Fran's hand. 'I'm sorry, lass. I'm just a selfish old man. But, I'll miss him!'

Gently, Fran squeezed his hand in hers, saying. 'Let's have another cup of tea.' Will nodded, leaning back in his chair. They sat in awkward silence. Fran thought she must talk to Isabel about their father's health. If she came to care for Will, how would they spend their time? Bickering or what? Her thoughts had been so full of Michael that she had given no thought actually to coming to live permanently at High Bank. Was it such a good idea to return to her roots and to care for an aged parent?

'*Oh, Michael!*' she whispered silently. '*If only it was you I was coming to care for. I would gladly come.*' She fought back tears, the lump in her throat making her cough. Taking a gulp of the tepid tea, she tried to think rationally instead of emotionally, but couldn't quite manage it. Should she tell Michael that she was his mother, not Isabel? Would he welcome her with open arms? Or would he hate her? What a mess! She didn't want to ruin his life, his chance and his future in Australia. Though did he have a future there? She didn't know anything about John Stanway, only what Isabel had said. But was she telling the truth? Fran wanted what was best for him, but why did it have to be with Isabel! Only now, with hindsight, did she realise she should have come back sooner and taken responsibility for Michael's life, to be part of his future, then he wouldn't be going off to the other side of the world. But she was determined he would learn the truth of his origins sooner rather than later. He would then be free to make his own decisions on his future. Fran heard the sound of the outside door unlatching. Isabel! Sighing, she fumbled under the chair for her shoes that she had kicked off earlier. Could she face living in a house that held such unpleasant memories? And Will, did she want to share her life with him?

The kitchen door opened, she rose to her feet and turned to face Isabel. But when she saw who was standing there, she swayed, almost falling backwards and a cry issuing from her lips.

Chapter Fifteen

Stunned by Michael's unexpected appearance, Fran was unable to respond to his greeting. She was only aware of Michael's dominating presence in the room.

He laughed at her startled expression. 'Aunt Frances, I'm not that bad. Am I, Shirley?'

Fran had been oblivious of Shirley's presence. Swiftly regaining her composure, and welcoming this unexpected pleasure, Fran smiled warmly at them both. Her dearest wish to see Michael again had come true and here she was behaving like a shy, tongue-tied child.

Shirley slipped her hand into Michael's, her eyes full of adoration. 'You're ace. Look,' she enthused, pulling a packet of her favourite jellybeans from her coat pocket. 'Mike's treat.' Letting go of his hand, she proffered the sweets to Fran.

Fran looked from Michael to Shirley and, laughing, she delved into the cone twisted white paper bag; she came up with a bright yellow jellybean. 'Thank you,' was all she could manage to say.

Will, not to be left out, demanded, in an amazingly strong voice, 'What about me?'

Shirley sauntered over to him. 'How are you, Mr Bewholme?' She bent down and kissed him on the cheek and rattled the sweets under his nose.

Will beamed at these two lively young people and Fran felt moved by the glowing transformation in him. The presence of Michael and Shirley changed the dull grey atmosphere to a vibrant, brilliant vermilion red, filling the room with warm vibes of pleasure. An experience to treasure, Fran thought, longing to hug Michael, but instead she fussed, 'Would you like tea?'

'It's okay, we'll have ginger beer,' Michael replied, striding over to the pantry. He came back with two glasses brimming and handed one to Shirley, and then he pulled up two kitchen chairs, forming a semi-circle: Shirley next to Will and Michael next to Fran.

As if in a trance, Fran handed round the biscuits, still unable to believe that Michael was sitting next to her. Her mind bubbled with joy. *This is my son!* How she wished she could say the words out loud. To tell him how she held him in her arms when he was just a few hours old. Now, though, it was hard for her to envisage. From such a tiny baby he'd grown into this tall, wonderful young man. There was so much she wanted to know about him. What was his taste in music? Did he play any sport or support football? What were his favourite books? She looked down at his feet, guessing he must be a size nine or ten. She knew he had a good appetite by the amount he'd eaten at dinner. And, she knew he wanted to undertake further education. When she'd written the cheque for him, she had no preconceived idea of what he would use it for and education was a bonus. No matter what Isabel said or did, Fran would have a part in his life, an important part: his education, the key to his future success. Proudly, she allowed herself the luxury of feasting her eyes upon her son.

Will was saying to Shirley, 'What do you think to our Michael gallivanting off to the other side of the world?'

Shirley, young, full of confidence, replied, 'We're going to keep in touch by letter, Mr Bewholme. After we've finished our education, we've promised to meet up and travel round Australia.' She gazed into Michael's eyes. He, full of admiration for the positive way in which she was taking his departure, kissed her full on the lips.

'Ah, you young ones, you have it all planned,' remarked Will, wistfully. Then he glared at Fran. 'Not like you. If you hadn't made a mess of things, Michael wouldn't be going away.'

Fran's body stilled. She felt the colour drain from her face at her father's harsh words. Michael and Shirley looked at her, unable to conceal their bewilderment at Will's outburst.

To cover her dread of what he might say next, she jumped up, collecting the empty tea cups, saying the first thing that came into her head. 'Don't be silly, Dad. Isabel is entitled to her happiness.' Whisking the tray across to the draining board, she leant against the stone sink to support her trembling body. Bleakly, she stared out of the window. How could he say such a hurtful thing? To be so insensitive in front of Michael, she just didn't understand her father's attitude. This was not how she remembered him. She didn't want to spend his remaining years at loggerheads with him, making them both unhappy. Isabel seemed to think Will wanted her to return, but Fran suspected her sister just needed to clear her conscience.

Her life was in limbo, and she was at a crossroad and wasn't certain which direction to travel. Not that she had many choices: Burton Banks or York. Then, a voice deep within her answered, '*You wanted a husband and children.*' A buried dream overshadowed by the fear of being in another wrong relationship. This fear she found more difficult with each passing year to shake off. As self-pity threatened to swamp her, she busied herself with the washing up.

Behind her, she heard the scrape of a chair and footsteps leaving the room. Instinctively, she knew they were Michael's. Enjoy these precious moments with him, she told herself.

His footsteps returned. 'Aunt Frances.' Her heart contracted at the sound of his voice and wished with all her heart that he was calling her 'Mother'. 'Come and look at these photos of Shirley and me in our school play.'

Turning, she smiled brightly at Michael and accepted the photos from him. What play it was she wasn't sure because her vision blurred, with threatening tears.

'That's me as a fairy, would you believe.' Shirley laughed, showing a photo to Will.

'Aunt Frances . . .'

Michael's hand rested on her arm, radiating warmth through her whole body. She could smell his freshness, breathe in his nearness, this young man to whom she had given life.

'Grandad's upset because Mam and I are going to Australia. He's not upset with you.'

She looked up into his concerned face. That touched her more than anything, to think he cared that she was upset by Will's harsh words. She nodded, not trusting herself to speak. But she knew her father blamed her because he believed it was her fault Michael was going to Australia. Will was right. If only she had been strong and fought to keep Michael.

But Agnes Bewholme had been a formidable woman and, after the birth of the twins and her grief when told her baby daughter had died, Fran had been very ill. Agnes had taken charge of Michael, which seemed helpful at the time. It had been six long months before she had felt fit enough to travel to Burton Banks, only find it was too late. Though the telephone calls she made to her mother asking about Michael should have warned her. 'Our Isabel is a natural mother.' And Fran thought Isabel was being a caring sister!

How could she forget that fateful September day? Desperate to see her baby son, she arrived back at her parent's home unannounced and found herself in the middle of Michael's christening party. Isabel was holding the baby with Agnes and Will, posing for photos for the family album, relations and friends looking on. She had screamed some incoherent words and, dashing up the stairs to the bathroom, had been violently sick.

Her mother followed, demanding, 'What are you doing here?'

Holding a damp flannel to her face, Fran retorted angrily. 'I've come to see my baby.'

'Don't you think you've done enough damage? Our Isabel is a fine mother. There's no place for you here.' She gripped hold of Fran's arm, pushing her. 'Now get yourself into my bedroom and stay there until the guests have gone, then you'll get on the first train back.'

Speechless, Fran stared at her mother, unable to believe what she heard. Then she managed to whisper, 'He's my baby.'

'You're not a fit person to care for the baby,' Agnes hissed, closing the door firmly behind her.

Slumping down on the bed, Fran sobbed with frustration and exhaustion. After a while, her tears spent, she slid off the bed and tiptoed onto the landing. Leaning over the bannister, listening to the voices below behind the closed front room door, she heard the faint cry of her baby. Hurriedly, she descended the stairs, her arms aching to hold her son, when a woman appeared. Seeing Fran, she called, 'Agnes!' Fran fled back upstairs . . .

'Aunt Frances.' Michael's voice jerked her back to the present. 'I've told Grandad I'll write to him, but his eyes aren't too good. Will you read my letters to him?'

She stared at Michael, not able to take in what he was saying. Before she could answer, her father's broke in. 'Please, Fran,' he begged. Will's eyes filled with unashamed tears.

'Dad,' she cried, hurrying to kneel by his side. She took hold of his trembling hands. 'Of course I will. Do you really want me to come home and look after you?'

Will nodded, his eyes never leaving her face.

'Grandad, I told you she would,' Michael said with confidence.

Shirley, tired of family emotions, said, 'Mike, want to walk me home?'

'Sure.' He stretched his long frame. 'See you later, Grandad. Aunt Frances, thanks.'

And Michael was gone.

'Australia,' Will muttered, 'I might never see him again.'

And nor will I, Fran thought. To be reunited with her son, then to lose him again was too much for her to bear. She started to sob, unleashing the years of suppressed emotions, hidden so deep within her.

Will stroked his daughter's hair, like he had when she was a child. 'Shush, it will be all right, love,' he soothed. But his caring words and gentle action made her cry even more.

After a while, when her tears subsided, she drew away from Will, saying, 'I'd better go and tidy myself up before Isabel comes or she will think I'm not capable of looking after you.'

The staircase was dark, but she didn't put on the light. She knew every inch of the treads and the fourth one up still creaked. The bathroom was as she remembered it, green-painted walls and the hard-water stains where the bath taps dripped. Leaning over the washbasin, she stared in the mirror, aghast at her blotchy, red face. But a quick freshen-up, a retouch of her make-up and her appearance was passable.

On the landing, she glanced to one of the open doors of a bedroom. Could it be Michael's? She tiptoed along the landing and stood on the threshold of the open door. Her eyes glazed over and her mind surged with hope. As her eyes focused, she saw that it could only be his room. She didn't enter, but stood there soaking up the atmosphere. Having no knowledge of teenager boys' rooms, except what she'd seen at the pictures, it was as untidy as she imagined it to be. Books lay scattered on the floor amidst cast-off clothing, the dried remains of a sandwich, posters of footballers adorned the walls and a whiff of aftershave reached her nostrils. She smiled. This was no ordinary room; this was a very special room. It was her son's room. For a long time, she stood, content to gaze, not intruding, but absorbing her son. Then, the sound of a car crunching to a halt in the yard below broke her reverie. Isabel.

One last look, then Fran turned away.

Chapter Sixteen

'Hello, Mike,' Tina called from a shop doorway in Market Place where she stood sheltering from the steady drizzle of rain.

Mike swung round, his face breaking into a smile when he saw her. 'Been stood up?'

'Joe said he might be late. Time for a coffee?' Her heart gave a queer lurch. Did she fancy Mike? She wasn't sure, but there was something about him that she couldn't quite fathom.

'Sure, I'm in no hurry.' The rich timbres of his voice were welcoming on this grey evening.

They walked a few yards to the cafe opposite the Market Cross that catered for the younger people, especially after six in the evenings and at weekends. Tina found a seat near the window where she could look out for Joe. Mike brought two steaming cups of coffee. She sipped the hot, tasty, frothy liquid, savouring it as it slipped down her throat and warmed her insides. 'That's good,' she said and, not wanting to waste a drop, ran her tongue along her lips, licking the froth from round her mouth. She gave a sigh of satisfaction and put down her cup, giving Mike her full attention. 'What's new?' she asked.

Mike eyed her over the top of his cup, put it down and leant back on his chair, stretching out his long legs. His voice was conspiratorial. 'I've just discovered this marvellous aunt who's given me a cheque for a hundred pounds.'

She grinned sardonically at him. 'You're making it up.'

'No kidding. It's true. She's my mother's sister and I've never seen her before.'

'How come, so why would she give you all that money?'

He shrugged. 'She said it was for my sixteenth birthday.'

'Is she about to pop her clogs?'

He dodged Tina's playful swipe. 'She's a lot younger than Mam.'

'You'd better introduce me. Say I'm a long-lost relation and she might take pity on me.' They both laughed.

Then Michael said, 'Seriously, I can introduce you to her. She's coming to take care of Grandad, and I don't think she has any friends here and you haven't got any family.'

Tina sat up straight on her chair and said hotly, 'I've got Joe and Nancy.' She wanted to yell, *and I've got a mother somewhere who doesn't want me.*

'Sorry, I didn't mean to upset you.' Michael pulled his chair round to Tina's and gave her an affectionate hug. 'It's just that . . .' His voice trailed, not sure what the right words would be. Then he knew. 'It's just that I care about you. And we're friends.' He hugged her again.

Tina felt the rapid beat of his heart through his bomber jacket and instinctively she drew closer to him, loving the nearness of his body to hers. Somehow it felt right. She slid her arm around his neck and kissed his cheek, feeling sharp stubble, which sent tingling sensations through her body. She let her leg rub against his, wishing . . . Suddenly, all too soon he moved away from

152

her. She lifted her head to look at him and saw he was waving to someone through the window. She glanced out and saw Joe.

Later, as Tina let herself into Nancy's warm, cosy kitchen, a delicious whiff of something baking in the oven greeted her. Tears welled up in her eyes again, a lump stuck in her throat. From the sitting room she heard Nancy give an answer to a question from one of her favourite wireless programmes, Wilfred Pickles' 'Have a Go'. Tina poked her head round the door. 'It's only me,' she said, her voice husky with emotion.

She was just about to disappear upstairs, when Nancy called, 'Tina.' Nancy was on her feet, standing in the doorway studying Tina. 'You look done in, lass.'

Tina's response was to burst into tears. As Nancy cradled her in her arms, Tina sobbed out her story. She and Joe had a row, all about nothing and of her search, or lack of it, for her birth mother, but she didn't mention the funny gut feeling for Mike. She didn't understand it and would find it difficult to explain, and what was the point when he would be so far away and out of her life? She was going to miss him though. Her sobbing intensified and Nancy's arms held her closer.

Later, sitting at the kitchen table, Tina drank hot, sweet tea with a liberal dash of whisky. She felt calmer but a little foolish for crying like a baby.

But Nancy was a great comforter. 'Lass, you've had a lot to contend with in your young life. Emotions can play funny tricks. I'll make you an appointment to see the doctor.'

'I haven't got a doctor.'

'You can register with mine. Losing your mam and coping on your own, you're a marvel. But everybody needs help sometimes.

As for young Joe, invite him for a meal at the weekend and I'll give him the third degree.' She smiled and said, 'Now, I'll tell you my good news. I've got myself another little job, starting next week so I can save a bit extra for my retirement. It's with a nice old gent, some kind of family mix-up.'

'I'm pleased for you,' Tina said. And then, from nowhere, the face of Maggie flashed through her mind and she remembered how hard she'd worked. If only she'd helped her more, Maggie might still be alive. 'Nancy, promise me you won't overdo it.'

Nancy laughed and said reassuringly, 'Don't you fret, lass, I'm fit and I like a challenge.' Then a mischievous twinkle came into her eyes. 'If it gets too much for me, I can always take you along for backup.'

'I'll hold you to that, Nancy Davis,' Tina replied, seriously.

Two days later, Tina left work early so that she could go home, have a bath and change her clothes before her doctor's appointment. Apparently, new patients can have a full medical examination. At first she wasn't sure about this, but Nancy said it was a good thing. Nancy gave Tina the most direct route to the surgery, but somehow she took a wrong turning and ended up down a narrow street called Dog and Duck Lane. If she was going to stay in this town, she'd better find her way around, she told herself, firmly. Standing for a moment, she breathed in the cooling air of early evening, catching the smell of dampness, of threatening rain. The sooner she had this medical, the quicker she would be home having her meal.

The surgery reception area was filled with bright lights, but the waiting room was empty, except for a couple standing at the desk giving the receptionist some details. Tina glanced around, she wasn't looking forward to being examined, being prodded. But Nancy said the lady doctor was very nice. The receptionist, still busy, didn't acknowledge Tina's presence. The couple started to move away, but then stopped to ask another question. Tina could see the agitation of colour rising from the receptionist's neck to her face. It was then that the receptionist looked up and fixed her with a frosty glare. Pressing her lips together to suppress a giggle, Tina lowered her gaze, fixing it on the woman's name badge.

Then, the floor came up to meet her. The lights of the room seemed to flash and dim in rapid succession. Her eyes refused to focus, but she forced them to read the receptionist's name again. *Isabel Renton, Isabel Renton, Isabel Renton.* The name echoed in her mind, reverberating through her whole body. Who was this woman? Surely, this wasn't her mother, this tall, dark-haired, sour-faced looking woman? She had no idea what her mother would look like, but she expected her to look pretty and have a caring manner, like Maggie.

'Name?' snapped Isabel.

Tina opened her mouth, but only an incoherent muffled sound came out.

'Come along. You mustn't keep the doctor waiting. Name?'

'Tina,' she whispered.

'Full name, please.'

'Tina Newton.' If she could have exerted her vocal cords, she would have yelled, 'Christine Renton.'

'The doctor will see you now, second door to the right along the corridor.' Tina continued to stare at Isabel who had dismissed her and was busy filing. Then Isabel glanced up and glared. 'The doctor has stayed behind especially to see you.'

Without a word, Tina turned away.

Chapter Seventeen

Fran was in a happy mood as she boarded the train at York, bound for Beverley. Mr Spencer, the bookshop owner, had engaged another assistant. Since the reorganisation of the shop and the start of the special themes, sales had risen, so Fran had one Saturday off each month. She had the whole weekend free to see Michael, a surprise visit. She decided not to contact Isabel as she would only make excuses. Fran's heart lightened at the thought of seeing her son again. She wondered about Isabel's intended marriage and whether it would take place now that John Stanway was back home. Maybe his intention to marry Isabel and provide a home for her and Michael would not come to fruition. Then, Michael could live with her. She felt certain that he would love York and its many attractions, like the castle, the railway museum, or join the rowing club situated by the banks of the River Ouse and the many educational and cultural facilities open to him. The possibilities were endless. She felt quite energised at the thought of Michael coming to live with her.

The rattle of the train drawing into the station and the hissing of the steam bellowing brought her back into the present. She felt good. Lightly, she jumped onto the platform. This time she had booked into a small guest house as she couldn't afford to stay at the large hotel. Outside the station, to her dismay, she saw the only remaining taxi drive off. She would walk, the exercise would stretch her body after sitting on the train. There was a sudden clap of thunder and rain began to pour down. Turning up her coat collar, she hurried to take cover under the station canopy in the hope of another taxi appearing soon. Soon puddles appeared and the rain, mixing with dry earth, gave off a damp musty smell. She pressed further against the station wall in an attempt to stop her best pair of stockings from being splashed and her shoes getting wet. She didn't see the man approaching. 'So, we meet again,' said a male voice.

She turned in surprise. 'Hello,' she said, looking into the rugged face of Rufus, her knight from her last visit to Beverley. He was dressed in rough tweeds, shirt and a tie, which was pulled loose in a casual manner.

'It's becoming a habit, us meeting outside the station. Waiting for someone?' he asked.

'No, I'm not expected. I was going to walk, but . . .' She held up her free hand to indicate the rain. 'So, I'm now waiting for a taxi.'

'There's no need. I'll give you a lift.'

She thought of the last time she'd visited Beverley and met Nick Saunders on the train, and Rufus had been there at the station to collect him and had given her a lift to the hotel. 'That's kind of you, but I don't want you to think . . .'

'It's not a problem. Besides, I like you.' He winked and she laughed. 'Where to?' he asked, taking her case from her hand.

'I'm staying at Mrs Stephenson's lodging house just off Grayburn Lane.' She settled in the passenger seat of the old Land

Rover, the dog dozing at her feet. They waited for the horse and rulley, stacked high with bags of coal, to pass by. Down by Lairgate, they were held up by a stream of cyclists racing home from the factory for their dinner break. The street was quite busy with pedestrians walking by and, while the Land Rover cruised, Fran searched faces in the hope that she might catch an unexpected glimpse of Michael. But she didn't and sighed deeply.

Rufus glanced at her. 'Are you here for anything special or business?'

'No, not business. Last time I was here, it was a sort of family reunion and now it's a prelude to a farewell . . .' Or not, she hoped, a lump struck in her throat. She gripped her hands tightly together in her lap and stared ahead. She hadn't meant to become emotional.

Rufus didn't speak again until he brought the Land Rover to a halt outside the lodging house. 'Let's book you in and then I'll buy you a stiff drink.'

Mrs Stephenson, a bustling woman, tall, with an angular figure, showed Fran to her second-best bedroom at the back of the house. 'Bathroom is shared with my permanent lodger, Miss Nicholls. She has her bath at nine sharp in the evening. I cook an evening meal for six o'clock. Was it just the two nights?'

'Yes, just a weekend visit.'

Mrs Stephenson pointed to a framed plaque hanging over the fireplace. 'A list of my rules. I don't allow gentlemen friends in the bedroom, but they can wait in my sitting room.'

Fran blushed, but didn't say anything. She suspected the woman had seen Rufus waiting outside for her and assumed he was a boyfriend. It was laughable – at her age she was now truly on the shelf, as she recalled her friend Maisie was fond of saying at their single status, before she herself married.

After changing her wet shoes and paying her advance lodging money, Fran escaped.

In the public house on the other side of Lairgate, Rufus guided Fran to a quiet corner in the snug and then went through into the noisy bar where workmen were having pints of beer and pork pies.

Feeling drained of energy, she leant back, resting her head on the back on the bench seat. Within a few minutes, Rufus returned carrying a goblet of brandy for her and a half pint of beer for himself. 'Drink this, Frannie. It'll help you unwind.'

'Thanks Rufus,' she murmured. Lifting the glass to her lips, she let the golden liquid trickle down her throat, feeling its warmth. By the time she finished the brandy, she felt more composed. She glanced across the table at Rufus and said, 'I'm sorry to be such a wet blanket, but I guess it's a bit of a sad time for me.'

He put down his half-finished drink. 'Want to talk about it, Frannie?'

She liked Rufus. He was a big, bear-like man, but with a gentle, caring manner. She felt at ease with him. After only the slightest hesitation, her words tumbled out. She told him everything: about Victor and Isabel; Michael and the loss of his twin; her mother's controlling ways and her bitterness, which over the years had caused Fran much heartache and misery; her reunion with Michael, but only as his aunt – and now Isabel was whisking him off to Australia.

Rufus listened intently, not once interrupting. When she had finished, he remained silent for a few moments then said sympathetically, 'You've had it rough, Frannie,' and, leaning towards her, he touched her arm, looking into her tense face. 'What I don't understand is why your mother remained so unbending, so distant. I mean, I'm not an authority on the mind of a woman, but you gave her a grandson. She should have been more supportive and recognised your suffering. After all, you were little more than a kid yourself.' He paused, then said, 'One day, Michael will have to know the truth.'

'I know,' she whispered. 'Much as I'd love to tell him, I don't think the time is quite right, not yet. Though, will there ever be a right time?'

'I'm sure there will be. Look, Frannie,' he said, taking a card from the breast pocket of his jacket. 'Here's my number. If you need me, call me anytime.' He glanced at his pocket watch. 'Sorry, business to attend to. Must fly.'

Fran ventured through into the bar, which was quiet and now empty of the workmen, to ask to use the public house telephone. 'End of the bar, love,' said the landlord, as he gathered up the used glasses.

She dialled the number. She would tell Isabel that she was going to take Michael on a day's outing, even if it was just to sit in the pictures or a cafe with him and his friends. At least she would be near to him. She wanted to cherish every precious moment with him.

On the twelfth ring someone finally picked up the phone, a woman out of breath.

A voice she didn't recognise, a stranger's said, 'Hello, High Bank House.'

'Can I speak to Isabel, please?'

There was a pause before the woman replied, guardedly, 'She's not here.'

'When will she be back?'

There was an even longer pause before the woman spoke. 'Can I take your name, please?'

'It's Frances. Is there something wrong? Is Michael all right?'

'Just a minute.'

The clink of the handset hastily put down, the woman's clattering feet on the parquet floor of the hall resounded in Fran's head. She clutched the phone in a vice grip so tight that her knuckles turned a bluey white. 'Hello, hello, are you there?' she demanded into the distant buzz on the line. Was Michael ill? Had there been an accident? She counted sixty horse brasses fixed around the bar structure before the woman returned, gasping.

'Mr Bewholme wants to know where you are.'

'I'm here, in Beverley.'

'Just a minute.' The woman went off again.

'For heaven's sake,' Fran shouted down the phone to the emptiness. 'What is wrong?'

Then, the woman answered, 'Can you come now?' The line went dead.

Bewildered, Fran turned from the bar to find the landlord looking at her.

'Everything all right, love?'

'I need a taxi, quickly.'

'Market Place's your best bet.'

In the taxi, she hardly dared to think what was wrong. Oh God, she thought, not Michael. On the road east towards Burton Banks, a farm tractor was shuffling slowly along the road and traffic began snarling up. Sitting on the edge of the seat, she cursed. 'Can't you go any faster?' she demanded to the driver. 'This is an emergency.'

Observing her through his rear-view mirror, he shrugged. 'Not a lot I can do.'

At last, the taxi turned off down the lane and she finally she arrived at High Bank House. She paid the driver and hurried round the side of the house and pushed open the kitchen door.

'Dad!' Will dozing in his chair jerked up his head as she burst into the room. 'Dad, what's the matter?'

Will did not reply. His face ash grey, his lips trembling, tears began to spill, coursing down his unshaven face. He just stared vacantly at her, speechless. Unable to move, she could only stare back at him. Then, fearing the worse, she closed her eyes for a moment.

Hurrying footsteps sounded and a homely looking woman entered the kitchen. 'Mrs Meredith, I'm so pleased you've come. I didn't know how to get hold of you. I'm worried about Mr Bewholme.'

Acknowledging the woman with a nod, Fran moved to her father's side and placed a hand on his thin shoulders, feeling his body trembling. Then she turned back to the woman. 'Where are Michael and Isabel?'

'They've gone.'

'Gone! Gone? Where to?'

'Why, Australia, of course.'

The colour drained from Fran's face and her whole body lurched and shuddered with shock. She leant heavily against her father's chair. 'When?' she whispered.

'Yesterday.'

Fran stared at the woman, her head in a whirl. Surely this could not be right?

Chapter Eighteen

Stunned, Fran felt her legs weaken. Somehow, she managed the few steps and slumped in the chair opposite Will. His head hung low and he was just staring at the floor. The woman went over to the stove and busied herself. Fran stared into the low embers of the fire. *Michael, Michael*, she said his name like a sad mantra. *He's gone. Isabel has taken him. I might never see him again.* A sob caught in her throat, but her eyes were dry.

'Drink this hot, sweet tea and you'll feel better.' The woman suggested kindly, thrusting a cup into Fran's hands.

She drank, not tasting anything. Her mind whirled, nothing made sense. She just couldn't take it in. All she could think about was Michael travelling to the other side of the world and she might never see him again. Foolishly, she had hoped against hope that circumstances would change and John Stanway would have misgivings about marrying Isabel and taking on Michael – a wild fancy, but not impossible. Never did she envisage Michael would be snatched so quickly and so cruelly from her for the second time in her life.

Her most cherished dream was to be reunited with her son, to hear him call her mother. Now all hopes were dashed. The cold reality of what had happened slapped her hard in the face, sending her reeling, shattering her expectations – the fulfilment of her life's ambition to be a real mother. The cup slipped from her fingers to clatter on the saucer and she buried her face in her hands and sobbed as if her heart was broken. And it was.

It seemed an age before her emotions calmed. Not looking at her father or the woman, she hurried up to the bathroom and drenched her red, blotchy face in cool, clear water. After this setback, would she be able cope with life, her future? What future? She closed her eyes, not knowing how she would be able to bear the intense pain. She turned away and slowly returned to the kitchen. The woman was standing by Will. She looked very concerned, her eyes fixed expectantly on Fran.

Fran found herself going through the motions of some kind of bizarre normality. 'I'm sorry, but I don't know your name,' she said in a trembling voice.

'It's Nancy, Nancy Davis. Now, you don't worry about a thing. I can stay until you're properly settled in. My Cyril is working away and my lodger can fend for herself. So I can stay.'

Fran made her first decision and sent Nancy by taxi to Mrs Stephenson's boarding house to collect her belongings and to cancel the room. Then she just sat with her father, holding his frail hand, neither of them speaking. Words couldn't convey the misery they both felt.

When Nancy came back, between them, they managed to take Will upstairs to his room. Fran sat by his side until he was asleep. Closing the bedroom door, she was surprised to see Nancy hovering on the landing. 'He's settled then.' Fran nodded.

Nancy rushed on. 'I've run you a nice warm bath and I've put a hot water bottle in your bed.'

'Bed.' Fran hadn't given any thought as to where she would be sleeping. The one thought that ran through her mind was her attic bedroom. The one where Victor had . . . 'Which room?' she whispered.

'Your sister said to put you in the spare room. Is that all right?' asked Nancy anxiously. 'And she said for me to use her old room.'

Sensing Nancy's unease, Fran replied, 'Yes, that's fine.'

'I'll make some cocoa,' said Nancy as she went downstairs.

The next few days dragged by in a haze. Fran was grateful for the presence of Nancy who saw to the running of the house and tempted them with tasty meals. But both Will and Fran had little appetite, though they made an effort to please Nancy. Fran rang Mr Spencer, at the bookshop, and explained, without too much detail, that there was a family crisis. 'Take the week off, Mrs Meredith. The new assistant is most capable, so don't you worry.'

She put the phone down. She knew a week wouldn't solve this particular family crisis, but it gave her time to think things through and then . . . What? She wasn't sure.

Will seemed to age within the few days she was there. His face was gaunt, his body more stooped and shaky. Concerned, she said, 'I'll ring the doctor to come and see you.'

'There's nowt he can do for me,' Will replied stubbornly, his eyes filling with tears.

Fran felt her insides quiver with pain. She knew only too well what he meant. There was no cure for heartbreak. Needing some fresh air, she slipped on her coat and went outside the back way and stared across at the derelict timber yard. She sniffed the air and caught the faint whiff of seasoned wood ingrained in the soil. She closed her eyes and she could hear the voices of yesteryear calling, the bargees unloading their cargo of timber. Her father had been a master joiner, mostly connected to farming projects, but the coming of the war and the terrible death toll of the nearby city of Hull meant that his skills were called upon to make coffins. Strong, forthright and much respected, Will Bewholme could always be relied upon by his fellow men. But not by his daughter, she thought, bitterly. When she needed him most, he wasn't there for her. He could have overruled Agnes and she, Fran, could have come home.

She spent restless nights and walks along the river bank before she came to her decision. 'Nancy, can you stay on a few more days? I have to go back to York to attend to some business.' It was Wednesday; they were in the kitchen sorting through the contents of the pantry.

Nancy pushed a curl off her forehead. 'I can stay until Friday afternoon, then my Cyril is home at teatime and I like to make him a nice meal. Is that all right Mrs Meredith?'

Fran suddenly realised what a treasure Nancy was and hugged her. 'Oh, thank you, Nancy. And, my name's Fran. Mrs Meredith makes me feel so ancient.' They both laughed.

Fran caught the afternoon train to York and went straight to her flat. Once inside, and without taking off her coat, she sat down on the sofa, her insides churning in knots as she thought, once again, of the magnitude of past events and their devastating effect on her life. Michael was now on his way to the other side of the world, lost to her for ever. Gone was her dream, her hope of being reunited with her beloved son, the child she'd only held as a baby. Even now, after all these years, she could still feel the warm softness of his tiny body as he snuggled close to her breast. That wonderful feeling was part of her being, the longing which kept her going, gave her something to plan for and to live for. Exhaustion overcame her and her eyelids begin to prick. She closed her eyes and fell into a shadowy half-sleep. The turmoil in her mind raced, dreaming of people passing through, trying to make contact but never quite there long enough to do so.

The damp coldness of the flat seeping into her body woke her. For a few moments, in that hazy time between sleep and consciousness, she wondered if she'd dreamt about Michael going to Australia. Her heart gave a quick leap and then dropped as she realised the cold reality. The confusion of her mind began to clear and she realised that the shadowy people in her dream were facets of herself throughout her life. She shuddered. A frightening thought.

Stiffly, she rose to her feet. Her life was in shreds and somehow she must piece it together. She set about sorting through the flat to see what items she would need and what could be discarded. Absorbed in her task, she hadn't noticed the semi-darkness, which now filled the flat. She was in the kitchenette, checking the top shelf of the food cabinet, when she accidently knocked over a jar of jam, which came hurtling down, smashing on the linoleum floor with a resounding crash. Fran just stood there, rooted, looking at the mess which seemed so like the state of her life at the moment.

The next morning Fran went to see Mr Spencer. As she entered the bookshop, the ambiance greeted her, allowing her to stand unnoticed for a few moments breathing in the wonderful atmosphere of the smell of old and new books. She felt joy at seeing a mother and two young children sitting at a table tucked in the corner, pouring over a volume of Arthur Mee's *The Children's Encyclopaedia*. She could feel the children's captivation as they listened to their mother. This pleased Fran, for such a book needed a parent's guidance. A lump rose to stick in her throat. Was she never destined to be a proper parent? Her attention was diverted as a thread of spring sunlight wove through the window display of books devoted to the Brontë sisters and crossed her line of vision to catch dust motes dancing around the back of an unsuspecting grey-haired man. She couldn't resist a faint chuckle. She felt a pang of abandonment, she would miss all this.

'Mrs Meredith, I didn't expect to see you so soon.' Mr Spencer breathed enthusiasm.

'The shop is doing well,' she murmured.

'Yes, pleasantly so.'

'Can I have a private word, Mr Spencer?'

His bushy brows arched. 'Come through to the office.' He turned and, in an authoritative voice, said, 'Miss Blanchard, take charge.' Fran followed him into the cramped office, which was more of an overflow storeroom. He gestured her to sit down and waited for her to speak.

She told him the barest necessary facts of how her sister had gone to Australia and her father, in Burton Banks, was old and failing, and needing her to care for him. 'So, it's with great reluctance that I must give you notice, Mr Spencer.' There was silence in the tiny, stuffy office and, for a moment, Fran thought he'd forgotten she was there.

He coughed, cleared his throat and looked kindly at her. 'Mrs

Meredith, I feel you are making too hasty a decision. Naturally, you are duty-bound to care for your father.' He paused, his brow furrowing and then, relaxing, he continued, 'Would you consider taking a three-month sabbatical? By that time, your father's health may be much improved. Alternatively, have you thought that he might like to come and live in York with you?'

Fran stared wide-eyed at Mr Spencer. Will coming to live here had never entered her thoughts. 'Mr Spencer, what can I say? Your offer is very generous. Three months . . .' Her voice faltered.

'On the other hand, if you decide to stay with your father and you wish to seek employment, I can recommend you to an excellent colleague of mine, Mr Barleyfield, who has two bookshops in Beverley.' He held up his hand as she began to speak. 'You are a loyal and trusted worker whom I value, Mrs Meredith. Take the three months and then let me know your decision.'

Back at the flat, she began packing her clothes, her few personal possessions and books. She would take what she needed for now and the rest could be sent on by carrier. She had paid the rent on the flat till the end of the month, but she couldn't afford to keep it on for the three months. Laura was going to move into it, if the landlord agreed.

'I'm so excited,' exclaimed Laura. 'A whole bathroom to myself, such luxury,' she enthused, as she and Fran enjoyed Babychams together.

The next day, Fran was ready to go. Laura was going with her to the station to help with the extra luggage. They hugged farewell. 'I'll send any post on to you,' promised Laura.

On the train, the thought which struck her most was that she was on her way home, after all these years of wandering, seemingly aimlessly, though this homecoming was not as she had often envisaged it. Going home to care for Michael, her son, had been the dream. But it was not to be.

Then, voices deep within her exclaimed, *Never give up hope.* And with that resolution firmly in her mind, Fran sat back in her seat.

Chapter Nineteen

Tina, home from work, let herself into the house and sniffed the still air. She stood for a moment, disappointed by the absence of the familiar aroma of cooking she had come to love. Nancy must still be at that house, she thought. How she missed her and they expected too much of Nancy. She went into the sitting room to grab an apple from the fruit dish and was startled to see Nancy stirring from a nap. 'Nancy, are you all right?'

'Hello, sweetheart, just a bit weary, had a busy day. Put the kettle on.'

Tina noticed the strained look on Nancy's face. Without a word, she went through into the kitchen. She wondered if Nancy was ill, and this filled her with dread. Nancy was so dear to her. She had never forgiven herself for not noticing when her beloved Maggie was so ill. She didn't want this to happen to Nancy. She placed the tray on the occasional table next to Nancy and poured the tea. She handed her a cup and sat on the comfy chair opposite.

'This is nice, love,' Nancy said, lifting the cup to her lips.

It was then Tina noticed she was having difficulty lifting her arm. 'Nancy, are you ill?' Nancy tried to plaster a smile on her face, but it turned to a wince. 'You don't look well,' she said coming to kneel by Nancy's side.

Nancy momentarily closed her eyes and then opened them to look up into Tina's concerned face. 'It's nothing. I must have pulled a muscle in my shoulder moving a wardrobe.'

'That's daft, shifting heavy furniture at your age.' Tina said, feeling panic rise in her throat.

Nancy tried to make light of it. 'Less of thinking I'm old. I'm in my prime.'

'You should still see the doc.'

'Tina, stop fussing. I'll be right as ninepence after a good night's sleep.'

'I hope you're not thinking of going to work tomorrow?'

'I must. I can't let Fran down. She's relying on me.'

'She can get stuffed.'

'Tina!'

'I don't care. It's you I'm bothered about.'

'But I've promised.' Nancy wished she hadn't, but wasn't one to break a promise.

Tina dropped to her knees again. 'Look, Nancy. If it makes you feel any better, I'll go. It's my day off tomorrow.' She placed a protective arm round Nancy's ample waist to help her to her feet. 'I'll help you upstairs and run you a nice hot bath. Then, I'll rustle us up an omelette.'

Nancy replied, 'You're a lovely girl, Tina. Your mum doesn't know what she is missing.'

The dark, cold face of that Isabel Renton flashed into her mind. *She can go to hell!*

Then, aloud, she said to Nancy, 'I'd rather have you any day.'

* * *

In the spare bedroom at High Bank House, Fran woke after another restless night, her body aching. She knew she was driving herself to physical tiredness, but she couldn't stop the process. Each night, she fell exhausted into bed, hoping this would quell her emotional pain. This was the theory, but, still, endless pictures and thoughts of Michael crowded her mind, torturing her. She loved him now more than ever, more than when she had first held him in her arms when he was the sweet-smelling baby. How she missed the vibrant young man her son had grown into. She sighed deeply at so many wasted years. Then, with an angry jerk, she flung back the blankets and jumped out of bed. The threads of the worn carpet were rough on her bare feet as she crossed the room and pulled back the curtains. She saw a grey day, which ironically matched her mood.

The bedroom, situated at the back of the house, looked onto the river. Skimming her eyes across the still water, her gaze rested on the distant rise of the Yorkshire Wolds where a tiny strand of blue sky caught her eye, lifting her spirits a notch. She moved away from the window and went along the landing to the bathroom where she managed to coax a temperamental flow of warm water from the antiquated shower fittings. The plumbing in the whole house needed updating. Her list of things to do was growing daily. At some stage, she would have to discuss with Will about finances for necessary improvements to the house, though, for now, the cleaning blitz would have to do. If her stay was to be permanent, maybe she would redecorate her dingy bedroom.

The bedroom Isabel had occupied overlooked the front of the house and was in reasonable condition, but it would have to be totally refurbished. But then, her sister might return with Michael (a thought forever on Fran's mind) so it would be left in abeyance. Michael's room was now devoid of any personal touches, except for marks on the walls left from hanging pictures and posters. Sometimes, she wandered into the room hoping for the feel of his presence; often, she would stand in the centre of the room with her eyes closed, conjuring up his smiling face. But nothing in the room reached out to her. It was as if he'd never been here.

Mentally, she shook herself as she stepped from the shower. She must try to stop dwelling on the past and think positively. She felt guilty about Nancy who had been caught up in this tangled web. Until the phone call the previous night, Fran hadn't realised the woman's loyalty to her. Suffering a pulled muscle, which affected her shoulder and arm, Nancy's sole concern was not to let Fran down. So, she had recruited a replacement, Tina, her young lodger. Though, Fran got the feeling that Tina disapproved of Nancy working so hard and Fran had to agree with her.

Dressing in comfortable slacks and a short-sleeved blouse, Fran went downstairs to the kitchen where she made a breakfast of tea and toast for her and Will. Neither of them spoke much. She sat alone at the table while Will sat in his chair staring, as usual, into the fire. Cleaning out the grate and making the fire each day was Will's only contribution to household tasks. Fran looked away from her father and sighed, her words forming, unsaid, *Yes, Dad, I miss Michael too*.

A knock on the door interrupted Fran's sad thoughts. 'That will probably be Tina,' she said to Will, but he didn't give any sign of acknowledgement. She composed her face, she hoped, into a welcoming smile and went to open the door. Tina was not what she expected, though she had no preconceived idea. But the sight of this petite young woman with spiky, bright-red hair, dressed in a black skirt and a daffodil yellow jumper, warmed Fran's heart. She was like a splash of welcome sunlight on this miserable grey day. 'You must be Tina,' she greeted her. 'I'm Fran. Come in.'

'Thanks,' replied Tina, stepping over the threshold, surprised. She had expected to see a much older woman, not one looking so slim with shoulder-length blonde hair. There were dark smudges under her sad looking eyes and Tina couldn't guess her age, maybe younger than she appeared. Nancy had warned her that Fran was a work-alcoholic. Better jump to it. 'Right, where do you want me to start?'

Taken aback by the girl's eagerness, Fran laughed spontaneously. 'You're keen.'

Tina laughed in response. 'You'd better make the most of me while I'm here.'

At the sound of their laughter, Will turned in his chair and stared at Tina. Then he blurted out, 'What have you done to your hair?'

Tina and Fran both jolted into silence gaped at him.

Will became agitated, cheeks flushed, his gaze still fixed on Tina. He spoke again, this time in a much louder, harsher voice. 'I said, Frances, what have you done to your hair?'

Fran frowned at Will's confusion and, standing slightly behind Tina, felt the girl tremble. Will's flush grew redder, spreading to his whole face and down to his scrawny neck.

Fran hurried to Will's side. 'Dad, what's the matter with you?' she said, resting calming hands on his arm, not sure what had caused his outburst.

His eyes wandered from Tina to Fran, bewilderment etching his face. Now, his voice barely audible, he said, 'But she's you. I don't understand.'

Fran put a cool hand on Will's forehead. He was burning to her touch. 'Come and have a lie down, Dad,' she said, soothingly. She helped him to his feet and said to Tina, who had not moved or uttered a word, 'I'm sorry about this. I won't be long.'

Fran sat by Will's bedside, listening to his laboured breathing and wishing he would give up smoking. Michael's departure had hit Will harder than he realised. She felt ashamed for being so wrapped up in her misery and self-pity that she failed to see her father's unhappiness. But what had caused his sudden flare-up, she had no idea. He seemed confused, mistaking Tina for her.

She glanced at the gilt-framed photograph of her mother on the bedside table, a young beautiful Agnes with flowing auburn hair, laughing green eyes and smiling. She could see why her father and married her, but beneath that loveliness had been a hard heart. Fran stared at the photo, she had never really known her mother, never understood her hateful attitude. How could she love one daughter and not the other? These questions had never been answered. Will moved restlessly in his sleep and Fran wondered if he knew the answers.

Agnes, who said she had no living relatives, came from the Yorkshire Dales to work as housekeeper for Will and his aged father. Before the year was out, they had married and a year later Isabel was born. Then, eleven years later, Fran was born. 'You were a mistake!' Agnes would often yell at her when angry. Fran would seek refuge in Will's arms, but he could never explain why she was a mistake, only saying, 'You must make allowance for your mother.' But she never knew what he meant.

Fran went down stairs and telephoned the surgery and then went back into the kitchen. Tina had washed and dried the breakfast dishes and tidied up the kitchen, and was now sorting through a pile of old newspapers.

'I could take the unwanted ones to the scout hut,' Tina offered, not meeting Fran's eye.

Sensing the girl's uneasiness, Fran replied, calmly, 'That is kind of you, Tina, maybe later. First, I'll put the kettle on and we'll have a coffee. You'll find the biscuit tin in the dresser.'

Fran placed two mugs of steaming coffee on the kitchen table and sat opposite Tina, who had taken the lid off the biscuit tin. 'My, you've got a good selection,' she said, cheerfully.

'Help yourself.' Fran smiled, liking the girl. 'Tina,' Fran said, tentatively.

'Yes.' She didn't look up but studied the intricate pattern of a custard cream biscuit.

'I'm sorry about my father's behaviour. I'm afraid he's not himself. He's missing his grandson very much. He's not really thinking what he's saying, hence the confusion.' Fran took a sip of the hot, revitalising liquid and said, 'As for your hair . . .'

'I'm not changing it,' Tina interrupted, biting on the biscuit.

Fran laughed, feeling the tension slip from her wound-up body. 'That's just it. I like your hair the way it is.' She nearly added, 'it's decorative', but that would be patronising.

Tina nearly choked on the biscuit. Then, thinking how much Nancy needed this job, she cleared her throat, took a gulp of coffee, then said, 'I'm sorry, I was rude.'

'Don't worry, I'm sure we'll get on just fine. Now, seeing that Dad is out of the kitchen, for the morning at least, we'll make a start in here.' Fran glanced around the room at the dull-green-painted walls and the wooden dresser in two shades of cream that had yellowed to burnt umber over the years. The bare window over the sink begged for some form of embellishment, perhaps curtains or a practical blind? She closed her eyes for a second and wondered, fleetingly, why Isabel had not maintained the house properly. Opening them, she found Tina looking quizzically at her. 'The paint work,' Fran offered. 'It's in a terrible state.'

Tina glanced around the kitchen, nodded in agreement and suggested, 'Have you thought of stencilling? It would brighten it up a bit. Me and my boyfriend are going to do my bedroom. He's gone stencil barmy.' She didn't add that Joe stayed with her when Nancy helped here. He had stencilled her back as she lay asleep in bed and she remembered the fun they'd had in the bath, scrubbing it off.

'That's an idea, but we'll save it for another day. Today, we will concentrate on turning out the cupboards and the dresser.' They worked in companionable silence.

Later on that morning, the doctor visited and examined Will, testing his blood pressure, he said, reassuringly, 'It is slightly high, but the tablets already prescribed will control it. Are you in any pain or discomfort, Mr Bewholme?' He knew of Isabel and Michael's departure.

'Can you mend a broken heart?' Will replied, dryly.

'No, but I can prescribe medication to help.'

'I take enough pills, thank you.'

'I think you are wise to rest today, but you need to have plenty of fluids and a light diet.' The doctor, a serious, caring man, sat down on the chair by Will. 'You need to take care of your health and top up your energy. I would like you to come into the surgery where I can give you a fuller examination.' Will just grunted.

Fran followed the doctor from the room and said, quietly, 'I'm worried about him.'

The doctor touched her arm, reassuringly. 'There's no cause for alarm. Let him rest for a few days then bring him into the surgery. And you take care of your own health. You look as though you've not been sleeping too well.' The doctor departed and Fran returned to the kitchen.

'Is he all right?' asked Tina. She closed the cupboard door, dusting her hands on her skirt.

'He just needs to rest and take his mind off things. I've got to think of a distraction.'

'Distraction? What for?' replied a slightly bemused Tina. 'The mind boggles.'

'Something to hold his interest to help to stop him missing his grandson, but I don't know what.' Sighing with despair, she sat down at the table, wondering just what she had let herself in for. She hadn't expected a rosy view – caring for her father was never going to be easy – but she hadn't expected this damned depression. Missing Michael was becoming a catching disease.

Then, Tina's clear, young voice cut into her thoughts. 'How about I make a bite to eat? There are tins of soup and bread rolls in the cupboard.' Fran nodded her agreement. 'Then, when we've eaten, I could teach your dad a card trick or two,' Tina offered. She bustled around the kitchen, mimicking Nancy's ways because she didn't know what to do for this sad woman. There was something about her Tina couldn't quite fathom. Still, it was none of her business. Some people led such funny, mixed-up lives.

Soon, the smell of tomato and vegetable soup, and warm bread rolls filled the kitchen. 'I'd better take Dad's up to him first,' said Fran.

'No!' commanded Tina. Fran stilled, surprised by the tone of the girl's voice.

'What I mean is . . .' Tina faltered. She was getting it all wrong. She swore under her breath. 'I'll start again. I'll take your dad's up, and stay and have a chat with him, while you take a break. But we'll have ours first. Is that okay?'

Fran sat back down with a bump. 'You're certainly an amazing girl.'

Tina served the meal and then sat opposite Fran. 'I hope you don't think I'm bossy, but things happened in my life and I've sort of got a second chance.' She shrugged, embarrassed at baring herself to a woman who was a stranger to her.

Fran studied the girl's serious face, seeing a faraway look in her eyes. Intrigued, she asked, 'How come?'

'I had a lovely mother, Maggie. She died . . .' Tina's violet-blue eyes misted. 'I just didn't appreciate her. She did everything for me and it wasn't until she went that I realised how fantastic she was . . .' Tina trailed off, her bottom lip quivering.

'She must have loved you very much.'

'Do you think so?' Tina asked, anxious to rid herself of the guilty feeling that swamped her.

'I'm sure. Now, tell me about your second chance.'

'It's Nancy. She's not exactly a second mother, but she's near enough.'

A lump rose in Fran's throat and her voice was a mere whisper. 'You're lucky – two women to love and care for you. A rare gift.' She thought of her own troubled relationship with her mother.

Suddenly, a thudding from above interrupted further conversation. 'That's Father,' said Fran.

Tina jumped up to prepare the tray and went up to Will. Fran tidied the table and was stacking the dishes on the draining board when a sudden wave of tiredness swept over her, sapping her energy. Tumbling into the easy chair by the fireside, she closed her eyes and dozed.

Fran woke up as Tina entered the kitchen. Stifling a yawn, she glanced at wall clock and sat up with a jerk. 'I've been asleep for over an hour.'

Tina shrugged. 'It's no sweat. Me and Will get on just great.

He was telling me about his joinery business and, when he's feeling better, he's going to show me around.'

Fran stretched and sat up. 'So, we haven't driven you away? You're coming back?'

'Yes.' Tina didn't mention that Will kept calling her Frances. Glancing about the tidy kitchen, she asked, 'Anything else you want me to do?' She'd stay if needed, for Nancy's sake, but she'd had enough of this house for one day.

Fran took in the flush of the girl's cheeks and the way she lowered her eyes to stare at the floor. 'Thanks, Tina, you've been a great help, especially with Father, but I think you've done enough for today. I appreciate you coming.'

'You mean it?' Tina looked up, startled.

'Of course I do. Come again, I can always do with extra help. And who knows, I might take up that offer of yours to teach me the art of stencilling.'

When Tina had gone, the house was quiet, empty. Fran stood in the centre of the large kitchen, already missing the sunshine mood Tina had brought into this house. Once, Fran reflected, she too had been a carefree spirit. Maybe that was why Will, in his confusion, had mistaken Tina for her.

Chapter Twenty

A few days later at the surgery, the doctor gave Will a thorough examination. Then he called Fran into the consulting room. 'Take a seat, Mrs Meredith,' said Doctor Lawson. She glanced at her father, but he didn't look at her. He continued staring down at his feet. She feared the worst. A terminal illness? She sat on the edge of the chair, her heart filled with anguish and concern for her father. The doctor was saying, 'I will arrange for Mr Bewholme to see an optician.'

She stared at him in disbelief, steeling herself to ask, 'Is Dad going blind?'

At this point the doctor noticed her pale, anxious face and replied kindly, 'No, my dear. But Mr Bewholme needs to wear spectacles.'

'Spectacles.' She almost laughed. 'I never thought – so simple.' Fran sighed with relief and reached out to clasp Will's hand. He lifted his head to look at her. 'I – Dad – we thought it might be something serious.' Will, his face etched deep with emotion, just nodded.

Outside, Fran tucked her arm in her father's. Slowly, they walked down the tree-lined avenue toward the town square. She could feel Will trembling and, as they approached a wooden bench seat, Fran suggested, 'Dad, we'll rest here awhile and you can have a smoke.' Although she didn't approve of his smoking, in this instance it would help Will to settle his nerves.

Later that afternoon, while Will was resting comfortably on his bed, she decided to go for a walk. She slipped on a waterproof jacket, because the weather was so changeable of late, and pulled on a pair of stout shoes. Stepping out, she breathed in the air, fresh after a shower of rain. Not wanting to go too far from the house, she stood for a moment, searching her memories of familiar walks of her youth for a short, circular route. Seeking solitude, she headed in the direction of the riverbank, remembering after a mile she could cross the field and return via the lane. By then, she would be back in time for Will's afternoon tea. The grassy bank was wet, quite sodden in parts, and she trod carefully to avoid slipping. Away from the drone of the distant tractor, the sound of the river was soothing and calming, filling her with simple pleasure. Further upstream, she came across an old upturned boat, long deemed unusable. Here, the river began to bend and she stopped to shade her eyes. Up river, just inland, hidden from view by overhanging trees and bushes of the pond, was a bird sanctuary. But today she didn't have time to rediscover it; instead, she turned and followed a footpath running parallel with a field, passing high hedges, rough scrub and a ditch where she had once fallen in as a child. She had been chasing one of their dogs at the time – or had the dog been chasing her? Enjoying the blissful, peaceful countryside, she meandered. This is how she remembered it, in often created pictures in her mind while she was exiled from home.

Suddenly, without warning, her foot caught in the bare root of a hawthorn bush and, unable to stop, she hurtled forward. She hit the ground hard on her knees, her arms spread-eagled, and her hands clutching at clumps of rough grass.

'Let me help,' said a masculine voice. Strong arms hoisted her up. Feeling shaken and dizzy, she leant against the taut chest muscles of the man who held her so securely in his arms. Within moments, the giddiness passed and then embarrassment filled her as she tried to disentangle herself from the man. But he held her firmly. 'It's Fran, isn't it?'

Surprised at the mention of her name, she found herself looking into the anxious brown eyes of Nick Saunders, Rufus's brother, whom she had first met on the train to Beverley.

'Hello,' she managed, weakly. He was the last person she would have expected to see.

'How are you feeling now?'

He still held her close and she was acutely aware of his physical nearness. She glanced down at the scuffed knees of her stockings and hastily pulled down her coat to cover them. 'I'm fine, no real harm done. Thank you for rescuing me,' she said, giving him a watery smile. His arms dropped to his sides and she wobbled slightly then righted herself. 'What are you doing here?' she asked. He didn't answer her. 'I'm sorry – I didn't mean to be rude.'

Then, he said, 'I'm staying in the area for a while, so I thought I'd explore the countryside.'

'You're staying with Rufus?'

A shadow passed across his pale, gaunt face and his eyes dulled, filling with sadness. 'It's not convenient for me to stay there,' he replied in a low voice.

'I see,' she murmured, but she didn't. He looked so downcast.

On impulse, she offered, 'I'm on my way home. Come and have a cup of tea and meet my father.'

His face lightened, but not his eyes. 'An invitation to tea, how could I refuse?'

Judging by the pain in his eyes, something seemed to be affecting him deeply. She wondered if her sadness, her loss of Michael once again from her life, showed in her eyes. Had Nick suffered a tragedy in his life? Her first reaction was to ask if anything was worrying him, but she didn't want to pry and she could be completely wrong. After all, she knew very little about him.

Silently, they walked side by side. She stole a glance at him, wondering if she should make polite conversation, but he seemed so lost in thought. They skirted behind Bloomsbury's old house and she remembered. 'Tall Chimneys!' she exclaimed with delight. Nick stared at her. 'I've just remembered the name of the house where my old school friend used to live.'

He followed her eye of direction and said in a flat voice. 'That's Rufus's house.'

She repeated, 'Rufus's house. I didn't realised he lived so near.' She was just about to say, 'Shall we call and see him?' when Nick's earlier remark, of it being inconvenient, flashed into her mind. She glanced at him, but he was staring straight ahead and she felt a touch of uneasiness. The last stretch to High Bank House seemed endless.

On entering the house, she was so pleased to see Will sitting in his chair by the fire. He greeted her by saying, 'Kettle's on,' and glanced questioningly at Nick.

'Dad,' Fran said, now wishing she hadn't been so impulsive with her invitation, 'I want you to meet Nick Saunders. We met recently on the train from York.'

'How do you do, sir?' Nick strode forward to shake Will's hand.

'I'll be all right once I get my eyes sorted out.' Then he proceeded to tell Nick about his visit to the doctor. Fran occupied herself with the tea tray.

Refreshments served, Fran listened to the men's conversation about the disused joinery shed and the yard. 'Yes,' Will was saying, 'it was a thriving business. My father started it up in the twenties and, when he died, I carried it on. I worked alongside him from being a youngster. Aye, many a day I'd skip school and help bargees unload. My dad was a great character, taught me everything I know. And me, I've nobody to teach,' he finished bitterly.

'Another piece of fruit loaf?' Fran offered, before Will could sink into remorse. 'Nick?'

'Please, it's delicious.' He winked at her and, taken by surprise, she laughed awkwardly. After that, Nick drew Will out, getting him to tell more of the heyday of the joinery trade.

At first, Fran sat on the edge of her chair, hoping her father wouldn't mention anything about Michael, but the conversation dwelt on the technical aspects of joinery. So, she leant back in her chair, feeling content to let their words ride over her until the scraping back of a chair startled her as Nick rose to his feet. She straightened up, feeling a little guilty – after all, she had invited him to the house and then practically ignored him. But he seemed unperturbed.

He held out his hand, so strong in her small hand. 'Thanks, Fran, for inviting me to tea. I've enjoyed it.' He smiled, but his eyes remained veiled.

She warmed to his politeness and, impulsively, again, she found herself saying, 'You're welcome to call anytime.'

'Actually,' he said, still holding her hand and looking in Will's

186

direction. 'Your dad's promised to hunt out a book for me on carpentry and joinery, and . . .'

Will assumed an obstinate face, his voice clear, 'I've asked Nick over for Sunday lunch. It's nice to have a yarn. I miss . . .' Here, his voice faltered.

Knowing what he was going to say, Fran said quickly, 'Dad! You know I'm not a good cook.'

'If it's going to cause a problem . . .' Nick said, withdrawing his hand sharply from hers.

Once again, she found herself apologising for her rudeness. 'Of course, you must come, but my cooking isn't great, I warn you.'

'What if we do it together, the preparation and the cooking – a joint effort?' He cocked his head on one side, looking at her like a woeful spaniel.

Surprised at his suggestion, she found herself agreeing. 'That would be nice.'

She walked with him to the front gate, conscious of its broken state. Nick eyed it, thoughtfully. 'I could repair that for you. That's if you don't mind,' he said, earnestly.

'Kind of you to suggest it.'

'Call it a thank you for lunch.'

'You haven't tasted my cooking yet.'

He laughed and she was given the delight of seeing his eyes light up. He waved goodbye and she watched him stride away in the opposite direction from Rufus's house. She still didn't know what to make of him, of his mood swings. At least Will enjoyed his company. Maybe, Nick was just lonely, and that she could understand. Nevertheless, she viewed this coming Sunday's lunch with some misgivings, wishing Will hadn't invited him – because cooking for a virtual stranger would be a burden she could well do without.

The next morning, as Fran came in with the post, Will asked, eagerly, 'One from Michael?'

Fran made an extra search through the letters, just in case she had missed anything. 'Sorry, Dad.' Under her breath she offered up a little prayer. *Michael, please keep your promise and write.*

For the rest of that week, Fran was quite busy in the house. Nancy was back and Fran loved her bustling warmth, which filled the house. Friday, she was sitting at the kitchen table, flicking through an old cookery book.

'Looking for anything in particular?' Nancy asked.

'Inspiration for Sunday lunch,' said Fran, pushing back an untidy strand of hair.

'Roast beef and Yorkshire pudding, can't beat it,' Nancy replied, matter-of-factly.

Fran replied, sheepishly, 'I'm not sure how to cook either.' Nancy feigned a look of horror. 'I'm fine with vegetables and stews, anything in one pot but beef and Yorkshire pudding!' Fran proceeded to tell Nancy about Will inviting Nick for Sunday lunch and his offer to help. 'I don't mind him helping, but I do need to know what I'm doing.'

'I tell you what, Fran, you come shopping with me on Saturday and I'll introduce you to my butcher. Then you can buy plenty of fresh veg from the market. I can come up early on Sunday morning and pop the meat into the oven and show you how to mix the Yorkshires.'

'Nancy, you are an absolute angel.'

So, on Sunday, the beef roasted slowly in the oven, its tantalising aroma filling the kitchen. As Fran weighed out the ingredients for the Yorkshires into a large basin, Nancy watched, commenting, 'Now, you whisk love into a Yorkshire, that's what makes it rise to perfection.' So, Fran whisked with vigour, enjoying the process. Nancy, after giving instructions on cooking, said. 'I must be off. Tina's boyfriend's coming for dinner.'

Fran looked up at the mention of Tina's name. 'I like Tina, a nice girl, she's fun.'

'She's just like a daughter to me,' Nancy said, proudly.

Nick arrived later on, carrying a box of Black Magic chocolates. He sniffed the air. 'Something smells good.' He was dressed casually in grey trousers, blue shirt and a navy sleeveless pullover. As he put the chocolates into her hands, Fran noticed the fragrance of his newly washed hair and the smoothness of his freshly shaved face. She was pleased she'd made an effort with her appearance, for beneath her blue apron she wore a soft pink cashmere sweater and straight black trews. It was rather daring for a woman to wear trousers, but she found them comfortable, having worn breeches and dungarees when she was on the farm. Her touch of lipstick was almost gone and her hair was damp and ruffled from the heat of cooking.

Will entered the kitchen. 'I thought I heard your voice. Nice to see you,' he greeted Nick.

Fran looked at him, surprised to see him dressed smartly in dark brown trousers and a cream shirt with a matching tie, clean-shaven and his sparse grey hair neatly brushed. She smiled, glad to see her father happy. Nick had certainly made an impression on him.

Will produced two bottles of beer from the larder and Fran looked enquiringly. Will grinned widely, showing his missing back teeth. 'Nancy fetched them' he said, handing one to Nick.

Fran made a start on peeling the potatoes, ready to roast them in the oven. 'Let me,' offered Nick.

'I can manage, thank you,' she replied too quickly.

'But I made a promise to help.'

She glanced at him about to say there was no need, but something about the way he was looking at her stopped her. 'You can scrape the carrots if you wish.' So they worked side by side.

The meal turned out reasonably well. 'I need more practice,' she lamented to the two men. 'Perhaps next time I'll try something different.'

'Next time, now that sounds promising,' commented Nick.

Not falling into that trap again, Fran said quickly, 'It won't be for a long time. I'm too busy.'

Nick looked at her, but didn't say anything. He rose from the table and began to collect the plates. She pushed back her chair, but he halted her, his hand on her shoulder. 'I'll do the dishes, you sit with Will.' Will was now sitting in the chair by the fireside, reading his newspaper.

'He likes to be quiet after dinner. You wash and I'll dry.'

Nick rolled up his shirtsleeves and she was appalled to see a jagged-looking red scar stretching from his elbow down to his wrist. At the sight of it, she flinched and threw him a glance, expecting him to explain how he came by it. But he didn't say a word.

They worked in silence and she struggled for something to say. She stared out of the window, seeking inspiration. 'The clouds are lifting. It looks as though it's going to be a fine afternoon.' He peered over her shoulder and she could feel his breath warm against her ear.

'You're right. Shall we have a walk later? That's if you've not planned anything,' he added.

'We could, I suppose.'

They sat round the fire for coffee. By the time they had finished, it was pelting down with rain. 'Let's have a game of dominoes?' suggested Will, anxious not to let their visitor go yet.

But Fran was finding the small talk a bit of a strain. She just wanted to curl up with a book. 'I haven't played dominoes since I was a child. I don't think . . .'

Will, cut in gruffly, 'Michael always liked a game. I wish he . . .'

'Of course we'll have a game, Dad,' Fran said too brightly. 'Okay with you, Nick?'

'Sure. I'm not certain who Michael is, but is he around to make up the foursome?'

An unbelievable surge of heat shot through Fran's body, reaching a peak in seconds then descending into a cold chill. Gripping the back of Will's chair for support, she cried inwardly, *Michael, oh, Michael I miss you so. Why don't you write and let us know how you are?* She gazed down at her father's balding patch, avoiding Nick's gaze.

It was Will, who answered, his voice calmer now. 'Michael's my grandson. He's in Australia.' Fran's hand slipped on to Will's bony shoulder, her touch soothing, comforting.

Chapter Twenty-One

Fran was outside, hanging washing on the line, when Nancy opened the porch door and called, 'There's a letter arrived from Australia. I don't think Will can wait a minute longer.'

'Australia!' Excitement filled Fran and she hurried into the kitchen.

Will was on his feet coming towards her, a sheet of thin blue paper outstretched in his trembling hand. 'It's from Michael!' he exclaimed, thrusting it at Fran. 'Read it.'

Will sat down on the edge of his chair and she stood by his side. Michael's untidy handwriting leapt across the paper. A warm sensation filled her and the image of him kissing her on the cheek when she'd given him the cheque illuminated her mind.

Impatiently, Will nudged her, urging, 'Go on then.' Fran took a deep breath.

Dear Grandad,
We arrived safely in Melbourne after a great voyage. I've
taken pictures with the camera you gave me and, when they
are developed, I will send them. Mam kept being sick. I was

fine. John's house is way out of the city in the country and in the distance you can see a range of hills and mountains. The house is so big, no upstairs and Grandad, can you believe, there are servants to cook and clean the house, so Mam's taking it easy while we are settling in. I am itching to see the vineyards and the winery. When John has time, he is going to show me everything.

It is winter here, would you believe. Not as cold as back home. It will take a bit of getting used to, the mix up of the seasons. Fancy having summer in December. You'd love the green-winged lorikeet, and red and blue parrots – so different from birds near the river back home. I miss you, Grandad. No one here plays dominoes, but I have a friend, Jarrod, and I'm going to teach him.

Hope you are okay, Grandad, and Aunt Frances is looking after you well. I hope she stays, she seems nice. Mam sends you her love and will let you know when she and John get married.

Cheers for now,

Your loving grandson, Mike

P.S. Write back soon

Fran sat very still, staring down at the letter, hearing Michael's strong, jovial voice so clearly in her head. She wished with all her heart she could be with him, sharing his experience of his new life, which he was obviously enjoying. She missed him now more than ever, but his happiness was her paramount thought. If he was unhappy he would want to come home, but his blissful joy radiated from the very words he wrote. How could she deny him that? A small consolation, she thought, but it gave her strength and from that strength, something stirred within her for, despite the thousands of miles separating her and Michael, she felt close to him, reading the letter.

She looked up to see Will wiping the wetness from his eyes with the cuff of his shirt sleeve. 'Well, he's enjoying it, I suppose,' he said, begrudgingly.

For the next few days, it rained persistently and the level of the river was unusually high for July. The house was built on higher ground and the river bank along this stretch of water was quite high. If the river broke its bank, it would only go into the old yard. Will reminisced about the times the riverside pub flooded. 'Many a time, Father and me sat in the bar, deep in water.'

Looking out of the window at the torrential rain, Fran asked again, 'Are you sure we're safe?'

Reassuring her, Will said, 'I've lived here long enough to know. The only place likely to have a problem would be Magpie Cottage up near ponds. It's low-lying there.'

'Who lives there now?' From her youth, she remembered the isolated cottage, inhabited by a retired bargee who was fond of whisky.

Will snorted impatiently, 'Well, you know!'

Puzzled, Fran said, 'I don't.'

'Nick's renting it. He must have told you?'

She shook her head. She'd never given a thought to Nick's accommodation arrangements. She didn't know why she should, but she felt a little guilty for her lack of concern.

The rains continued, and Will and Fran listened to the news on the radio. Both were quiet as the newscaster reported the devastation caused by rising rivers bursting banks, flooding homes and surrounding countryside. She looked across at Will, but he was dozing.

Restless, Fran stood by the kitchen window watching the rain, feeling hemmed in by the still silence of the house. She needed air. She propped a note for Will against the sugar bowl on the table, letting him know where she had gone. Pulling on her Wellingtons and waterproofs, she set off through the yard to the landing stage. Avoiding the rotten wooden planks, she eased down to the river bank. Her booted feet squelched and slithered, and she nearly lost her balance. She should have used one of Dad's walking sticks. Too late now, she would just have to take care. She stood still for a moment, the rain on her face, the smell, fresh and cleansing.

On the opposite side of the river, its banks were already broken, flooding farm land that now resembled miniature lakes. From this point, she wasn't able to see round the bend of the river to Magpie Cottage, where Nick was living. Suddenly, she had an attack of conscience and decided to find out if he was all right.

Determinedly, she trudged along the sodden bank in that direction, but she didn't get very far because it was so waterlogged and she was in danger of slipping down the bank. The only other way to reach the cottage was to backtrack, go down the lane and follow the path around the back of Tall Chimneys. 'Rufus!' Why hadn't she thought about him before? He would know. So, to ease her mind, she splashed on, hurrying towards Rufus's house.

She knocked on the front door and waited, but there was no answer. She was wondering what to do next when she suddenly heard a scraping noise from within the house. The door opened to reveal a woman in a wheelchair, Helga, Rufus's wife. 'I'm sorry to disturb you but—'

'What do you want?' the woman interrupted, coldly.

Fran drew a deep breath. 'I'm concerned about Nick and I was wondering if Rufus could contact him.' Fran hugged nearer to the wall of the house to shelter from the rain.

'You're concerned about that scum? I wouldn't waste my breath on him. He's a killer!'

And before Fran could utter another word, the door was slammed in her face. Stunned, she just stood there, shocked at what Helga had said.

A cold fear seeped into her body and she shivered involuntarily. She turned quickly and headed for home, thinking what a lucky escape she had that Rufus wasn't home. She must warn Dad not to encourage Nick to come to the house ever again. The wind whipped at her face as she hurried down the lane. She kept her head down, thinking of the warmth of the welcoming fire.

She was almost upon the house before she saw, parked near the back door, Rufus's Land Rover. Entering the porch, she wondered what had brought him here. Surely, not a social call? Shrugging off her boots and waterproofs, she pushed open the kitchen door and was stunned to see Nick sitting in front of the fire, shivering and sneezing.

'Fran!' Rufus came bouncing towards her. 'We were getting worried about you.'

She stared at him, anger welling. 'What's happening?' she demanded.

Before he could answer, Will butted in, 'We've plenty of room. I've said Nick can stay.'

In disbelief, Fran rounded on Will. 'You've what?'

At the harshness of her tone, Nick glanced up at her. His face flushed, he began a series of sneezes again. At this point, Rufus came and put an arm about her shoulder.

'I'm sorry to impose this on you, but Nick's home is flooded and he's not well. In fact, he's running a high temperature and I'm loath to bung him into a hotel. It's just for a few days until he's feeling better.' He looked pleadingly into her eyes. 'Nick said you've been kind and friendly towards him. You'd be doing me a great favour. Things are rather difficult at home.'

I bet! she thought. *Having a murderer under your roof it would be.* Though, looking at Nick sitting huddled into himself, he looked pitiful, not a threat. But then, who could tell?

When she didn't answer, Rufus said, hastily, 'If there's a problem, I'm only down the road.'

'Oh yes, I know where you live.' She couldn't keep the aggression from her voice.

He glanced sharply at her. 'Are you all right?'

She sat down heavily on a chair. 'I'm tired, cold and wet, and in need of a hot bath,' she said, feeling all her energy draining away.

'Poor you,' Rufus said, sympathetically. 'You go and have your bath. I'm going into town to collect Nick's prescription from the chemist and on the way back I'll call at that new Chinese takeaway.' Pulling on his green waxed jacket, he winked at her. 'And I'll call at the off-licence and buy something to make a hot-toddy.'

Fran, feeling totally exhausted, both mentally and physically, just nodded. She closed her eyes. Nick sneezed, the fire hissed, Will muttered to himself and she? She was unable to believe the scenario that had unfolded before her.

* * *

Joe whistled Perry Como's 'Magic Moments'. He couldn't believe his luck. A whole two weeks alone with Tina at Nancy's house. Cyril had taken Nancy to Scarborough for a holiday. 'Keep an eye on her, Joe, but no funny business,' Nancy said. He'd pretended to be shocked. But he and Tina agreed, it was an opportunity not to be missed. He turned the sizzling bacon in the frying pan. He glanced at the clock on the cabinet, ten minutes and Tina would be home from work and, as soon as she came through the door, the eggs would be cracked and in the pan. There were two bottles of beer cooling on the pantry stone floor. The tiny kitchen table was set for two with a plate piled high with bread and butter. Tina had a ravenous appetite for someone so slender. His whistling wobbled as fat from the pan spurted, spraying his bare arm. That didn't bother him, but the shrill ringing of Nancy's new-fangled telephone did.

'Who the hell's that?' He listened a moment because Nancy had said they were on a party-line and shared with another household. But the ringing seemed to become more persistent.

Lifting the pan from the stove, he went into the sitting room, picked up the handset and held it near to his ear. He bellowed, 'Who's that?'

'Can I speak with Nancy?' a woman's voice replied.

'She's away.'

'Tina?'

Joe caught the anxious note in the woman's voice. 'She's at work.'

'When she's home ask her to ring me, Fran Meredith, please.' She gave the number.

'Sure.' He let the receiver drop back on its cradle. But as soon as Tina came home, the meal was ready and he forgot about the phone call until much later.

* * *

They were cuddling up in bed, mulling over their day, when it jolted into his mind. 'A woman rang you on Nancy's telephone. She sounded a bit upset.'

Tina untangled herself from his arms and raised herself on her elbow to gaze into his honest eyes. 'What did she want?' She sounded casual, but inside she trembled. Was it her mother, Isabel Renton? Had she discovered from the medical records that Tina was her daughter?

'Didn't say.' He kissed the tip of her pert little nose.

She wriggled away from him. 'Well who the hell was it?'

'Fran something or other.' He made to gather her back into his arms, she resisted and sat up.

'I was supposed to ring her about some stencilling, but it wasn't anything important. It's my Saturday off tomorrow, I'll ring her then.' She snuggled back down in the bed, pulling Joe down with her, entwining her legs around his warm, appealing naked body.

When Joe woke up the next morning, it was to the sound of Tina vomiting in the lavatory He pulled the blanket over his head and closed his eyes, but sleep was lost to him. He scrambled out of bed to see a white-faced Tina coming back into the bedroom.

On the defensive, he said, 'You've got a bug. It isn't my cooking or I'd be sick as well.' Ignoring him, she tumbled back into bed and lay moaning. Joe stared at her. He had no idea what to do with an ill woman, so he quickly dressed and went down the stairs.

In the kitchen, he put the kettle on to make tea and, while he was waiting for it to boil, he popped two slices of bread under the grill. The kettle sang and his attention was diverted to pouring the water into the pot, so he forgot about the toast. He was thinking about his motorbike. She needed a good clean and polish. He'd do that this afternoon after he finished work at one. And, tomorrow, he and Tina would go to the coast for a spin. Suddenly, the kitchen was full of smoke as the toast burnt to charcoal. At once, he turned off the grill, opened the window and wafted the room with a tea towel. He scraped the black off the toast, but it just crumbled. So he poured out the tea and was just about to take Tina hers, when she dashed passed him into the lavatory. The sound of her being sick again mingled with the burnt toast made him feel nauseated as well.

Tina was back in bed again so he crept up to peep at her. Peaky-faced, her half-closed eyes glared at him from the pillow. 'Shove off,' she muttered, wearily.

'Will you be okay?' She didn't answer, but sank lower in the bed. He sighed, glad to be dismissed. He'd ask the boss if he could use the office telephone and ring her at break-time.

Tina woke to the insistent ringing of the telephone. She wished that Nancy had never had the damned thing installed. She lay for a moment contemplating getting up to answer it when it stopped. She turned over and it began ringing again. She stretched out her body, surprised that it didn't ache. Pushing back the blankets, she padded downstairs into the sitting room, picked up the receiver and, thinking it was Joe, said, 'Now what do you want?'

'Tina, its Fran. I'm sorry to disturb you, but with Nancy away, I wondered if you are free to come down. I . . .'

'Fran, you sound worried. It isn't Will?' Tina thought of the old man's confused state.

'Dad's fine. It just that I've got someone staying whose home is flooded and he's not feeling too well. I could use a pair of extra hands and if you could stay over for a couple of nights that would be a great help.'

Tina took a deep breath; she didn't feel queasy any more. 'Sure, I'll come on Nancy's bike.'

'Take a taxi. I'll pay.'

As Fran put down the phone, she breathed a sigh of relief. Slowly, she went into the kitchen. She hadn't slept much last night. The very thought of Nick Saunders tucked up in bed in the room next to her filled her with dread. She didn't know how to deal with violence. For the moment, she was safe. He was ill with a heavy cold and running a high temperature, and she had to nurse him. There had been no chance to speak to Rufus yesterday, no chance to voice her fears, to ask for confirmation of what Helga had said. She sighed. Was she overreacting?

Will interrupted her thoughts. 'Are you going to help me write this letter to Michael?'

'Tina's coming soon and then I'll have time.'

Will's face brightened. 'She can help me.'

'No!' Fran snapped. 'I want her to look after Nick.'

'You sound just like our Isabel – bossy,' he muttered, reaching for his baccy tin.

'Dad!' she admonished. Sometimes there was no pleasing him. She made an effort of normality and, when Tina arrived, the kitchen had a delicious aroma of warm muffins and coffee.

'Gosh, I'm hungry,' were Tina's first words as she sniffed the air.

'Help yourself,' said Fran, so pleased to see the girl that she could have hugged her.

'How are you today, Will?' Tina asked.

'Middling. You come and sit near me, lass. Careful what you say to Fran, she's got an edge on.'

'Oh, yeah,' she said saucily. 'Have you been naughty?'

'Not me. I reckon it's him upstairs.'

Tina looked questioningly at Fran. 'We have a guest staying. Nick Saunders is ill – nothing serious – but I would appreciate your help with nursing him.'

'I wanted you to help me write my letter to my grandson, but . . .'

'Dad! You know I want to do it.'

Tina jumped up from her chair, sensing the need to escape from family quarrels. 'That's filled a corner, great. This bloke who's ill, what's he having to eat, Fran?'

As Tina left the kitchen, carrying a tray of hot soup and orange juice upstairs to Nick, Fran sighed. She fetched pen and writing pad from the dresser and sat next to Will at the table. 'What shall we write?' she asked, knowing what she would dearly like to write, but couldn't.

She began writing, mentioning the appalling weather and Will's need to wear spectacles. Will contributed a few ideas he had for the joinery shop and yard, and what did Michael think about them. Will mentioned Nick, so Fran countered by writing about what a lovely girl she had helping her. She was just sealing the envelope when Tina came bursting into the kitchen. 'Fran, come quickly. Nick's fallen out of bed.'

Later, after they'd settled Nick back into bed, Tina telephoned Joe.

'Where are you?' he demanded. 'What do you mean, you're at Fran's?'

'If yer stop shouting, I'll tell yer. She's got this fellow staying, been flooded out of his place and he's got a bad dose of flu and I'm helping to nurse him. I thought I might stay the night, not much point in coming home then having to come again in the morning.'

'You what? Who's this bloke?'

'Don't worry, he's old enough to be me uncle.'

'I thought you weren't well, so don't you go too near him, catching his bugs.'

'I'll be okay. Sorry for messing up the weekend. What are you going to do?'

'I'll go home, then to the pub, see me mates.'

Tina went back into the kitchen. Fran asked, anxiously, 'Everything all right?'

'Yes.'

Fran breathed a sigh of relief. Earlier, she didn't know how she would have managed without Tina's help in getting Nick back into bed. She didn't mind getting up during the night to see to Nick if need be, but she felt happier, safer, with Tina staying. Then she wrestled with her conscience – should she tell Tina what Helga had said about Nick been a killer? She didn't want to alarm her if it wasn't true, so, best to remain vigilant until she confronted Rufus.

Fran uncurled her legs and rose from the chair. 'I'll just pop up and see how Nick is.' Tina made to get up from her chair, but Fran stopped her. 'You relax and keep Dad company.'

Fran climbed the stairs and tiptoed into the room Nick was occupying, Michael's old room. He was sleeping soundly after his earlier mishap and the restlessness and high temperature had subsided. How soon would he leave? She noticed the deep jagged scar on his arm that she had seen earlier and wondered how it had occurred. Then 'murder' flashed through her mind and she gasped. Hurrying down the stairs, she picked up the telephone and dialled Rufus's number, praying that he would answer and not Helga. He answered.

'Rufus,' she gabbled, 'I need to ask you an important question.'

His voice cut in. 'Is Nick all right?'

'Yes, he's sleeping. When I saw Helga, she said Nick was a killer. Is it true?'

Chapter Twenty-Two

'Christ!' bellowed Rufus. 'What the hell has she been saying?'

'What I just said. Rufus, I need an answer now. I have Nick in the next bedroom to me.'

'Frannie, you have nothing to fear from Nick.'

'But why did Helga say that?'

'Her mind's twisted. Look, I can't explain over the phone and I'm rather tied up with a business deal at the moment. But as soon as I'm free I'll come and explain.'

Fran banged down the receiver, muttering, 'It had better be convincing or he will be out.'

She went back up to look in on Nick. He looked innocent in sleep, but then looks can be so deceptive and, despite what Rufus said, she wasn't reassured.

Downstairs, Will was listening to *The Goon Show* on the radio. Fran poured out Will's nightly tot of whisky, adding hot water, and took it over to him. She felt like a drink too. 'Whisky, Tina?' she asked, raising the bottle.

Tina looked up from the large book she was flicking through.

'No, thanks.' She continued, 'This is a stencilling book I've borrowed from the library. It's got some swell ideas.'

Fran glanced at the open page, liking what she saw. 'A Mexican styled bathroom. I love the warm terracotta colour wash and deeper tone stencilled pattern. So cosy and inviting,' she added, thinking of their drab bathroom. 'But it's not practical at the moment to start there.'

Tina flicked back a page. 'What about the kitchen?'

'That's a better idea. The kitchen could do with livening up,' she said, looking round. 'We could start with the walled area above the cupboards. What do you think?'

'You've got plenty of space, so if you make a mistake it won't be noticed.'

'Thanks for that vote of confidence.'

Later that night, Fran thought about the decorating venture that Tina suggested and was mildly surprised at her surge of enthusiasm, despite having Nick under the roof. She'd taken him a hot milky drink and biscuits before giving him his medication. He'd managed to walk to the bathroom unaided, a shuffling figure dressed in a pair of her father's pyjamas, which were too short in the leg for him. She wished Rufus would hurry and clear up the situation and explain the meaning behind Helga's accusation.

Once back in bed, Nick was soon asleep and Fran went into Isabel's old room to see if Tina had settled. Knocking, she popped her head round the door, asking, 'Do you need anything?'

Tina was sitting in the middle of the big bed, her knees drawn up to her chin. 'No, this is swell. It's a big room and I've got some fab ideas for decorating it. Whose room was it?'

'My sister's.'

'I'd strip off all this yucky wallpaper for a start.'

Fran laughed. 'Tina, I just might keep you to your word.'

'Do you know, until I met Joe and Nancy, I'd never given decorating a thought. My mam used to do ours. I should have helped her. Poor Maggie,' she whispered, her eyes filling with tears.

To distract Tina from her sadness, Fran said, flirtatiously, 'I think I'd like to meet this boyfriend of yours. You've kept him to yourself for far too long. Bring him over for Sunday dinner. Not this Sunday, but next.'

Instantly, Tina perked up. 'Do you mean it?'

'Of course I do. It's a date.'

The next day, Fran awoke early to the sound of birds chirping. Hopping out of bed, she drew back the curtains to reveal a dry, bright summer's day. She pushed up the sash window and leant out, breathing in the fresh air and experienced a feeling of pure delight and happiness. The weather certainly helped and, if it continued, she would take a trip into town, visit a hardware store and make a start on decorating the kitchen.

She shrugged on her dressing gown, she opened her bedroom door and heard the terrible sound of someone being sick in the bathroom. Nick? But he was still asleep and so was Will. She tapped on the bathroom door. 'Tina, are you all right?'

'No,' she replied, feebly.

Immediately, Fran pushed open the unlocked door to see Tina bent over the lavatory basin, retching. Fran rinsed a clean facecloth in cold water, dropped onto her knees and placed it on Tina's burning forehead. *My God*, she thought, *I hope she hasn't caught Nick's symptoms*. Guilt racked her. How could she have been so selfish as to involve this young, innocent woman?

Eventually, Tina stopped being sick and Fran helped her back into bed, alarmed at the girl's white, pasty face and dark sunken eyes. 'I must ring the doctor.' Tina let out a low moan.

The doctor agreed to call on his way to the surgery. After a quick examination, he came out of the bedroom where Fran waited anxiously on the landed. 'Has she got the same as Nick?'

'No. There's nothing to worry about, though I do need her to make an appointment to come into the surgery to have her pregnancy confirmed.'

'Pregnancy!'

The doctor smiled at the disbelief registered on Fran's face. 'Apart from the bouts of morning sickness, Tina is a healthy young lady.'

When she'd seen the doctor out, Fran made her way slowly up the stairs, thinking back to the time when she was pregnant and her bouts of morning sickness.

Propped up on the pillows Tina looked crestfallen. 'What am I going to do?' she asked woefully. 'And Joe, he'll go bananas.' She began to sob, her body heaving.

Fran sat on the bed and cradled Tina in her arms, whispering soothing words, but not able to give an answer.

When Tina tears subsided, Fran disentangled herself, saying, 'I'll run you a bath. Have a good soak and I'll make you an appointment.'

As she rose from the bed, Tina grabbed her arm. 'Will you come with me?' she pleaded.

Fran stroked back the girl's tousled hair and without hesitation said, 'Of course I will.' As she went out of the room an image flashed from nowhere into her mind of her baby daughter. If she had lived, she would have been about Tina's age.

Tina was glad of Fran's presence as they went to the surgery. The examination proved positive and an appointment was made for

Tina to see the area midwife at the clinic. 'And, before you ask,' Fran said to a still stunned Tina, who was clinging on to her arm, 'I'll come with you.'

Later, back at High Bank House, Tina sat huddled in a chair. 'What am I going to tell Joe?'

'Tell him the truth, that you are pregnant and don't forget it takes two to conceive,' said Fran. Though, when she became pregnant, according to her mother's views, it only took one to conceive, namely Fran.

'I never thought about getting pregnant. It was just nice to have someone to love me.' Tina's eyes filled with tears. 'I'm making a right mess of my life.'

'Look, Tina, it is not your fault. I'm sure Joe will understand and, from what you've told me about him, he sounds a nice young man. Now, I'm going to send you home in a taxi and if there is a problem with Joe, you ring me. Okay?'

'Okay,' Tina muttered.

'And don't forget, you're bringing him for lunch next Sunday.'

Back at Nancy's, Tina rang Joe to say she was back and was he coming because she had something to tell him. Then she went to work and was kept busy, putting out new haberdashery stock.

On her way home from work, Tina popped into the butcher's shop, down Toll Gavel, for a pound of best sausages and a quarter stone of potatoes from the fruit and vegetable shop. Sausage and mash, and Oxo gravy would make a nice meal and she bought a raisin pie from the baker's for afters.

She arrived home before Joe, so she was able to remake the crumpled bed and tidy up before cooking the tea. She heard him whistling as he opened the back door and her heart lifted a notch.

This took her by surprise, for, although she liked Joe and his lovemaking, she still thought about Mike. But he was many miles away and out of her reach.

'Hello, Joe,' she said, smiling at him.

He strode the few steps to reach her and hugged her tight. 'I've missed you, Tina.'

She could smell the familiar smell of grease on him, her smile wobbled and tears welled in her eyes. Before she could stop herself, she blurted, 'Joe, I'm pregnant!' She had meant to tell him later after, they'd eaten. Tears trickled down her cheeks.

Joe gasped, now holding her at arm's length. 'Do you mean pregnant, as in babies?'

'You dumbo, that's what pregnant means. What do you think?'

'Dunno. I'd better sit down.'

The sausages were sizzling and spluttering, so she pulled the frying pan off the heat and sat down at the kitchen table opposite him, her eyes downcast. Neither spoke. Outside, a couple of lads were kicking a football in the street and calling to one another. The kitchen became hot and stuffy so Tina got up and opened the back door. Next door's cat was sitting on the fence, his beady eye on a couple of blackbirds foraging around Nancy's sweetpeas. She sat down again, waiting for Joe to speak, her heart racing madly and her thoughts full of confusion.

'Does it mean I'm gonna be a dad?' His voice was gentle.

She looked at him, surprised. She had expected him to be angry. 'Do you want to be a dad?'

He shrugged. 'It can grow on yer, why not?'

'But how will we manage?'

'Easy,' he said, as he drew himself up tall. 'I've got a good job. I know I'm only an apprentice, but there's always plenty of overtime. And you've got a job.'

'Yes, but when the baby's born, what then?' Another thought struck her, something she'd overheard two customers discussing in the shop. 'What if you get called up?'

'Oh, that. I'm exempt, the boss saw to that.'

Tina let out a sigh of relief. If Joe was sent away to do his National Service, she didn't know what she would have done. 'Still, it'll be tough and we'll be frowned upon.'

'Who by?' he asked, indignantly.

She shrugged. 'The authorities could be nosey.'

'We won't tell 'em.'

'Where shall we live? Cos Cyril won't want a baby in the house.'

'Our Maureen's bloke's lodging at our house so there's no room.' He scratched at his tufts of ginger hair for inspiration. 'I don't know what we're gonna do.'

They both fell silent again, both deep in thought as to their interpretations of what problems a baby would bring into their lives.

Joe broke the quietness. 'I'm starving.'

Tina was glad of the ordinariness of his words. 'You have a quick wash and I'll dish up.'

Left on her own, she placed a hand on the small swell of her belly and unexpectedly, she felt her first surge of delight. At least her baby would know who its mother was.

Chapter Twenty-Three

Rufus was here at High Bank House upstairs talking to Nick, who was now feeling much better. Fran was in the sitting room, waiting to speak to Rufus. She glanced round the drab, cheerless room. *A neglected room*, she thought. The kitchen was more cheerful, but she didn't want Will to overhear what Rufus had to say about Nick. She stood by the window, looking out on the equally neglected front garden.

A knock on the door and Rufus entered beaming, saying, in a jovial voice, 'My, you've done wonders with Nick. I can't thank you enough. I . . .'

Fran spun round. 'Rufus, please! Tell me about Nick.'

He came and stood before her. 'Yes, Frannie, I will. Do you think I could have a drink first? Whisky, if you have it, please.'

There was her father's whisky in the kitchen, but she didn't want him asking any awkward questions. She found half a bottle in the sideboard and, hoping it was still drinkable, she poured him a generous measure. She watched him gulp it down as she seated herself on one of the dining chairs. She gestured for him to sit on a chair opposite her. She wanted to see his face as he explained about Nick, but he sat sideways on the chair, not looking at her.

He began in a flat voice. 'There was an accident. Nick was driving. His wife, Zeta, was next to him, and Helga, her cousin, was in the back of the car with Jamie.' Rufus stared into space and Fran stared at him.

'Who's Jamie?' she heard herself say.

It took Rufus a few seconds to answer. 'He was Nick and Zeta's son.'

'Was?' she whispered.

He nodded, continuing, 'The roads were icy, so Nick needed to concentrate on his driving, but Zeta had been drinking heavily, which wasn't unusual for her. Helga, Zeta and Jamie had been to a village concert and Zeta won a bottle of vodka as a raffle prize and drank it all. Nick went to pick them up and Zeta, the worse for drink, kept arguing with Nick and hitting him. He tried to remonstrate with her, she grabbed the wheel, he lost control, the car hit an icy patch and crashed into a tree.' Rufus turned to face Fran and there were tears in the big man's eyes.

Fran could smell the sweat which soaked his shirt, hear his laboured breathing as he fought to regain control of his emotions. She thought about offering him another drink, but it didn't seem appropriate. She waited for him to continue but, in her heart, she guessed the outcome.

Rufus mopped his brow and ran his tongue around his dry lips. His voice croaked and was scarcely audible. 'Zeta was killed outright and poor Jamie died two days later. Nick was in a coma for over a week and two years on he still hasn't fully recovered. Helga lost the use of her legs, so you see why she is so bitter towards Nick. She blames him totally. Nothing that anyone else says, or that I say, will make her think any differently. And I love them both.'

She felt tears prick at the back of her eyes and gently she touched Rufus's arm and said, 'It's so tragic. I'm sorry for nagging you about Nick. He can stay as long as it takes for him to recover.' Relief filled her that Nick wasn't the cold-hearted killer Helga had inferred.

The next day, Nick ventured downstairs to sit and chat with Will. As she stirred the milk into the mugs of coffee, Fran glanced across the kitchen at Nick's thin frame dressed in a pair of faded jeans and navy-blue pullover. She stifled a yawn. She hadn't slept much last night, her mind still too full of Nick and his tragic background. He hadn't spoken about it and she wasn't sure if Rufus had told him that she knew. Watching as he relaxed in his chair, listening to Will yarning, she felt genuinely pleased that Nick was improving. She felt ashamed of her black thoughts now that she knew the reason behind his sad-looking eyes. They reflected his grief at the untimely death of his wife and young son. What a terrible weight to bear, and more so as he was driving the car.

She shuddered; at least she had Michael, even though he didn't live with her and only regarded her as his aunt. But then, she'd had her share of pain: the loss of Christina, her baby daughter. Biting on her lip to suppress a sigh, she knew from bitter experience that life could be very cruel. Though she had been happy in her working life in the bookshop, her personal life was a sham. She seemed to be forever searching for a deeper, inner happiness, which somehow eluded her. Like rushing into marriage, only to find out he was the wrong man for her. But the saddest regret of her life was that she'd left it too late to be a satisfying part of her son's life. Now, she was playing nursemaid to two men, who, for their own reasons, seemed to need her.

'Isn't the lovely Tina around today?' Nick's quiet voice broke into her thoughts.

Fran handed him his mug of coffee. 'She'll be here for Sunday dinner with her boyfriend.'

'Will I still be here?' Nick asked, a serious expression on his drawn face.

Fran felt her heart contract. Was it the emotional strain of the last few days that had weakened her? Because, all of a sudden, she wanted to take him into her arms and tell him it was all right. A motherly instinct, she told herself. But, before she could answer Nick, Will did.

'Of course you will be.'

'Thanks, Will.' But his eyes were fixed on Fran's face.

'Dad's right. You need to be back to full strength before you think of moving on and Rufus said it will take some time for your cottage to dry out.'

Immediately, Nick's face lost its seriousness as relief shone from his pale features. He caught her hand, pulling her towards him. 'You don't know what this means to me, to be here as part of a family. I really do appreciate it.'

For a moment, Fran thought he was going to kiss her. Confused, she hastily drew away from him and found, to her horror, she was blushing. 'Good,' she replied briskly to cover up her feelings. 'Now that's settled, I'd better start planning the menu for Sunday lunch,' she said, realising, to her dismay, she had five people to cook for. Worried now that she might not be able to cope, she went to the dresser and pulled out one of the well-thumbed cookery books.

'Fran, may I use your telephone, please?'

She looked up from the page where she was reading, with some disbelief, of an old-fashioned recipe called 'washday pie', to see Nick leaning on a chair opposite her.

'Yes, of course.' She flicked over the pages, looking for an easy recipe.

A smiling Nick came back into the room, his voice sounding much stronger, like before his illness. 'I think I may have solved your menu for Sunday lunch.' She looked at him in surprise. 'All will be revealed within the next couple of hours.'

Later, as she was pegging out sheets on the line to dry, she smiled wryly to herself. Satisfied with her work, she stepped back to admire the billowing white sheets contrasting against the background of the azure blue sky, so easy to imagine them as yachts in full sail on the sparkling Mediterranean Sea. If anyone had suggested to her a few months ago, when working in York, that she, a supposedly dedicated working woman, could have been contented with such a menial task as washing bedding, she wouldn't have believed it possible.

'Quite a fetching domestic scene for a city girl,' commented a voice.

Startled, she spun round. 'Rufus, I didn't hear you come. What have you got there?' she said, eying the huge cardboard box he was carrying.

'I come bearing bounty for a damsel in distress.'

'Rufus.' She laughed. Intrigued to see what it was, she followed him into the kitchen.

'Special delivery,' he announced placing the box on the table.

'Excellent,' said Nick, a mischievous grin on his face.

Even Will was curious and pulled himself up from his chair and ambled across to peer in the box and sniffed. 'Smells like pheasant to me.'

'Right, straight from my freezer and the other goodies are from Nick,' Rufus explained.

Fran pushed in between Will and Rufus. 'What's all this for then?' she asked, puzzled.

Nick, sitting opposite at the table answered. 'It's a thank you. Five people to cook Sunday lunch for is no mean feat and, if I'd been fit, I would have helped. So, I've done the next best thing, hopefully.' He looked at Fran, waiting for her to say something.

'But I don't know how to cook pheasant,' she blurted.

'I do.' Astonished, she stared at Will. 'Your mother never liked pheasant, but when I was a young man, I often cooked it.'

'Well I never,' she said, kissing him on the cheek. 'You're a dark rascal.'

Rufus emptied the box containing a brace of pheasants, an assortment of freshly dug vegetables, a wedge of Wensleydale cheese and a freshly baked apple pie, still warm.

'Who baked this?' Fran asked.

Rufus put his finger to the side of his nose, saying, 'I have my sources.'

He continued unpacking bottles of beer and cordial, and a box of mint chocolates.

On Sunday morning, both astride the bike, Joe asked Tina, 'Where does this woman live then?'

'High Bank House, Burton Banks.'

He turned round to face her. 'High Bank House, are you sure?'

'Of course I'm sure – I've been there.'

'Well, in that case you'll know who used to live there!'

'Who?' But Joe's answer was blown away by the roar of the engine.

Within ten minutes, Joe brought the bike to a halt outside the back door of High Bank House. Nick and Will were drinking beer, sitting on a makeshift bench of a plank of wood on two piles of bricks. Joe swung off the bike and went towards the two men. 'How are yer, Mr Bewholme? Long time no see.' Tina stopped to adjust her skirt so didn't hear Joe call Will 'Mr Bewholme'.

Will, held up a hand to shield his eyes from the sun, squinting though blurred vision. 'Well, if it isn't Michael's old pal. How yer doing son?'

'Just fine and you?'

'Better when I get my eyes sorted out.'

Tina strode up to the men. 'Hello, Will.'

Will smiled at Tina, saying, 'He's a good 'un is Joe.'

'He's not too bad and neither are you,' she said, kissing the old man on his cheek. Then she turned. 'Nick, this is my boyfriend, Joe.'

Nick shook Joe's hand. 'Fancy a beer and you too, Tina?'

'Yes, please.'

Fran came out, her face flushed from cooking, her blonde hair scraped back and held in place with a ribbon. 'I've come for a breather and a beer.' She joined Will and Nick on the bench while Tina and Joe perched on the low-sided wall of the old timber yard. 'So, you're Joe. I've heard you're good at stencilling,' she said, pleasantly.

He looked at Tina and grinned, 'I hope she hasn't told yer too much.' Tina nudged him. All five chattered about different topics, and then Joe said to Will, 'Shirley says Mike's having a great time and it's their winter. Fun with the snowballs.'

'Snow?' asked Will, 'I thought it was warm in Australia, even in their winter?'

'You're right, but it's cooler and it suits Mrs Bell because she doesn't like the heat.'

'Who's Mrs Bell?' asked Fran.

'Mike's mum, Isabel. Just a bit of fun I had with Mrs Renton's name.' He felt Tina stiffen by his side and when he turned to look at her, he saw her face was a pasty-grey colour.

Her lips trembled as she forced out the words. 'Mike's mum is Isabel Renton?'

Fran notice Tina's discomfort and she answered. 'Isabel is my sister. Do you know her?'

Tina felt her body sway as a dark dizziness enveloped her. It was Fran who caught her, stopping her from falling off the wall.

'Tina!' Joe cried, as Tina's half-full glass of beer splashed his best white shirt.

'Quick, Joe, take her other arm and let's get her inside where it is cooler,' instructed Fran.

They took her into the sitting room away from the heat of the kitchen and laid her carefully on the old sofa. 'Will she be all right?' asked Joe anxiously, not certain what to do next.

'You hold her hand. I'll be back in a minute,' said Fran, hurrying off. Returning in seconds with a glass of cold water and a damp facecloth, she dropped to her knees, gazing down at Tina's white face and closed eyes. Gently, she dabbed Tina's temple and cheeks with the cloth until, after about thirty seconds, which seemed like hours, Tina opened her eyes. Joe looked to Fran for advice. 'Support her into a sitting position.'

More used to lifting machinery than fainting women, Joe gingerly put an arm around Tina and lifted her up, and Fran placed a cushion behind her back. Holding the glass of water to Tina's lips, she whispered, reassuringly, 'Come on, have a drink and you'll soon be all right.'

Slowly, Tina drank all the water and the colour began to return to her face.

'Feeling better?' Fran asked.

Tina nodded, saying weakly, 'Sorry if I gave you a scare. I think it must have been the heat.' But, even as she spoke, the name 'Isabel Renton' reverberated in her head.

'She's pregnant!' Joe exclaimed, laying a protective hand on Tina's arm.

'Yes, I do know, but it's not an illness, just some things might make her queasy. Perhaps staying off alcohol might help?' Fran offered, sympathetically.

'Do all pregnant women have this sickness and fainting thing?' asked a serious-faced Joe.

Laughing, Fran replied, 'Some do. I did.' Instantly, she felt her body freeze.

Tina, now feeling a little better, stared at Fran, 'I didn't know you had any children.'

Fran, her legs feeling weak, groped for a chair and sank on it, unable to reply.

Joe rushed from the room and brought Fran a glass of water. Two fainting women in one day – it must be the heat. Time for him to retreat.

Fran sipped the water, feeling a little foolish. What must Joe and Tina think of her? She looked at Tina and said, 'I'm feeling better now.'

Though Tina had known Fran for only a short time and knew she was divorced, she had never mentioned children before. For a moment, her own problems forgotten, Tina felt curious and asked, 'Are your children with your ex, is that why you are upset?' Fran stared at her. Quickly, Tina said, 'You don't have to answer me.'

Fran's eyes stung with unshed tears as she grappled with what Tina was saying. 'My ex! We didn't have children. I wasn't married when . . .'

Now it was Tina's turn to be the comforter. She rose, went to Fran and put a soothing arm about her shoulder. 'I'm sorry, Fran, I can see it's upsetting you so forget I asked the question.'

Fran forced a smile, but her lips trembled as she said, 'It was a long time ago and I was a foolish young girl. You are lucky, you have Joe. I had no one.'

There was a knock on the door and Joe's head peeped round. 'Just to let yer know, grub's up.'

'Gosh!' exclaimed Fran, rather too brightly, 'I'd quite forgotten lunch. Give me five minutes.'

Tina, seemingly recovered, went off with Joe and Fran went to the bathroom. She splashed her face with cold water and patting it dry with a soft towel. She stared at her reflection in the mirror, feeling annoyed with herself. One unguarded moment and she'd revealed her shadowed past.

In the kitchen, an unbelievable, surprising scene greeted Fran. Will was carving the pheasants and Joe was handing round the plates, Nick was pouring the cordial and the piping hot tureens of vegetables were already set on the table. Fran felt a wonderful happiness flood her body.

The day after its rocky start, proved a great success and much later, too tired to sleep, she lay in bed, her mind playing over the happenings of the day. One particular segment of a scene seemed to stick. It was when Tina had asked, '*Did you say they called Mike's mum, Isabel Renton?*' And she had answered, '*Isabel is my sister. Do you know her?*' It was at this point that Tina fainted and she thought it was because Tina was pregnant. Perhaps that was the reason, but something puzzled Fran and she wasn't sure what it was. The scene kept replaying until sleep finally caught hold of her.

* * *

Back at Nancy's, Tina snuggled next to Joe, but she couldn't sleep. Her mind was too active. A picture of Isabel Renton flashed vividly before her, the ugly, angry face of the doctor's receptionist. Was it possible, after all, that woman was her biological mother? She had seen Isabel Renton only the once and didn't like what she saw, so she had dismissed her from her mind. A thought struck her and she sat bolt up, paying no heed to Joe's mumbling as she jerked the bedclothes off his bare body. Could it be possible there was more than one Isabel Renton? Then she sank back onto the pillow. This Isabel Renton was living in Australia and she was Mike's mother, but she couldn't be her mother because Mike was the same age as she was. In the next instant she sat bolt up again. What if . . .

'What's up with you?' Joe grunted. 'You've woke me up again.'

'Sorry,' she pacified, slipping from the bed. She pulled on a nightie, not to cover her nakedness, but to soak up the cold sweat swamping her body. Downstairs in the kitchen, she leant against the table for support. Breathing in the solitude, she let out her burning thought.

What if she and Mike Renton were twins?

Chapter Twenty-Four

Fran watched for the postman. They were due to have a letter from Michael. Although he wrote to Will, Michael knew she read the letters, so he included her in them. For her part, she wrote of day-to-day happenings and, despite the miles separating them, Fran felt close to him. There was no longed-for letter today.

In bed that night, the weather was still humid, too hot for sleeping. The window was wide open, but the room was airless. Naked, Fran lay with just a thin sheet covering her, listening to the night sounds: the water gently lapping against the broken jetty, the hoot of an owl in a distant tree. She thought of Nick in the next room and her body generated new heat. The more she thought of him, the more she wanted to be desired. She wrapped her arms around her body; it had been a long time since a man held her in his arms and made love. Now, why was she thinking of that? She was no good at relationships with men. She didn't need them, she reaffirmed to herself, though she wasn't sure if she was cut out for a life of celibacy. In this confused state of mind, she drifted off, only to be woken up by moans coming from Will's room.

Hastily, she scrambled from the bed, pulled on a thin cotton robe and rushed to her father's side. To her surprise, Nick was already there. He was massaging one of Will's legs.

'What's wrong?' she asked, rubbing sleep from her eyes.

'He's got cramp, but it's getting easier,' Nick answered.

Fran glanced at her father's face and saw it visibly relax as he closed his eyes. Then her gaze went back to Nick. He was wearing just a pair of pyjama bottoms and, though his body was long and lean, she could see the flexing strength of his shoulder muscles as he massaged Will's leg. Her insides gave a strange flutter and she began fussing with Will's pillows. Will went back to sleep and Nick stopped massaging. 'I guess he'll be all right now.' He gently replaced the quilt over Will. Stepping back, he rested an arm about Fran's shoulders and led her from the room.

Fran asked, anxiously, 'Is he going to be all right?'

'Yes, I'm sure he will be. He was probably just lying awkwardly and got the cramps.'

His arm felt comforting, protective, and she felt his fingers playing with loose tendrils of her hair in the nape of her neck. He drew her closer and through the thin cotton of her robe she felt the tantalising heat of his body. Instinctively, she leant into him, her robe slipping off one shoulder to reveal a glow of pearly, satin skin. 'Fran,' he whispered, 'you're so beautiful.' She wasn't sure how it happened, she was in his arms, his lips caressing her smooth skin. Then, gently moving his lips up her slender neck he sought her lips with engaging tenderness. At the same time, his hand cupped her breast, circling the hardening nipple. Wild dancing flames sent sensation after sensation through her tormented, starved body. Reaching out, she clung to him, her lips parting as his tongue found the intimacy of her mouth, arousing in her a long-forgotten passion. Startled by the deep intensity of his kiss, but more startled by her matching response, she moulded into his body, pressing against his arousal, wanting him, desiring him. Her robe slipped further down her body dropping at her feet. Swaying slightly, his hands kneaded the roundness of her buttocks. His breath, warm, feathery, fanned across her breasts and she gasped with pleasure. Intoxicated by the smell of his masculinity, her hands explored the taut muscles of his back.

'Nick,' she whispered, throatily, her passion ablaze.

Then, as if her voice had pressed a button, he stilled, drawing away from her. His face full of anguish he stared down at her. Shrinking from her, he muttered, 'Sorry! Forgive me.' And without another word, he turned from her and went into his own room and closed the door.

Stunned, bewildered, frozen in the heat of the night, all she could see in the dimness of her mind was the replay of Nick's retreating figure. Her only awareness was the terrible ache. She had bared her body, and her soul, to this man and he had rejected her.

Sleep eluded her until the early hours of the morning and then she only slept for a couple of hours. She heard Nick get up and go downstairs and let himself out of the house.

She persuaded Will to spend the morning in bed, pampering him with bacon and egg, and the morning newspaper. She busied herself and, for the umpteenth time, she wondered where Nick was. Feeling restless, she went outside and round to the front of the house to look down the lane for any sign of him. The day was dull, the sky, grey – one of those useless summer days. In her confused mind, she tried to analyse why he should reject her so, but she couldn't think of an answer – nothing which made sense. Or was it that he found her repulsive? *To hell with him*, she thought, angrily brushing away a hot tear. Back in doors, she settled down to write to Michael. It didn't matter that he owed them a letter, she just felt better writing to him. Mostly, she told him about Will's visit to the optician's and what a difference wearing spectacles had made to his eyesight, but also about the visit of Tina and Joe, the weather and Nick staying with them because of the flood damage to his cottage. If she didn't mention him, Will would think it odd. She went up to Will's room so he could read the letter before posting it.

'Where's Nick?' Will asked when she entered his room.

'Out for a walk,' she replied, which was partly true, though where, she had no idea.

Later, after a snack dinner, Will was still in his room, settling down to have an afternoon snooze, and there was still no sign of Nick. Fran decided she needed some fresh air.

'Dad, I'm going down to post Michael's letter. Can I get you anything from the shop?'

Drowsily, he replied, 'Just some baccy.'

She strolled down the narrow lane with its hawthorn hedge and grassy edging abandoned to the wildness of nature, among tall grasses, feathery with seed, the yarrow with its clusters of white and pink blooms. This beauty was lost on her because her mind was on Nick and what happened last night. Or, what didn't happen. The rejection hurt more than she cared to admit. She had been overwhelmed by Nick's unexpected attraction to her and surprised how eager her response was to his ardour. He'd aroused her sensuality and she'd loved it, and so had he, she felt it. So, why had he drawn away from her? She couldn't fathom that out.

After posting the letter and buying Will's baccy, she hurried back home, expecting Nick to be there, but he wasn't. This surprised her as she knew from talking to Rufus that his home was still uninhabitable.

'Cooee!' Fran turned to see Nancy entering the kitchen. 'Thought I'd drop by to tell you that Tina's, the silly girl, got herself pregnant. I told her she won't be the first or the last. They're saving like mad to get a place to rent, but housing so scarce. I'll keep my eyes open and ask my ladies if they know of anywhere.'

'Tina seems a survivor.'

'She's had to be since her mam died.' Nancy's usual pleasant voice was sharp.

'Sorry, I didn't mean to be insensitive,' said Fran. Then, a thought struck her. 'Why did she come to live in Beverley? I've not heard her mention anything about family living here.'

Nancy was about to say something, then changed her mind. 'It's not for me to say.'

Fran glanced at the older woman, wondering what the mystery was. 'Let me know if I can help.' Her thoughts turned back to Nick and she voiced her concerns to Nancy.

Nancy said, 'I'll stay with your father, you go down to Nick's cottage and see if he's there.'

The quickest way to Nick's was along the riverbank. The recent floods had receded, but the banks were rather muddy. Exchanging her shoes for wellington boots, Fran squelched along the bank. It had been years since she was this far up river. From here, she could see quite clearly across the river, the great expanse of farmland that stretched for miles towards the distant village and the airfield, which, during the war, had been a Bomber Command base. Passing the bird sanctuary, she saw Nick's cottage round the next bend.

Nestling by the riverside, its small plot of garden was a quagmire and the rickety wooden gate swayed on its broken hinge.

She walked down the silt path to the front door and knocked. There was no reply, so she followed the path round to the back of the cottage. Her heart contracted as she saw Nick dragging a wet carpet across to the back fence. She stood for a moment, expecting him to look up and see her, but he was too intent on the task in hand. She caught a sideward's glimpse of his face and saw deep lines etched that she'd never noticed before.

She could see that the sodden carpet was heavy and would need two pairs of hands if it were to make it onto the fence to have a chance of drying out. 'Let me help.'

He half turned at the sound of her voice to look at her, raising an eyebrow of surprise. 'Thanks,' he said wearily.

Together, they heaved and tugged until, finally, the carpet rested on the fence. Getting their breaths back they both stood, eyeing the carpet, and then Nick's voiced what Fran was thinking, but didn't like to say. 'I think it's had it.'

She just nodded in agreement, then added. 'Did you take the cottage furnished?' He nodded. 'Then the owner will be responsible for replacements.'

'I'm afraid not. You see the cottage was up for sale and Rufus persuaded the owner to rent to me with the proviso that I will be responsible for any damage that occurred.' Shrugging, he turned and walked towards the back door of the cottage and Fran followed him inside.

In the tiny sitting room, Fran saw a reluctant wood fire splinter and hiss in the grate, its weak flames attempting to heat a saucepan of water.

Nick followed Fran's gaze. 'I was going to make coffee, but I guess the water is never going to boil,' he lamented, his shoulders sagging.

She should forget last night, she chided herself, and think about now, so she took a deep breath and said, lightly, 'I don't think you can do any more here. Best put the fire out of its misery and we'll go back to High Bank. Nancy might be making us something tasty for tea.'

His gaze met hers full on and they locked for all of three seconds, then he broke into a grin. 'You mean it?' he asked as if he was a school boy who had been offered an unexpected treat.

'Of course, and we don't want to disappoint Nancy.'

He made the fire safe and locked the cottage. Once on the bank path, he took hold of her arm and gently turned her to him. She looked into his sad, tired eyes, trying to find a glimmer of hope. 'I just want to clear the air. I'm sorry for last night. I'm a guest in your house and I took advantage of you. It shouldn't have happened.'

While he was speaking, she just stared, mesmerised, as she watched his lips moving. Then he stopped speaking, leant towards her, and with his long fingers he lightly dusted away the specks of soot clinging to her cheeks. She wasn't certain how it happened but there she was in his arms again, their lips seeking and finding. The kiss was soft, sweet and full of glorious passion that made her breathless, desiring more.

'Wow!' She exclaimed her body still in tremor as she clung to Nick for support.

'You okay?' He looked at her, a little uncertain, as if he couldn't believe what had just happened between them.

'Yes. It's just that I'd never before experienced such intense feelings of . . .' She wanted to say love, but she wasn't a youngster in the throes of her first love, but she did know that her feelings were strong. 'Such joy,' she finished.

He grinned at her. 'Then last night wasn't a mistake?'

'No,' she replied firmly, slipping her hand into his.

When they reached home and deposited their muddy boots in the porch, they found Nancy in the kitchen popping a meat and potato pie in the oven. She looked up, her swift glance taking in their happy faces. 'Everything all right?' she queried.

'Fine,' Fran answered.

'And, before you ask, Will's up and getting a shave and he'll be down for tea.'

Fran went up to Nancy and hugged her. 'You're a treasure.'

As Nancy slipped on her cardigan, she said casually, 'Been having a mud bath?'

For the first time, Fran noticed her dirty blouse and mud splattered skirt, and laughed.

Later that evening, after supper, Fran and Nick left Will listening to the wireless and went into the sitting room. They sat side by side on the old sofa, laughing as the broken springs pinged and groaned under their weight. Sharing a bottle of cool beer, they talked, finding out about each other, how they both enjoyed the countryside and Fran confessed that in spite of living near the river she'd never taken to boats, not since she and a school friend were toppled from their rowing boat to end up in the murky water of the river.

'I'll take you out on the river,' Nick offered. Fran's face creased in horror.

After moments silence, Nick said, 'Rufus mentioned he'd told you a little of my background.'

Here, Fran felt guilty. 'He was clearing up a misunderstanding. Something Helga said.'

'I can guess. She still blames me for the accident and she's right. I shouldn't have let my wife's argumentative mood distract my driving or I should have stopped the car.' His voice was sad, almost painful. 'If only I'd known it would have cost the life of my son.'

Fran thought of Michael, oceans away. She waited to see if Nick was going to say any more about his tragedy, but he didn't. So they talked about nothing in particular. By this time, darkness was falling and they were both feeling rather tired. 'I'll make the cocoa and see Dad off to bed.'

When she came back with their bedtime drink and biscuits, she said, 'Shall we have an early night?' He just nodded. And, wanting to take away his hurt and to ease his pain, she said softly, 'My bed is the most comfortable one.'

And the joy on his face gladdened her heart.

Chapter Twenty-Five

Tina lay in bed, looking up at the zigzag crack in the ceiling. It was like a crazy path, mirroring her life. She was supposed to be finding her birth mother, Isabel Renton, who could be Mike's mother. That was enough to unravel in itself and now she'd added another complication: she was pregnant. She stretched out her arm to the empty side of the bed. The sheet was cool, smooth, unwrinkled. How she missed the warm bodily comfort of Joe. He had gone from her bed now that Nancy had returned. She thought of Nancy as a mother figure, though at first she had been upset on hearing Tina was pregnant. Fran had been helpful and kind, but she wasn't family.

Tina pulled herself from the bed and it was only when she was dressing, that she realised she hadn't been sick that morning, which was a relief. She fastened her dirndl skirt placate with a safety pin to accommodate her thickening waist line and wore her blouse loose.

She'd worked her lunch hour and left the shop early so she could be home before Nancy. This would be the only time she could talk to Nancy because Cyril would be home this evening.

First, she put the kettle on to boil, and then took from her shopping bag two Yorkshire curd cheesecakes – these were Nancy's favourites. And, by the time Nancy arrived home, the kettle was singing.

Taking off her head scarf and shaking her permed curls, Nancy exclaimed with surprise, 'This is a treat.' Tina smiled and poured out the tea. She felt guilty because of her ulterior motive. Her stomach churned with tension. Was it fair to land Nancy with another one of her problems?

'You should be eating for two.' Nancy said, watching Tina nibble at her tartlet. Tears pricked Tina's eyes and she fought them back, giving a gulp. 'Sweetheart, are you worried about the baby?' Nancy asked. Tina shook her head. Baffled, Nancy asked, 'What then?'

'It's my mother.'

'Your mother?' Nancy repeated, thinking of the dead Maggie.

'Isabel Renton,' Tina whispered the name as if she was frightened of it.

'You've spoken to her?'

'She's in Australia.' Nancy reached out to hold Tina's hand. From the warmth and comfort of Nancy's touch, Tina found the courage to continue. 'I think Michael Renton is my twin brother.'

'Michael?' Nancy looked puzzled. 'Do you mean Joe's friend? Are you sure?'

'Not really. I feel so confused.' Then she related to Nancy when she and Joe had gone to High Bank House for Sunday lunch and she'd found that Isabel Renton was Michael's mother. 'Mike's my age. It connects, don't you think, Nancy?'

Nancy pondered a moment and offered, 'I'm not sure, love. You'll need more details.'

'Nancy! I've just got to know. I can't think straight. I need to know.' Her face screwed with uncertainty, she pressed her hands to her throbbing temple.

Nancy rose, went to Tina's side and hugged her closed. 'There,' she soothed. 'I think the best thing is to talk to Fran. She might be able to help.'

Hope touched Tina's heart. 'Oh, Nancy, do you really think so?'

Early evening, Tina and Nancy caught the bus to High Bank House. 'This is a lovely surprise,' said Fran opening the door to them. Then she noticed Tina's subdued look and red rimmed eyes. 'Is there something wrong?'

Nancy answered, 'Fran, there's something we need to talk to you about.'

Nick and Will were in the kitchen, so she said, 'Come through to the sitting room. Sorry, but the sofa is not very comfortable. Pack the cushions behind your back, Tina.'

Thinking they wanted to talk about the expected baby, Fran smiled reassuringly at Tina, but Tina kept her eyes downcast. So, Fran looked to Nancy and waited.

Nancy gave Tina a gentle nudge. At that very moment, Tina thought of her beloved Maggie and her heart cried. *Oh, Mam, Mam.* She swallowed hard and the heat from her body clung to her blouse. She gave a deep sigh and her voice quivered. 'It began when my mother, Maggie, died. It was so sudden. There were only the two of us and we were happy.' She closed her eyes for a moment, thinking of those cherished memories. Then she continued, her voice gathering momentum, becoming stronger. 'There was a lot to see to, documents and things, and the Reverend Fairweather was very helpful. He gave me good advice, but I didn't always take it.' She took in a great gulp of air and said quietly, 'Until she died, I didn't know Maggie wasn't my real mother, that she was my foster mother and until I'd left school a "Mrs Bewholme" paid Maggie to look after . . .'

Fran interrupted, 'Which Mrs Bewholme?'

Tina thought for a moment. 'Agnes Bewholme, I think.'

The colour drained from Fran face. 'How do you know this? Did you see her?'

Tina gasped at Fran's harsh tone and the strange way she was looking at her. A feeling of uneasiness filled her, but she had to carry on. How else could she find out the truth? She stumbled on, 'There were letters from Mrs Bewholme. I've left them with the Vicar. I think I saw her once, but I didn't know who she was. Maggie said she was an aunt. She was well dressed, wore a hat and talked posh, but with a funny accent. That's all I remember about her. She didn't come to Maggie's funeral.'

That was her mother, she felt positive. But what had she been up to? What was her connection with Tina? Fran sat on the edge of the chair, bracing herself. For what, she wasn't sure.

Nancy took up the story. 'Tina came to Beverley to find her real mother.'

'Her real mother,' Fran repeated, not sure where this situation was going and why Agnes Bewholme had been involved. 'Do you know her name?'

Tina felt everything in her body turn and twist, and her nerve ends tingle. She drew a deep breath and forced out the words. 'Isabel Renton!' The name was out, but it hung in the air like a bird trapped on an unseen wire.

Fran felt as if the room was revolving. From the kitchen came the sound of distant laughter. Both Tina and Nancy were staring at her, waiting for her to speak. She forced out the words. 'Agnes Bewholme was our mother, that is, Isabel's and mine. But I don't know anything about Isabel having a daughter.' She tried to get her head around what had been said and if Isabel had had a daughter it must have been after Michael was born. Or could it have been before?

'Fran,' Tina spoke softly, feeling afraid for upsetting the woman, as she clearly was. Perhaps it wasn't such a good idea of Nancy's after all to ask Fran about Isabel. 'I'm sorry.'

Fran felt ashamed at seeing the distress in Tina's eyes and she knew, whatever the situation, it needed to be resolved. 'Don't be sorry.' Thinking logically, she asked, 'What makes you think Isabel is your mother?'

'Her name's on my birth certificate.'

Her head spun. Was it possible, Isabel had a daughter? Fran stared at Tina in disbelief and said, 'Are you sure?'

'I can bring my birth certificate to prove it.'

Nancy rose quietly and left the room, leaving Fran and Tina alone together.

'There's no need for that.' Fran forced a smile. This girl had just presented her with an emotional shock. But then what about Tina's feelings, finding out that Isabel was her mother and, worse still, not even to be acknowledged as her daughter.

Feeling emotionally drained, but needing to qualify further her birth mother's name, Tina said, 'I did see Isabel once, when I went to the doctor's. She was the receptionist.' Tina didn't add that she didn't like the woman on sight.

Fran searched Tina's troubled eyes. 'You didn't speak to her?'

'No, it was late and I think she was tired. I didn't see her again.'

'And now she's in Australia,' Fran said, failing to disguise her hopeless tone. 'I doubt if she's ever going to come back.' Was there more to Isabel marrying in haste than just to whisk Michael away? Was her past catching up to her?

Suddenly, feeling so overcome, Tina burst into tears.

'Oh, my dear.' Fran went to Tina and knelt beside her and held the sobbing girl close. Soothing her, she stroked her red hair, seeing the light roots showing through. Fran thought fleetingly, she's blonde beneath that mop of red. What a bitch Isabel was to desert such a lovely girl. But, why had she done it? And why had Agnes been involved? Something wasn't making sense, but she couldn't think what.

Tina stirred, raising a tear-stained face and mumbled, 'Sorry.'

'Don't be. It's your hormones acting up. You're pregnant. Now, your top priority is to take care of yourself. You are going to be a mother. Think of that.'

Tina brightened. 'I'd love a little girl. I'd call her Maggie, after . . .' Her lips quivered.

Fran gave Tina her handkerchief. 'Dry your eyes.' Then, kindly, she said, 'Go home and rest. We can talk again later if you wish.' Inwardly, she cried, *Isabel! What have you done?*

Later that evening, in their bedroom, Nick said, 'What's on your mind?'

Wearily, Fran got into bed. 'It's where to begin.' Fran told Nick of Tina's revelation and how she came to Beverley to find her birth mother. 'Naturally she's very upset and it doesn't help matters that Isabel is on the other side of the world. It came as a shock to me. I knew nothing about it. Not that Isabel and I were ever close.'

Nick cuddled Fran, saying, 'It's a pity this didn't come to light before Isabel departed.'

'That's the funny thing. When Isabel worked as a doctor's receptionist, Tina saw her but didn't make herself known then. Perhaps it's something to do with her being pregnant now. Where you come from and who you are, are important bases in forming relationships and . . .' She suddenly thought of Michael. He didn't know the truth. He was living a lie and she allowed it to happen.

Suddenly, she remembered something about Tina which had puzzled her earlier. Then it came to her in a flash, startling Nick. 'It's impossible!'

'What is?' Nick asked, not following her line of reasoning.

'As far as I knew, Isabel was unable to conceive so Tina cannot possibly be Isabel's daughter!'

'But you said . . .'

'I was giving Tina the benefit of doubt, but I have no proof.'

'What proof do you require and why would she make up such a story?'

'I don't know, but what I do know is that Isabel was unable to have children.'

'But I thought she had a son!'

'Michael is my son!' Fran exclaimed, experiencing a short spurt of exhilaration. Then she covered her face with her hands and sobbed. Nick held her trembling body close, stroking her hair and, gradually, the soothing movements released her tension and she felt able to look into his face. He must be wondering what kind of woman he had become entangled with. She owed him an explanation – if she had any kind of future with Nick, she must be honest with him.

'Nick.' She looked deep into his eyes and quietly told him everything. How Isabel's late husband had got her drunk when she was in a vulnerable, emotional state of mind; Michael's birth and the death of his twin sister; her mother's cruel intervention in taking Michael away from her when she had been so ill; her disastrous marriage; her failure to win Michael back; and the final breaking point – Isabel whisking Michael off to Australia and Michael wanting to go.

Nick hugged her tenderly. 'One day Michael will come to you when he learns the truth.'

'Do you really think so?' Fran felt a slight surge of hope.

'Yes, I think the truth will come out eventually,' he said, reassuringly. He frowned, pondering thoughtfully before saying, 'Fran, did you ever visit your daughter's grave?'

'Why, no. I was so ill at the time my mother told me of Christine's death. And afterwards, I just focused on Michael.'

'Your daughter was called Christine?' Nick sat up with a jerk. 'Have you considered that Tina might be your daughter and not Isabel's?'

Fran closed her eyes briefly, then opened them, staring at Nick. 'Of course I did, deep down, but I couldn't admit it to myself. I was frightened to hope.'

'Isabel's name is on is on both Michael's and Tina's birth certificates. How did that come about?'

Fran sat up and gasped in realisation. 'I'd forgotten until now, mother booked me into the hospital as Mrs Isabel Renton. She said it was to save further disgrace and better for me if the nursing staff thought I was married. She wasn't thinking of me, only of herself and the scandal it would bring if the full story was told. Damn, damn my mother for interfering,' she retorted angrily. She flopped back on the pillow, emotionally drained. 'How can I put it right?'

Nick lay down beside her and said, 'You tell Tina what you believe to be the truth and take it from there.'

Overwhelmed by the support and compassion of this wonderful man who had come into her life, she flung her arms about him in a loving embrace, kissing him passionately.

That evening, Tina met Joe in the coffee bar in the Market Place. It was early, so the usual crowd of lads and lasses were not yet in. They were both subdued. Tina wondered if Joe was regretting becoming a father. He was young and so was she. With parenthood came a great responsibility and neither of them was really ready for it. He sat next to her and was wearing the aftershave she'd bought him. Even with the aftershave, she caught the odd whiff of grease and petrol. 'It's ingrained in my soul,' he told her, dramatically.

Just then, one of Joe's mates came in and waved to them. He stopped to select a tune from the jukebox. Tina said, quickly, 'I need to talk to you before he comes over.'

He glanced at her and took a swig of his ginger beer, then said, 'Okay.'

She charged in. 'I've been to see Fran today. You know I'm looking for my real mother?'

'Yeah. I can't see the point if the woman abandoned you. Besides, you've got me.'

Ignoring what he said, she continued, 'When we were at Fran's for dinner, you mentioned that Mike's mother was Isabel Renton.' Joe cocked an eye at her. 'Isabel Renton is my real mother's name, it says on my birth certificate. And I'll tell you something else. Mike has the same birthday as me. We could be twins.' She finished breathlessly.

'You're making it up.' He tore open a packet of crisps to find the twist of blue paper containing salt and began sprinkling it over his crisps.

'I'm not!' she yelled, swinging her arm and knocking the packet of crisps flying. Joe's mate who was approaching made a hasty retreat in the opposite direction. 'I'll show you my birth certificate.' She raked in her handbag and withdrew it, thrusting the certificate in his face. 'Read that,' she commanded.

He glanced at it. 'So what?' He drained his glass. *Women*, he thought, *are strange creatures*. He needed male company, to have a game of billiards and crack a few jokes.

'It means that Mike is my brother, don't you see?'

'Sure, but he's hardly going to jump on a ship and come back from Australia just to see you.'

Sunday was the first day Tina had had off work since Fran had rung her to say she had some news to tell her, but not over the telephone. She dressed carefully in her new flared skirt and blue blouse, and slipped on a pair of ballerina shoes. Brushing her hair smooth, like she had done when going for her job interview, she added rose-pink lipstick. She eyed herself critically in her dressing table mirror. Her insides felt full of butterflies, wondering what Fran had to tell her. Was it about Isabel Renton?

She caught the bus to High Bank House and alighted at the top of the lane. As she walked along, she kept rehearsing what she would say to Fran when she presented her birth certificate. Fran had said that there was no need for her to see the document, but, in spite of that, Tina felt this irritating niggle at the back of her mind that Fran didn't all together believe her.

As she neared High Bank House, her heartbeat raced as if she'd just swam the full length of the river. Rubbing her clammy hand, down her skirt, she walked down the path to the back door and, for one wild moment, she thought of fleeing. But the baby kicked her as if to say, 'don't run'. She placed a protective hand on her belly and then she knocked loudly on the door.

Fran opened it. 'Come in, Tina,' she welcomed with a smile. Tina glanced round the empty kitchen and looked at Fran. 'Dad and Nick have gone down to the pub, so we won't be disturbed. Sit down,' Fran said, and sat opposite her at the table. She cleared her throat. 'You must be wondering why I asked you to come.'

Tina nodded. Then she pulled from her handbag her birth certificate and passed it across the table to Fran. 'This is the proof of my birth.'

'There was no need.'

'I want things to be clear.'

Fran unfolded the document and read. A similar, unbelievable, chill to that which had gripped Tina when she first read it now gripped Fran. *Mother: Isabel Renton. Father: Victor Renton. Christine Renton. Date of birth: 8th March 1942.* She stared at it for what seemed an eternity, her eyes brimming with tears.

Tina spoke quietly, 'I didn't know I was Christine until Maggie died.' Her voice caught in a sob.

Fran looked up, her voice trembling, she said, 'Tina, on 8th March 1942, I gave birth to twins: a son, Michael, and a daughter, Christine.' Tears ran unheeded down her face as she looked across the table into the stunned face of her beloved daughter, Christine.

'You are my mother! But why did you let me go?'

'Oh, Tina.' She gulped back more tears. 'I was told you had died.'

'Well, I hadn't,' she said indignantly. 'But, how did Maggie get me?'

'I think it was entirely my mother's doing. She was ashamed of me. I was unmarried and had brought disgrace to the family. Isabel couldn't have children, so my mother gave her my son, Michael, and she must have given you to Maggie.'

'What a wicked woman. Didn't your father know?'

'Yes, about Michael, but not you.'

'Does Michael know?'

Fran shook her head.

Suddenly, realisation gripped Tina as she blurted, 'So, Mike is my brother. I hoped – I knew there was something between us, but I wasn't sure of my feelings. I felt so mixed up.' She smiled, her face lighting up with joy. 'I've got a brother.' Then she burst into tears.

Fran pushed back her chair, nearly toppling it in her haste to be at her daughter's side. Fran gathered Tina into her arms and hugged the trembling girl close, whispering, 'Tina, my darling daughter, I will never let you go again. Never!'

Chapter Twenty-Six

After hugging and kissing, and eyes wiped dry, mother and daughter just sat quietly for a few moments. Then Fran jumped up, saying, 'I have something to show you, Tina.' She went over to the dresser where her handbag was, opened it and drew out the well-worn leather wallet, soft to her touch. She felt her heart contract as she held it in her hands, so precious it was to her. She went back to Tina and sat on the chair next to hers. All the time, Tina was watching her, her eyes unsure. Fran smiled, reassuringly, and flipped open the wallet to reveal two compartments holding the cherished photographs of two babies, one of her son and one of her daughter, and placed it on the table in front of Tina.

Tina gazed at the two photographs, her eyes wide with wonderment. She picked up the wallet and, caressing it, she traced her finger tenderly over each photograph and whispered, 'Is this . . . is me and Mike?'

Fran, her voice barely audible, replied, 'Yes, taken when you were both only a few days old.' She wanted to say more, but words would not come, so she just watched her daughter's beautiful face and saw the joy and the happiness in her eyes.

Tina held the wallet for a long time, not wanting to let go of her new-found past.

'There's more,' said Fran, reaching out for the wallet, which Tina was reluctant to let go of. On the other side of the pictures was a single closed compartment. Fran eased it carefully open, her heart beat faster and she caught her breath. She hadn't looked at this photograph for such a long time, because it always tortured her.

'What is it?' said Tina. Fran handed her the wallet. Tina stared at the photograph of a young girl, in bed, with a baby resting in each arm. 'It's you!' she exclaimed in surprise, 'and Mike and me. It's amazing. Oh, Fran, you were so young.'

Suddenly, both mother and daughter were laughter and crying at the same time.

'What's all this?' Both women turned to see Nick and Will standing in the doorway of the kitchen and, by the look on their faces, not sure whether to enter or not.

'Why are you both crying?' asked Will. His face etched with bewilderment, he ran a trembling hand through his sparse hair.

Fran answered, 'Because we are so happy. Come in, don't stand there.' Both men came in.

Then Will's face lit up and he muttered, 'I don't understand the ways of women, everything teks them so long.' He shed his coat and shoes, put on his slippers and sat in his chair and lit his pipe.

Nick, guessing what had happened, didn't comment, but wisely went and filled the kettle to make a pot of tea. Tina slipped upstairs to the bathroom and Nick looked across at Fran who was still sitting at the kitchen table. She smiled at him. He turned back to pour the tea.

Tina returned, her face fresh and pink. She was not sure what to do or say, though there were so many questions she wanted to ask – but, at the moment, they were all racing around in her head. She sat down next to Fran and watched as Nick carried the four mugs of tea to the table. She was just about to say she would take Will's to him when Fran said, 'Dad, can you come over here for your tea. I—Tina and I have something to say.'

'Um, just when I'm comfy,' he muttered, knocking out his pipe. But he creaked up from his chair and ambled to the table. He surprised them all by saying, 'I know what you're going to say.' Three pairs of eyes were fixed on Will's.

Fran said, 'How can you?'

'Ah,' Will replied. 'You say, lass, and we'll see.' With that he took a long sup of his tea.

Mystified with her father's riddle, Fran coughed and cleared her throat, and found herself blurting out, 'Tina is my daughter.' She reached for Tina's hand and squeezed it tightly.

Nick smiled and gave Fran a wink, to say 'I told you it would be just fine'. She returned his smile and looked to Will.

'Dad.'

Will beamed and said in a loud voice, 'I was right – I always thought she was yours, because, Fran, Tina reminded me of you when you was young.' He leant back in his chair with a degree of satisfaction. Then he startled them by sitting bolt upright. 'What I don't understand is how she came to be.'

Tina turned to look at Fran, waiting.

All eyes were fixed on Fran. She sat erect and held her head high. Her voice was soft but clear. 'Tina is Michael's twin.'

Will gasped. Fran looked directly at her father. 'Did you know, Dad?'

Will's ruddy complexion had blanched. He stuttered out his words. 'No, I never. I only saw Michael and there was no talk of a baby girl. Agnes never said. I would have remembered, surely.' He glanced bewildered at Fran. 'What happened?'

Fran's voice was cold and harsh. 'Mother told me that Christine, my baby daughter, had died. I was heartbroken and ill for months. Why would she do that, Dad, tell me that my baby was dead?'

Will, unable to take it in, just shook his head, looking shocked.

It was Nick who intervened. 'Fran, I think it is best if we let Will have a rest.'

Fran slumped back, emotionally drained.

Tina waited for Nick and Will to leave the room before speaking to Fran. 'Why do you think Agnes hid the fact that I was alive? She must have been ashamed of me.'

Quickly, Fran sat up and reached from Tina's hand. 'Oh, my darling daughter, you must never say that. Agnes was only ashamed of me.'

'And I had Maggie to love me.' Tina sighed, thinking of Maggie still as her mother. Suddenly, a thought jolted her. 'How did Maggie come to get me?'

'I wondered about that. All I can think was that when I was confined with you and Michael, there was a woman whose baby was stillborn and I remember how sad she looked. On the day we were waiting to leave the hospital, she was also in the waiting room. She came to look at you and Michael and there was this longing in her eyes. I think that woman was Maggie and knowing her grief at the loss of her baby, Agnes took advantage of the circumstances.'

The two women were silent, both deep in their own thoughts and memories. The silence was broken by Fran when Nick entered the kitchen. 'Is Dad all right? I really thought he knew about Christine.'

Nick came and put an arm around Fran. 'He'll be all right. Said he was just having a nap and he'll be down in an hour or so.'

Tina stood up. 'I'd best be going now. I'll catch the four-thirty bus.'

Fran moved away from Nick and rose to her feet. 'I'll walk down the lane with you.'

Mother and daughter, arms linked, strolled down to the bus stop. 'Life is strange,' said Fran. 'The years I've spent longing to be reunited with Michael, for him to call me "Mother".' She paused, remembering those lost years. 'Unrequited love is hard to bear. But in all my years of longing, Tina, I never dreamt that I would be reunited with you, my daughter. It is a miracle.' Fran stopped in her step and so did Tina. Fran held Tina's gaze. 'You are happy?'

Tina averted her eyes from Fran, saying, 'Yes, but I'm not sure if I can call you mother. You see Maggie . . .' Her voice trailed away, her eyes brimming with tears.

Fran drew her close, saying, 'All those years Maggie brought you up and you called her mother, which was only right. You and I know we are mother and daughter, and that is all that matters to me. Tina, I am happy for you to keep on calling me Fran.'

'You don't mind? I was worried.'

'Now the air is clear, we'd better move on or you'll miss the bus.'

At the bus stop, Fran said, 'Can you come tomorrow after work?' She saw the look of uncertainty in her daughter's eyes. 'Bring Joe, come for a meal. I'll have a talk with Dad to see if he can remember anything more.'

Tina flung herself into Fran's arms. 'I'm so glad I found you.'

'Me too. Bus is here.' Fran quickly kissed her daughter on the cheek. 'See you tomorrow.'

Fran waved until the bus was out of sight then turned to retrace her steps down the lane. She walked slowly, as if in a trance. So much had happened in such a short space of time. It seemed a surreal situation, for never in her wildest dreams could she have imagined that her daughter was alive, the daughter she had been told by Agnes had died in infancy. Silently, for years, Fran had mourned the loss of her beautiful baby girl. What if Tina hadn't been searching for her birth mother, would she have ever known? She shuddered at such a thought.

The next morning, Fran was woken up sharply by banging and bumping coming from Will's room. She glanced at Nick, but he was sleeping deeply. She slipped out of bed and reached for her dressing gown and slippers, and went to tap on Will's bedroom door, calling, 'Dad, are you all right?'

His gruff voice echoed, 'Course not.'

She pushed open the door, gasping. 'Dad, what on earth are you doing?' She couldn't believe what she saw. The dressing table drawers were all open and the contents were scattered across the floor, and her father was on his knees, his head and upper body inside the huge Edwardian wardrobe, where he was rummaging. Treading carefully, not wanting to damage anything, Fran crossed the room and dropped to her knees to see what Will was doing.

'It must be somewhere,' Will muttered.

'What are you looking for?'

'Your mother's box of tricks,' he wheezed.

'Dad, you get up and let me look. Come on.' She put her hand under his elbow to help lever him to his feet and he came up, panting for air. 'You shouldn't be doing things like this,' she admonished. 'I don't want you to trip, so mind where you put your

249

feet,' she said, leading him to a chair. He wheezed and panted some more, and Fran went to fetch him a glass of water.

When Will had his breath back, Fran asked, 'What is so important about what you were looking for?'

Will looked glum-faced. 'It's Tina. I didn't know about her.' He looked at the chaos scattered about the room then at Fran. 'Agnes used to have a fancy chocolate box with all her bits and pieces in. I wanted ter see if there were anything about Tina, but I can't find it.'

She thought that Isabel had probably thrown it out, but to humour him she asked, 'Do you want me to look?'

Will's face brightened a little. 'Please, lass.'

First, she tidied up the room and then Fran went over to the wardrobe and, hitching up her dressing gown, she dropped to her knees. The interior was dark and gloomy. A torch would have been useful, but she was here now so she fumbled, moving shoes and belts and a pair of trousers, and she tugged at something wedged in a corner. A box. She eased it out and blew off the dust, coughing as she did so. It was a square, flat box with a faded picture on the lid of a cottage with a garden and a stream. Once, it must have been bright and colourful, now it was a dull green and yellow. It was fastened with a bow of ribbon, once white, now grey. Fran felt a prickly tingling of her spine. This was Agnes's box. Carefully, she rose to her feet and turned to Will. She didn't say a word, but handed it to him.

He stared at the box, a fearful expression on his face. He looked to Fran and said, 'I can't, lass. I can't open it. Will you?'

Fran did not want to unlock what Agnes had stored in her box but, nevertheless, she took the box from Will's shaking hands. Slowly, she untied the ribbon, not wanting to discover what lay beneath the dusty lid. To her mind, nothing that Agnes did was good. She just wanted to forget about her, the woman she once called Mother. She was dead and had no part or future in her life. But, here she was . . . Fran squeezed her eyes tight. She could never forgive Agnes for her cruelty in keeping Fran away from her beloved Michael and the lie of saying that Christine had died, the yearning years of longing for her children and the suffering of unbearable grief, all caused by Agnes. She opened her eyes and, with a mighty pull of anger, the ribbon snapped, releasing the lid, which fell to the floor.

Fran stared down at the contents of the box, a damp, musty odour secreted from the brittle paper, making her stomach turn, nauseating her.

'What do they say?' Will asked, his voice not more than a whisper. She looked at him, startled for a moment because she had forgotten he was there in the room with her.

'I'm not sure.' She rose, crossed the room and tipped the contents of the box onto the bed. She winced inwardly, feeling loath to touch them. Will, his knees cracking, struggled over to stand by her side and stare down at the bundles of letters. They both stood in silence for what seemed an eternity.

Will broke the uneasy stillness. 'What shall we do with them?'

Fran pushed her own feelings away and replied. 'We'll have to read them for Tina's sake and Michael's. To see if they explain anything.' She rubbed the bridge of her nose, trying to gather her thoughts. 'Tina's coming for tea today, and Joe. If there is anything she needs to know, the sooner the better to tell her.'

Chapter Twenty-Seven

After breakfast, Will and Fran sat at the kitchen table. Nick busied himself upstairs, painting the spare bedroom, leaving father and daughter to peruse their findings. The bundle of letters was now undone and each one lay separately on the table. Fran looked at them and then let her gaze wander around the kitchen, searching for anything to delay the task ahead. She didn't want to probe into Agnes's past. Fran would always hate her, no matter what was revealed. Taking a deep breath, she forced herself to pick up the first letter, aware that Will was watching her.

The envelope was faded white to beige and from it Fran extracted the single sheet of paper. The date at the top of the page was 12th May 1925. *So long ago*, she thought, and glanced down to the bottom of the page, squinting to decipher the scrawling signature as she read out loud, 'George Spring.' She looked to Will to see if he recognised the name. He shook his head. Fran went back to the beginning of the letter, her voice held a tremor as she read.

Dear Mrs Agnes Bewholme,
Just to let you know that my dear friend, your mother, Martha
Boswell, passed away on 10th May. Martha made all her
own funeral arrangements before she died and asked that I
inform you. The service takes place on the 20th at 2 p.m. at the
Methodist Church in the village, prior to her interment in the
family grave. Her last words were to ask for your forgiveness.
You know what that means.

Fran looked to her father, her voice now touched with sadness. 'Was Martha my grandmother?'

Will's eyes held a faraway look, as if trying to remember, and it was a few moments before he answered. 'Aye, she was, lass, but I never met her. Your mother left home when she was fifteen and never went back.'

'Why ever not?' Fran asked. Will closed his eyes. Was he trying to remember or trying to forget? 'Dad,' she said, impatiently.

'I'm not sure your mother would want you to know,' he prevaricated.

She leant across the table towards him, her patience waning. 'Look, Dad, we're doing this for Tina's sake and Michael's. Agnes is dead,' she said bluntly.

Will reached for a cigarette and lit it. 'Sorry, lass,' he said. He inhaled deeply, letting out a halo of smoke. He said, quietly, 'Your mother was illegitimate.'

Fran gawped at her father, feeling stunned by this revelation. It was not what she was expecting to hear, if anything. Thankfully, today the stigma of being born illegitimate had diminished a great deal. But Agnes had been born in 1896 when it must have been considered a terrible sin for both child and mother.

Will continued, 'Your mother had a very unhappy childhood, living with her mother and grandparents who were strict Methodists. Both Martha and Agnes were confined to the house and garden except for church on Sundays. When Agnes went to school, she was ridiculed by the other children for having no daddy and the terrible fact that her mother had sinned. Agnes was never allowed to forget.' Will drew on his cigarette, not happy to be disclosing his late wife's past. As far as he was aware, she never told anyone else of her past and they never discussed it, so he dismissed it from his mind. But now it seemed to matter.

Fran, though sorry for what the young mother and daughter had to endure, could not relate it to Agnes, the woman who had so cruelly denied Fran the right to bring up her own children. At least, Martha had kept her daughter.

The rest of the correspondence was to do with Christine. There were letters to Mrs M. Newton, which mostly were about the welfare of Christine and of Agnes's intended visits to see Mrs Newton and Christine, and letters to solicitors, Fawcett & Farrow, regarding the financial arrangements for Christine's care. Fran looked to see if there were any of her letters which she had written, over the years, to Agnes, but there were none.

In anger and with an uncomfortable feeling of bitterness, Fran blurted out to Will, who was just about to light another cigarette, 'Why didn't you write to me?'

Will held the lighted match, letting it scorch his finger before he blew it out. He screwed up his face, searching his memory, and then he frowned and said, 'I did write. It was you who never answered. I wanted yer to come home. I missed yer, lass.'

She flung back at him, 'You didn't write to me, it was I who wrote to you and Agnes. Neither of you made an effort to reply.'

The flow of hot tears ran unheeded down her cheeks and her voice rose to a high pitch. 'I was lonely, far from home, missing Michael and grieving for Christine. No one showed me any love or compassion. And yet, here I am, caring for you while my so-called sister has taken my son to the other side of the world.' By now she was sobbing, uncontrollably.

Will's slumped back in his chair. The hand which held the unlit cigarette shook and his ruddy complexion blanched grey. His eyes, once the bright blue of his youth, now faded, were damp with threatening tears.

Suddenly, the kitchen door burst open and Nick came rushing in. 'What's happened?' he asked. 'I heard shouting.'

'Oh, Nick,' Fran cried, flinging herself into his arms.

He held her trembling body close. Over the top of her head, he saw the dejected figure of Will and the letters scattered about the table. He gave a swift glance around the room, half expecting to see someone else. It was a strange feeling.

Nick felt Fran's body relax a little and her sobs ceased. 'Come and sit down, love.' He guided her back to the chair opposite Will. Quickly, he went over to the dresser and found a small bottle of brandy, which was kept for medicinal use, and poured out two liberal measures. He gave one to Fran and the other to Will, and then he waited, watching both their faces until they were visibly calmer. Then he broke the silence. Addressing them both, he asked, 'Do you want to talk about it?'

It was Will who answered, his voice barely audible. 'A misunderstanding. Mix-up of letters not received. Post was all ter pot during war.'

Fran stared at him and he caught her look, and, in that instance, Will knew that Fran knew it was Agnes's doing, her meddling, her heartless ways that had caused untold misery and grief. No words were spoken between father and daughter, and Fran knew on that subject they never would be. Agnes was dead and so was her past.

By the time Tina and Joe arrived for the evening meal, peace was restored, and both Will and Fran were in calmer minds. It had been decided by father and daughter that no useful purpose would be gained by keeping Agnes's correspondence. The letters had all been burnt in the kitchen fire except for the one from George Spring and an old photograph.

Fran told Tina that Agnes was born illegitimate and had an unhappy childhood, which narrowed her view on life, and added, 'I supposed she thought that her actions toward me and you, in her eyes, were justified.' Then it struck Fran that neither Tina nor Michael had the stigma of illegitimacy attached to them, but, then, Fran had never been given the chance to make a life for her and her children. She dashed the bitter thoughts away and smiled, saying, 'Read this.' Fran passed George's letter to Tina.

They had gone outside and were sitting on the wall outside the kitchen while the men were inside having a beer and talking rugby. The early evening air was still, the wind having dropped to give that balmy effect of being in another world. Tina took her time reading the letter as if she was digesting every word. When she looked up, her eyes were wet with tears. 'So sad, I never knew of her, she was my great-grandma Martha.' Then, through her tears, she smiled, saying, 'I'm part of her family.'

Fran reached to take hold of Tina's hand and said, 'I didn't know of Martha's existence either. Agnes never talked about her mother or any of her family. So strange,' and added wishfully, 'I would have liked to have met Martha, but I think she died the year I was born.'

'I wonder what she looked like,' Tina said softly. 'You know, if you or I look like her.' She turned her face to Fran, looking directly into her eyes. 'We have the same deep blue eyes and now I come to think of it, Michael has too.'

Fran's heart beat faster at the mention of her son and she turned away from Tina's intense gaze, thinking there was a lot more to be talked about and resolved regarding Michael, but for now she was happy to have her daughter close by. Cheerfully, she said, 'I have another surprise. Take a look at this.' Fran reached for the envelope by her side on the wall and handed it to Tina. She watched her daughter's face, so beautiful and yet solemn, as she opened the envelope and drew out the contents, and gasped in admiration, saying, 'What a pretty girl.'

Tina held the brown sepia photograph in her palm and gazed in wonderment. The girl must have been about twelve with long fair hair and wide expressive eyes. She was wearing a lovely summer gown. The hem of the gown was trimmed with little frills held in place by bunches of satin forget-me-nots and peeping out from beneath her gown was a pair of shining laced boots. In her hand, she was holding a Bible. Tina looked to Fran and saw her eyes sprinkled with tears. 'Is this Martha?' she asked softly.

Fran moved closer to Tina and looked down at the photograph, taken so long ago. 'Yes, this is Martha, my grandmother, your great-grandmother and my mother's mother. It's hard to believe that Agnes was the daughter of this, kind-looking and beautiful young girl. But then I've never seen a photo of the young Agnes.' Fran's voice trailed away. Both women were silent, both lost in their thoughts.

'Are we eating or what?' Joe's voice broke the silence, making both Tina and Fran jump.

The day, unnoticed by mother and daughter, had drawn to a close and stars were twinkling in the dusky blue sky. 'I'm starving.' He held the door open for them and they entered the kitchen, which was filled with the delicious aroma of the casserole simmering in the oven.

Will looked anxiously at the two women and Tina caught his eye. 'You alright, Will, Mr Bewholme?' And then she laughed. 'Can I call you Grandad?' Will's face lit up with pleasure and love. Tina went to his side and, sitting on the arm of his chair, leant forward and kissed his grizzly cheek and said, 'Hello Grandad.'

Much later that evening, when the young people had gone and Nick had gone for a pint with Rufus, Fran and Will sat by the fire, both deep in their own thoughts. Suddenly, Will said, quietly, 'What about our Michael?'

It was as if he had been reading her mind, for Michael was very much in her thoughts. Tina now knew she had a twin brother, but Michael didn't know that he had a twin sister. 'I know, Dad.' She sighed heavily. 'He should know about Tina, but then he will have to know about everything else. If only I had told him before he went to Australia. I thought there would have been time to get to know him, build up a relationship, but Isabel whisked him away too fast,' she lamented. But her father's voice pulled her up, sharply.

'Now, my girl, we'll have no self-pity. First thing in the morning, you phone our Isabel and tell her about Tina.'

Chapter Twenty-Eight

October 1958, Melbourne, Australia

'Telephone, Mrs Stanway. It's your sister from England,' announced the housekeeper, Edith.

Isabel, relaxing out on the veranda, frowned and looking up from the magazine she was reading, and said, more to herself than Edith, 'What on earth does she want?' Reluctantly, she went indoors, thinking it must be something to do with Father for Frances to ring. She glanced at the carriage clock on the hall table – nearly five. Good gracious, she thought, it must be early morning back in Burton Banks, though she had yet to fathom out the approximate time difference. Now Michael, he could work it out in a flash. She picked up the phone, aware that the local telephonist might be listening in. 'Hello,' she said, lightly.

'Isabel!' Fran's words came spurting out like an icy waterfall. 'Michael has a twin sister, Tina. Why didn't you tell me she was still alive? How could you be so cruel and wicked? Now Michael must be told the true circumstances of his birth, that I am his mother and Tina is his twin sister.'

Isabel couldn't make sense of what she was saying. 'Frances, what are you gabbling on about?'

Fran repeated and Isabel listened, her body turning cold despite the heat. She replied sharply, 'I know nothing of this Tina. You're making it up.' She laughed a high-pitched noise. 'If you think I'm going to fall for your little scheme, you are mistaken. I am Michael's mother, not you.'

Fran's righteous voice shouted across the miles. 'No, you are not. I am Michael's mother and Tina is my daughter and Michael's twin sister. Nothing you say can alter that fact.'

Her voice shaking, Isabel said, 'You can't do anything. We are too far away.' And, with that, she banged down the phone.

Stunned, Fran just stood there in the silence. Isabel's words and reaction had shaken her, horrified her, but then what had she expected of Isabel? For her to renounce her claim on Michael? She was not sure what the next move would be, but what she did know was that Tina should be acknowledged as Michael's sister. Michael, now more than ever, needed to be told the whole truth. For her to discover Tina and for them to be reunited as mother and daughter, and Will as her grandfather, the family would not be complete without Michael.

It was difficult for her to accept that the bond existing between Isabel and Michael could not easily be broken. How could she explain this to Tina? And would Tina be content?

'Penny for them,' murmured a husky voice in her ear.

Fran twisted round into the warm security of Nick's arms. She leant into him, her head resting on his shoulder, breathing in the comfort of his male freshness. 'It's Isabel.' She told him of her conversation with Isabel and her reaction.

Nick listened quietly and didn't speak until Fran had finished. 'Not an easy situation,' he said.

'Tell me, Nick. What should I do?' She turned to look earnestly at him.

'My darling Fran, from what you tell me there is no quick fix. But, I think you are going to have to sit down with Tina and talk it through. Let her ask you questions. Answer them truthfully.' She gave him a hard look. 'Sorry, I know you will, but it could be painful for you, but necessary if you and Tina are going to build a solid relationship together. And tell her the outcome of your telephone conversation with Isabel.' He looked steadily into her eyes and held her gaze.

Then she spoke. 'Nick Saunders, what would I do without you?' And before he had a chance to reply she kissed him, a long, passionate kiss.

It was Saturday afternoon, Tina's half-day off from work, and they had agreed to meet in the Market Place. As Fran stood on the bus running board, waiting to alight, she caught sight of Tina waving to her and she felt her heart quiver with love and pleasure as she waved back. She couldn't help but say to the woman standing next to her. 'That's my daughter.'

Fran and Tina hugged and linked arms as they headed towards the colourful array of market stalls, which were thronged with shoppers looking for bargains. They passed fruit stalls piled high with polished apples and shining oranges, always a treat to see them after the austere years of the war – now a distant memory, Fran thought, not wishing to dwell on her lost years. If only Michael was here. She sighed heavily.

'Are you alright?' Tina asked. There was so much she wanted to ask Fran, but she was scared to break the fragile relationship which existed between them as mother and daughter.

'I was thinking of Michael,' Fran replied. Tina just nodded.

'Excuse me, missus, are you buying or what?' boomed a loud masculine voice.

Both Fran and Tina, not realising they had stopped walking, stared at the wet-fish stallholder, who was wearing a large striped, blue apron over his white coat overall. Their gaze dropped to the cold eyes of a large cod on a marble slab and they both giggled. 'Sorry,' Fran muttered, as they quickly moved on.

'Tina, were you shopping for anything in particular?'

'Not really. I'm saving up.' She didn't add what she was saving up for, later she would tell.

Fran suggested, 'Shall we find a cafe and have a talk?' Tina nodded her approval. They negotiated through the busy shoppers, crossings the cobbles to the bakery and tea shop next to the Green Dragon public house. They managed to find a quiet table tucked in a corner and ordered a cream tea for two.

'This was delicious,' Tina said with satisfaction, licking from her lips the last of the cream doughnut. 'Now I'm no longer sick in the mornings, I can eat most anything.' She wrinkled up her pert nose, 'Though, the smell of liver and onions cooking turns me.'

Fran watched her daughter's animated face, loving this intimacy. She put down her tea cup and felt her insides quiver with uncertainty. She took a deep breath and smiled, saying, 'Tina, I guess there must be things you want to ask me.'

'Do you mind, Fran? Because there are.' She shrugged her shoulders, not wanting to upset her. Fran nodded for her to continue. Tina spoke in a low voice, not wanting the people at the next table to overhear. 'My father – on my birth certificate, it says his name is Victor Renton. Is that true?'

At the sound of that name, Fran felt a cold shudder run through her body, but she braced herself, her head held high. 'Tina, I want to be honest and truthful with you. Victor Renton was your father and Michael's. He was also married to my sister, Isabel.'

Tina gasped. 'Wow! Did you love him?'

Fran was taken aback; no one had ever asked her that question before. She thought for a moment and then drew a deep breath. 'Tina, there is to be no more deception. I will tell you the truth about how you and Michael were conceived. My boyfriend at that time had just publicly ditched me and I was terribly upset. Along came Victor. I was surprised how kind and understanding he was to me, but what I didn't realise was that he plied me with alcohol to make me drunk.' She paused for a few seconds, thinking of the right words to say. 'He took advantage of my vulnerability.' She couldn't bring herself to say, 'he raped me'. Tina's eyes widened, but she didn't interrupt. 'When my mother found out, she was very angry. In her eyes, I had committed a mortal sin and I was sent away to distant relatives.' She thought of the unhappiness and the loneliness she had endured while been forced to remain at the farm. But most of all, it was the lost years, the heartbreaking longing to hold her son in her arms again, the waiting to be reunited.

An uneasy silence stretched between them as both women became lost in thought. Then an angry Tina exploded. 'Agnes sounded a terrible woman.'

Fran laughed, dryly. 'That's putting it mildly.'

'So she got rid of me, but why couldn't you look after Michael?'

Fran leant heavily back in her chair. It wasn't something she could explain in a few sentences. 'I was shut away in a nursing home and both your births were difficult. I had an emergency Caesarean and afterwards I was ill for a long time.' Tears threatened as memories came flooding back, but she dashed them away. 'Agnes said Isabel was looking after Michael until I was better, or so I thought, but Agnes had other ideas. It was said that Isabel and Victor had adopted a baby boy, Michael. I was the girl who had run away from a good home to seek bright lights and goodness knows what else was said about me. I did try, often, to make plans to bring Michael up, but Agnes always thwarted me and, as he grew older, it became more difficult and I agreed, naively, to stay out of Michael's life until he was sixteen. I had it all planned and wrote to Isabel to tell her I was coming. I never dreamt she would be like Agnes, set on preventing my plans. I was devastated when she wrote back, telling me she was marrying again and taking Michael to Australia. By then, I was desperate to tell Michael the truth, whatever the outcome. But when I finally saw him after all these years, I saw a young man who viewed Australia as an adventure. He was so full of enthusiasm, how could I spoil his happiness, shatter his dream? He would hate me.'

Tina interrupted, 'What about me? Michael is my brother.'

Fran felt her heart pound with failure as she looked into the deep blue, hurting eyes of her daughter. 'I'm sorry, Tina, he has every right to know that you are his twin sister. I rang and spoke to Isabel, but she seems to think I'm making you up and it's a ploy to get Michael to come home. I can write to him.'

Tina reached across the table to touch Fran's arm. 'Leave it for a while, I want to get to know you properly.' Her voice soft, her eyes shining, she said, 'Since I found out that I was fostered, I wanted to find my real mother. I thought I'd found her once – your sister, Isabel – and I didn't like her.' Her touch on Fran's arm tightened. 'But you are my true mother and I don't want to lose you.' Her beautiful eyes swam with tears.

'Would you like more tea, madam?' enquired the waitress as she stopped by their table.

Fran looked to Tina who shook her head. 'No, thank you.'

Leaving the cafe, they slipped down Wood Lane, away from the market and the hustle and bustle of shoppers, and made their way to the open green spaces of the Westwood, where children were flying gaily coloured kites. They walked along in companionable silence, breathing in the scented air of late summer, which held a hint of approaching autumn.

Her legs suddenly aching, Fran said, 'Shall we sit down for a while?' They found a patch of dry grass beneath the gentle swaying branches of a tree.

'I often used to come up here with my school friends,' said Fran. 'I was a bit of a tomboy, often in trouble for dirtying or tearing my dress.'

Tina laughed and said, 'I was a tearaway, so Maggie was fond of telling me. She spoilt me rotten. She was a good mother and I never really appreciated her until she went and . . .' Her voice broke.

Fran slipped an arm around her shoulders and hugged her close. 'Maggie sounded a truly wonderful woman and for that I'm eternally grateful.' She dreaded to think if Tina had been fostered by an uncaring person. Gently, Fran smoothed Tina's hair, inhaling its freshly washed fragrance and realising with a terrible pang that she had never bathed her children. She had forfeited that simple pleasure.

Mother and daughter talked non-stop about their pasts, trying to achieve the impossible, cramming years into hours and enjoying every minute.

Chapter Twenty-Nine

Things were moving fast. Fran accompanied Tina to the antenatal clinic. She would have wanted more for her daughter, for her not to have a baby so young, for her to have a life, a career, but Tina was happy and loved Joe, and was looking forward to having the baby, so Fran was happy for her. She was blessed to find her alive when she thought her dead, and to be part of her daughter's life and the comings baby's. She breathed a huge sigh of contentment.

When Fran wrote to Michael, she found it difficult not to tell the wonderful news about Tina, her daughter, and that she was expecting a baby and he would be an uncle. It frustrated her not being able to tell him of the forthcoming marriage of Tina and Joe. It made her feel so sad not to be able to communicate all this wonderful, happy news to Michael.

Weeks later, when Michael replied to the letter there was no mention of Tina being his twin sister. Fran thought that Isabel might have had second thoughts about the situation. Tina didn't complain, but Fran knew her daughter must also have the same ache within her heart as she had.

The good news was that Tina and Joe had found a flat to rent over a tobacconist shop. So they decided on a Christmas wedding, a quiet affair at the register office and, later when the baby was born, a church blessing to be performed by Tina's friend, the Reverend Fairweather.

Everyone rallied round to help decorate and furnish the flat. Nancy made curtains and covers, Fran wielded a paint brush, Joe and Tina scoured the second-hand shops, Nick repaired tables and chairs, and Will made a crib for the expected baby. While all this activity kept Fran busy, in her mind, she outlined the letter she was going to write to Isabel.

Leaving Tina and Joe's flat one day after, painting the bathroom a delicate shade of sea-green, Fran arrived home, calling out, 'It's only me, Dad.' On entering the kitchen, she found Will hunched up in his chair staring thoughtfully into space, his newspaper and glasses discarded. 'Penny for them, Dad,' she said, shrugging off her coat.

Will looked at her, answering quietly, 'I was thinking of Michael, wondering what he's doing. I wish he was here lass. I really do.'

Fran felt the lump rise in her throat and swallowed hard, and it was a few seconds before she could speak. 'I know just how you feel.' So, that evening she wrote the letter to Isabel.

John Stanway collected the post when he was in Melbourne. 'Letter for you, Isabel,' he said, as he came out on to the veranda, where Isabel was sitting in the shade, away from the heat of the hot Australian summer. He placed the letter on her lap and dropped down into the chair next to hers, stretching out his long limbs. 'There's one for Michael from his grandfather.' She glanced at his hands. 'I've left it in his room.' Michael was still away with his friend Jarrod and the last postcard received said they were heading for Green Island on the Barrier Reef.

Isabel picked up her envelope, turning it over in her hand, reading Frances's name and address on the back. The letter lay burning in the palm of her hand for what seemed an eternity. She didn't want to open it. Her insides churned as the old fear returned.

'I've a headache. I think I'll have a lie down before supper,' Isabel said.

John looked with concern at her. 'You go and rest, darling.'

In the bedroom, she sat on the edge of the bed and ripped open the envelope and read.

Dear Isabel,

I am sorry if I upset you when I telephoned you last, but it was rather an emotional time for me, to find out that my dear daughter, Christine, whom I thought had died as a baby many years ago, is alive. You can imagine this was a great revelation to me. As she is the twin of Michael I thought you should know and, I believe, so should Michael. Isabel, you cannot keep the truth from Michael for ever. He is now old enough to understand. Christine knows the truth and she is anxious to get to know her brother, though they were friends before he left for Australia.

Whatever cruel thing our mother did is now buried in the past. It is only the future which concerns me. What does John have to say? Surely, he understands the situation.

Please, Isabel, give the matter your most urgent consideration for all concerned.

I wait to hear from you.

Frances

Isabel's face hardened. She had no intention of replying to Frances. And never would she tell Michael anything. She tore the letter to shreds.

Today, Tuesday, Christmas Eve 1958, her wedding day. It seemed unbelievable, thought Tina. So much had happened in less than a year. From being on her own after Maggie's death, to meeting Joe, expecting his baby, finding her true mother, Fran, and now she and Joe were to be married. Her heart beat with happiness. The one shadow on her life was Michael. Would they ever be reunited as brother and sister? It was an unanswered question. For now, she was going to push it to the back of her mind.

She turned over in the bed, listening to the sounds of the river, the water lapping the bank, the swoop of wings as the geese flew in for their morning fodder. High Bank House was a heavenly place. 'It's fitting for the bride to leave from her mother's house,' Fran had said. Tina thought of Maggie, her mother for the first sixteen years of her life. If only Maggie hadn't died. If only she hasn't been fostered. Tina let out a sigh, recalling the past only made her sad. She must look to the future and today was her wedding day.

She propped herself up on one elbow to view her wedding outfit and caught her breath. Her heart filled with love and joy for finding Fran, the woman who had given her life. Like any mother for her daughter's wedding, Fran had been more than generous, buying her the dress, hat and shoes. Tina gazed in wonderment as the early morning light caught the shimmer of the satin dress – it was like a lake of clear, blue transparent water overlaced with a gossamer coat of delicate organza. Her hat was bandeau styled, a garland of white daises, her high-heeled sandals were white and strappy, not really suitable for winter, but Tina couldn't resist them. Her gloves, white lace, were a gift from Miss Draper. Nancy and Cyril gave her a pair of the finest, seamless nylon stockings. A knock on the bedroom door broke Tina's reverie.

Fran entered carrying a breakfast tray: a pot of tea, boiled eggs and toast. Tina felt her tummy lurch. She didn't feel hungry.

Fran smiled and, as if she'd read Tina's mind, she said, 'You'll need a good lining in your stomach today.'

'But there's all that food you and Nancy have been making,' Tina protested.

'You've hours before the wedding tea,' Fran said, placing the tray on the bedside table and, pouring a cup of tea for Tina and one for herself, she sat on the edge of the bed. Tina eased herself up, sipped her tea and nibbled at a piece of toast. Both women were silent, both deep in thought.

Fran broke the silence. 'It's strange,' she reflected, 'this time last year I never dreamt I would be preparing for my beautiful daughter's wedding.' Tears glistened in her eyes.

Tina reached across to hug Fran, whispering, 'I do love you.'

'And I love you, my darling daughter, with all my heart.' Suddenly, from outside on the landing, came the tuneless whistling of Mendelssohn's 'Wedding March'. Tina and Fran looked at each other and broke into fits of giggling.

At last it was time to go to the register office. Joe's boss, the garage owner, arrived in his gleaming Bentley to collect the bridal party. Nick produced his camera and everyone smiled. 'One of the bride and her mother,' he said. He fussed, arranging Tina's posy of white roses and winter greenery, a gift from Joe's father and sister.

The wedding ceremony was a haze for Tina. At the reception at High Bank House, she drank juice and ate a delicious tea.

Afterwards, someone provided a Dansette record player and lots of LPs of swinging music. Soon, the dining room, its carpet rolled back, rang as everyone sang and danced to Elvis Presley's 'All Shook Up', Cliff Richard's 'Move It', and Lonnie Donegan's skiffle group. Fran and Nick watched the happy couple dance and the other young people: Tina's friends from the department store and Joe's mates from the garage, and his sister Maureen and her fiancé, Keith. Occasionally, Fran and Nick joined them. Joe's father sat next to Will, both enjoying a smoke, a drink and a yarn. Then the tempo changed and Nancy and Cyril took to the dance floor, waltzing to the silver music of Victor Sylvester and Nat King Cole.

When everyone had gone home, including the happy couple, Fran had started to collect empty glasses, when she felt hot breath on her neck and the rich timbre voice of Nick say, 'May I have the pleasure of this waltz?' The next second, she was in his loving arms, feeling the strength of his body as it dove-tailed with hers as they glided around the room, to the tune of 'Unforgettable'.

Chapter Thirty

One day in early April, the phone rang. Fran was reading, curled up on the new sofa in the sitting room. 'I'll get it,' said Nick. In a few moments he was back. 'Tina's gone into labour.'

'Oh, my dear Lord!' exclaimed Fran, jumping up, panic rising within her. 'I must be with her.' In her mind's eye flashed a picture of the birth of her babies, no one to hold her hand or whisper words of comfort. She lurched forward, catching her heel on the edge of the rug.

Nick steadied her. 'Joe's going with her and Cyril's driving them to the hospital. There's no need for you to worry. Joe will ring as soon as the baby is born.'

Fran sat back down on the sofa with a thud. Her eyes bright and shining, she whispered, 'It's incredible, I find my darling daughter and she is now about to present me with a grandchild. This time last year, I wouldn't have believed that I could have been saying this. It's a miracle.'

Nick sat down by her side and hugged her. 'And, you're my miracle.'

After a few moments she said, 'We'd better tell Dad the news.'

'I'll make a pot of fresh coffee. I've a feeling it's going to be a long night.'

Will was all set to stay up with Fran and Nick, but Fran insisted he went to bed and, as soon as there was any news, she would wake him.

The night was long and Fran dozed fitfully, woken at six in the morning by the phone ringing.

It was Joe. 'Fran, you have a beautiful granddaughter.' He was laughing and crying at the same time, and so was she.

'When can I come and see them both?'

'She's fast asleep and so is little one. Best come in the afternoon.'

Fran turned to Nick who was by her side. 'A baby girl.' And to Will who was just descending the stairs, she called ecstatically, 'Dad, you have a great-granddaughter.'

'That's wonderful news,' Will cried with joy.

Julie Margaret Miller was born on Wednesday 7th April 1959 and weighed in at 6lbs 2ozs. Her tiny face was pink and wrinkly, her hair soft, downy auburn, with a hint of blonde. 'She's gorgeous,' exclaimed an emotional Fran, brushing away tears of delight as she gazed at her granddaughter lying sleeping in her cot. She went round to the other side of the bed and hugged Tina, saying, 'My darling daughter, I'm so proud of you.'

Tina smiled, responding to Fran's affection. She was still tired, but, looking lovingly at her mother, she said, 'The pain was worth it. She's a little beauty.' Then her smile was replaced with a look of anxiety. 'She's so tiny and I'm frightened I might drop her.'

Fran soothed back a tendril of Tina's hair. Now, no longer dyed red, it was natural blonde, just like hers. 'Babies are tougher than you think and as long as you love Julie, she'll feel secure.'

Tina's eyes widened. 'Do you really think so?'

'Yes, I do. And you have me and Nancy to help you.' She took hold of her daughter's hand. 'Tina, don't ever be afraid to ask for my help if you should need it. Promise?'

'I promise.' Tina sank back on to the pillow, fighting to keep her eyes open.

Fran kissed her tenderly on the cheek. 'I'm going now, love. See you tomorrow.'

One more peep at her granddaughter, then she turned to wave to Tina, but she was already asleep. Overcome with emotion, Fran sat in the empty waiting room, her head resting in her hands and wept. Oh, how she wept. She had so much wanted to pick up baby Julie and hold her in her arms, but something held her back. All she could think about was her babies, Michael and Christine. She could feel them now, cradled in her arms, smell their baby fragrance, so warm and sweet. And, as she lay so desperately ill, her babies were cruelly taken from her. The void in her life had been heartbreaking. All those lost years. Her years of longing, yearning, to hold her son.

Her tears spent, she made a vow. No more looking back. Look only to the future. Tomorrow, she would hold her precious granddaughter in her loving arms.

Ten days later, Tina and her baby were ready to leave the maternity hospital. Both Fran and Nancy offered for mother and baby to stay with them for a while, until Tina felt stronger.

'Ta ever so much,' said a waxen looking Tina, 'but Joe's taken a week off week.'

Joe, the protector, taking his role as father seriously, hoisted Tina's bag and baby's holdall over his strong arms and said, 'I'll take care of them both, don't worry.'

Arriving at the flat, Joe had switched on the electric fire earlier so the tiny living room was warm and cosy. Tina, still holding the baby, sank thankfully onto the sofa and closed her eyes. Immediately, Julie started to cry, a soft whimper at first and then she hollered.

Amazing, thought Tina, for one so tiny to make such a noise. She half opened her eyes and, unbuttoning her blouse, she put Julie to her breast and baby quickly latched on to the nipple.

Joe entered the room. 'I've put the bags in the bedroom.' Then he saw Tina and baby. He stood in the centre of the room with open admiration on his face and tears in his big brown eyes.

'A happy little family,' Fran said wistfully to Nick later on, when they were in bed.

Nick didn't say anything, but responded by cuddling Fran close. He thought of his son, lost to him for ever. He would love to have children with Fran. But she had never conceived with her ex-husband and she seemed to think she was unable to have any more children. He sighed deeply.

'Nick?' Fran leant back from his arms to gaze into his face.

He pulled her back close and, not wanting to look into her eyes, said, 'I'm so happy with you.'

And he was, it was just that children made a family complete.

Joe returned to work, and Nancy and Fran took over for the next two weeks, helping Tina get into a routine with the baby. Nancy did the morning stint, washing and cleaning, making Tina a snack. Fran came in the afternoons and ironed the laundry, and then took Julie for a walk in her pram while Tina rested. When Joe came home from work, Tina had a meal waiting for him. This was working well until the middle of the third week, when Fran went down with a heavy cold. She didn't want to give the germs to mother and baby, so she phoned Nancy, but there was no reply. So, she rang Miss Draper to leave a message with her, asking for Tina to telephone.

'You can speak to her now, she is right beside me.'

'Oh, Fran, don't fuss,' Tina said jauntily. 'You just get yourself better. We'll survive. I'm taking Julie to the baby clinic tomorrow.'

'If you're sure, love,' said Fran, anxiously.

'Yes.' She didn't tell Fran that Nancy had gone away to nurse her sick sister.

Back home in her flat, Tina fed Julie and laid her down in her cot. Alone, she suddenly burst into tears. She didn't know why. She'd done everything: the washing and ironing, and tidied the flat. Through wet lashes, she glanced round the room, feeling its walls crowding in on her. The suffocation overwhelmed her, sending waves of desolation flooding over her, leaving her feeling so afraid and lonely. It would be hours before Joe came home. She sank back on the sofa and sobbed and sobbed, until exhaustion lulled her into a fitful sleep.

It was Julie's lusty cries which woke her. Stiffly, Tina pulled herself off the sofa and wearily padded into the bedroom, where her daughter lay in her cot, legs and arm flaying. She picked her up. For one so tiny, she had such strength, arching her body away from Tina in an attempt to keep her arms and legs free. Julie didn't stop hollering until she was firmly latched onto her mother's nipple and sucking away greedily. It took ages for Julie to settle back down. Tina looked down in dismay at her shrunken breasts. She didn't seem to have enough milk to satisfy the baby and she didn't know what to do.

The next day she still felt lethargic. She bathed and fed Julie, but didn't seem to have the energy to wash her clothes. She put her down in her cot, went back into the sitting room and flopped on the sofa, dead beat. She lay there until Julie's next feed and, after putting her back in her cot, felt even more shattered and fell sleep on the sofa.

When she awoke, the room was in darkness and she squinted at the clock on the mantelpiece. It was gone five. She let out a low moan. She'd forgotten to take Julie to the clinic and she'd promised Joe to cook his favourite meal of steak, mushrooms and chips. But she hadn't been out shopping and now it was too late.

Joe put his motorcycle away in the lock-up garage. He'd worked late to earn more to save for a deposit on their very own house. Whistling a cheerful tune, he strode across the yard, his thoughts on food – he was starving. He bounded up the stairs, remembering not to shout, 'I'm home', because the baby might be asleep. 'Tina,' he whispered, entering the darkened sitting room. From the stray shaft of light from the street lamp he could see Tina's sleeping figure on the sofa. He wrinkled his nose, no lovely aroma of his steak, only the stink of a dirty nappy.

He snapped on the light. Forgetting his good intention, he yelled, 'Tina, where's my tea?'

Startled, she gaped at Joe through half-open eyes. 'What time is it?'

'Gone seven. Where's my tea?' he repeated.

She levered herself up into a sitting position. 'I didn't feel up to going out, sorry Joe. You can go ter fish shop,' she said, brushing damp, greasy hair away from her face.

He looked down at her, anger welling up. 'I've been bloody

well working hard all day and you've been lazing about.' He felt like slapping her, but, instead, he turned away and stomped from the room, down the stairs, banging the outside door as he left. He heard Julie start to cry.

After a pint, a couple of pickled eggs, a chat to his mates about cars and football, Joe enjoyed himself in the pub until he felt guilty at storming out on Tina. 'Night, lads,' he called, dashing off.

Quietly, he let himself into the flat and crept up the stairs. He thought the baby would be in her cot and Tina would be watching the television he'd hired for them. He was going to tell her how sorry he was. The sitting room door was open and he stood in the doorway surveying the scene. The light was glaring down on a sleeping Tina with the baby held loosely in her arms.

In a few strides he was by their sides. Gently, he eased his sleeping daughter from her mother's arms and carried her carefully into the bedroom and tucked her into the cot. He gazed down upon her, it never ceased to amaze him that he, Joe Miller, was partly responsible for making this tiny being. He touched Julie's outstretched hand with his little finger and she grasped it tightly. This brought tears to Joe's eyes. Now, he felt so ashamed for being angry with Tina. This little mite was dependant on them both, her parents. Back in the sitting room, Tina hadn't stirred and Joe noticed for the first time how worn-out she looked. Tenderly, he made her comfortable on the sofa, lifting up her feet and covering her with a blanket. He kissed her on the forehead, his heart full of love for her. Cursing himself for being such a chump, he went to an empty bed.

The baby woke him around six in the morning with her bellowing cries of hunger. He picked her up and she dripped. He held her aloft. This was to be his first nappy changing venture. He was terrified as he gently and scarily manoeuvred the tiny wriggling body, making Julie dry and secure. When he finished and sat back on his heels for a breather, she stared up at him, her eyes twinkling as if to say, 'You took your time.' Then she bellowed for her food. Tina was now awake and Joe smiled at her, eager to tell her of his achievement. Tina nodded her appreciation.

Joe made tea and toast, and they sat on the floor eating and drinking, and a now-contented Julie was lying on a blanket between them, testing her limbs.

Joe glanced at Tina. 'Sorry about last night. I'd had a hard day.'

Tina, feeling a little better, laughed it off, saying, 'So am I. Let's have a fresh start.' She leant across the kicking baby and kissed Joe.

'You go and have a bath,' he said, 'and we'll go out for dinner.'

So, the proud parents walked through Saturday Market, thronged with a multitude of stalls and shoppers. An even prouder Joe pushed the pram, stopping occasionally to talk to people who wanted to admire the baby. Finally, they arrived at The Magpie, which boasted an annexe where children were welcome. They tucked into pie and peas, and Joe kept a tender eye on Julie.

They were just finishing eating when a familiar voice said, 'Hello, you two.'

'Shirley,' said Joe. 'I thought you were still on your travels.'

She looked tanned and sported an air of sophistication. 'I've been back a couple of weeks.'

Just then, Julie stirred and whimpered and Joe hoisted her out of the pram and onto his lap.

'Whose baby is it?' asked Shirley, not seeing Joe as the babyminding type.

Eyes shining, chest expanding, Joe announced, proudly, 'It's our baby, mine and Tina's.'

Shirley stared in amazement and promptly sat down on the chair next to Tina. Unable to keep the surprise out of her voice, she said to Tina, 'You've had a baby?'

Wiping her lips with a serviette Tina smiled, serenely, for the first time feeling rather superior over Shirley who always seemed much better than her. 'Yes, this is our beautiful daughter, Julie.'

'She's gorgeous,' Shirley enthused. 'Mam never mentioned it in her letters and come to think of it neither did Mike. Does he know you've got a baby?'

Tina and Joe exchanged a quick glance. Joe said, 'Keeping in touch isn't my thing.'

Suddenly, Shirley caught Tina's left hand, touched the shining gold band and exclaimed in astonishment. 'You're married as well!'

Tina slipped her hand into Joe's, saying, with such pleasure, 'Yes, we're married.'

Shirley was silent for a moment, as if to take it all in. Then she said cheerfully, 'I've kept in touch regularly with Mike – letters and the odd postcard. I'll write and tell him your good news.' Someone shouted her name. 'Gotta go, bye.'

They watched her as she left and Tina wondered what the outcome would be if Shirley told Mike.

Chapter Thirty-One

Fran was over her cold and was looking forward to seeing Tina, Joe and baby Julie, so she invited them over to share a meal. Now, as they were all gathered around the kitchen table to eat, Fran scanned the happy faces, though, she thought, Tina looked a bit peaky. Julie, having been fed, now by bottle, and made comfortable, was sleeping peacefully in her carrying cot.

The meal was a happy occasion and there was plenty of beer left, but, surprisingly, Joe opted for soft drinks. Nick set up his camera on a tripod, unobtrusively in a corner, but in an excellent position to capture everyone. *Michael will love the pictures*, thought Fran, especially seeing baby Julie, his niece and his sister, Tina. A moment of sadness flickered across her eyes. Isabel still hadn't replied to her letter. Across the table from her sat Tina and Fran noticed that she wasn't eating very much. She watched her toying with food, pushing it around the plate. *Tina's not well*, she thought. Then Joe said something to Tina, Fran couldn't hear what, but he looked concerned. Later, she would see if Tina wanted any help with the baby. Then, right on cue, Julie let out a loud cry, kicking back her blanket, her tiny fists punching the air.

Wearily, Tina made to rise from her chair, but Joe was on his feet and by his daughter's side. He lifted her from her cot, holding her at a safe distance he said, 'Phew, she pongs.'

Swiftly, Fran went to Joe. 'I'll take her. You finish eating.' She took her granddaughter into her arms and whisked her from the room before anyone could blink twice. She collected the baby bag from the hallway, all the time crooning to Julie, soothing her as she went up the stairs. As she changed the baby and made her comfortable, she thought of Isabel doing the same for Michael and Maggie looking after Tina. Deep down, the hurt was still with her. She stood for a moment, reflecting, and then, looking down at her cooing granddaughter, thought, *This is what matters.* She picked up Julie, went into her bedroom and sat down on the basket chair. With Julie resting in the crook of her arm, Fran nuzzled the soft, downy hair, smelling the fresh warmth of this special baby and, as she did so, experienced the most wondrous feeling of contentment.

After a few precious minutes of pure bonding, she said to her granddaughter, 'Come on my lovely, let's go back to your mammy.'

Downstairs, she placed the sleeping baby in Tina's arms. 'Thanks,' said Tina, holding her daughter close. 'I didn't realise a baby so small could demand so much attention, but she's a beauty.' She leant forward, kissing Fran on the cheek, and said, 'I'm so glad I found you.'

Fran felt a lump rising in her throat and tears of joy sprinkled her lashes. 'You're the best thing that ever happened to me. Now, you and Joe go and relax in the sitting room.' Tina placed the baby back in her cot and Joe carried it.

'Coffee's ready,' called Nick, as he turned from the stove.

Fran took Tina and Joe's into the sitting room and was just about to leave when Joe said, 'Fran, would you mind Julie while I take Tina for a spin on the bike? Fresh air will do her good.'

'Of course I can, Joe. Anything to help.' So Joe went off to fetch his bike and, in a short time, the young couple set off.

Nick and Will were chatting in the kitchen and Fran settled in the sitting room with the sleeping Julie. She picked up the *Lady* magazine which she'd bought earlier but, soon, her eyes grew heavy and she half slumbered, remaining conscious of the baby in her care.

It was the faint whimper of Julie which stirred her. Opening her eyes, Fran was startled to find the room filled with dark, gloomy shadows. Rising from the sofa, she flicked on a table lamp, not wanting the harsh glare of the ceiling bulb to startle her granddaughter. She picked up the tiny, warm bundle from her cot and crooned, 'My darling little angel.'

In the kitchen, she found Nick making a pot of tea and Will listening to Hancock's Half Hour on the wireless. Surprised not to see Tina and Joe, she asked, 'Haven't they come home yet?'

'No,' replied Nick, looking through the window at the darkening sky, a frown on his face.

Fran glanced at the wall clock. 'They've been gone over three hours.'

Sensing her anxiety, Nick soothed, 'I expect they went further than intended.'

Fran busied herself preparing the baby's feed. The cup of tea Nick gave her was untouched.

Another hour passed. Julie was fed, changed and now asleep in her carrycot, close to her doting great-grandfather. 'We'll just go out into the lane, Dad, won't be long.'

Rufus answered the loud knocking on his door and exclaimed, 'Well, what an unexpected pleasure.' Then he saw their anxious faces. 'What's wrong?'

'It's Tina and Joe; they're out on the motorbike and haven't come home yet. We're worried.' Fran's voice trailed off. She felt near to tears.

'What direction did they go in?' asked Rufus.

'The coast,' Nick answered.

'Right, you two go home. I'll take the Land Rover and head in that direction.' He shouted his intentions to Helga, and grabbed his jacket. He said, 'I'll be in touch.'

As they walked back down the lane, Fran said, hopefully, 'They could be home sitting in the kitchen and we've worried unnecessarily.' Nick didn't speak, but tightened his hold on her hand.

Back home, the kitchen was quiet. Julie was sleeping. Will looked up expectedly. Fran shook her head, not trusting herself to speak. She sat down near to Julie and stared at the sleeping child. The fire in the grate spat and crackled, and Fran shivered. She dared not think.

'They could have stopped off to see friends and lost track of the time,' Nick said, optimistically.

Fran jerked her head up, a ray of hope in her eyes. 'Do you think so?'

'It's a possibility.'

'But I don't know who their friends are.' She jumped up, saying, 'I'll ring Joe's sister.'

'Fran, sit down, I think it's best to wait until we hear from Rufus.'

Rufus travelled slowly along the coast road. Traffic was light, eerily so. He strained his eyes. Ahead, he could see lights flashing and whirling: an ambulance, a police car blocking the road, figures moving about. Approaching nearer he saw it. His heart went cold. It was a motorcycle, spread across the hard surface of the road. Quickly, he brought the Land Rover to a halt and jumped out, running to the scene of the accident, his breathing heavy. He'd seen that motorbike earlier, when the couple on it passed him down the lane and waved to him.

A policeman came towards him. 'Sir?'

Rufus, his voice hoarse, blurted. 'The accident – is it a young couple?'

It was Fran who heard the Land Rover arrive as its tyres spurted gravel. She jumped up and went to the door, throwing it open. 'Rufus, I . . .' Then she saw his face, tense, sad. 'What is it?' she asked, her voice barely audible. His answer was to put his arm about her shoulders and draw her back into the house. Nick came to stand by Fran and Will shakily got to his feet.

In the light of the kitchen, Rufus' face was ashen and his eyes glistened with moisture. His voice faltered. 'I think we'd all better sit down.' Silently, the four sat round the kitchen table, sombre faced, so very, very different from the dinner party earlier in the day.

Rufus cleared his throat. 'There's no easy way to say this.' His eyes were fixed on Fran's across the table from him. 'There's been an accident and Joe is dead.'

'No!' cried Fran, a cold shiver ran the length of her body. 'Joe dead, but how?' But before Rufus could answer, Fran cried out again, 'Tina?'

Rufus wiped his sweating brow with the back of his hand. 'She's injured and in hospital.'

'My darling daughter!' Fran cried, jumping up. 'I must go to her.' She sobbed.

'I'll take you,' Nick said, drawing her into his arms, comforting her. Then he looked over the top of her head to Rufus. 'The baby?'

'I'll take her to Helga. She'll cope with the infant.'

On the nightmare journey to the Kingston General Hospital in Hull, neither she nor Nick spoke. The only sound in the car was the swish, swish of the windscreen wipers, grating, making her head ache even more. They pulled into the bleak car park and, shoulders hunched, they ran to the reception office, where they were told that Tina had been admitted to ward ten, the emergency ward that evening. Inside the ward, lights were low and nurses were quietly going about their tasks. Fran and Nick hovered just inside the door, both still in shock, uncertain what to do, when a nurse came to show them to the ward sister's office.

'You are?' said the sister, briskly.

Fran opened her mouth but no sound came out. A lump welled up in her throat. It was Nick who spoke. 'This is Mrs Meredith.' He gently eased Fran forward. 'Her daughter, Christine Miller was admitted following a road accident.'

The sister's face softened. 'She is being attended to and the doctor will come to speak to you later. For now, I will take you both along to the waiting room, where a member of staff will come and take Mrs Miller's details.'

Formalities dealt with, an auxiliary nurse brought them two cups of hot, sweet tea. They sat near a window, oblivious of the ink-stained sky turning into a grey dawn.

Finally, a weary young man wearing a creased white coat approached them. 'Mrs Meredith?'

'Yes.' Fran looked up, searching his eyes, seeing no clue. Simultaneously, she and Nick rose.

'I'm Doctor Patterson. Your daughter, Christine Miller has regained consciousness and her condition is stable. However, she has serve bruising to her forehead and the right side of her face. She has a fracture of the right arm, her ulna, and to the right ankle.'

Fran gasped and Nick said, 'Can we see her?'

The doctor looked at Nick. 'You are Christine's father?'

'No, but I'm a close family friend.'

The doctor replied, 'For now, just Mrs Meredith and only for two minutes.'

Nothing could have prepared Fran for the sight of Tina. Her face was ragged and greyish-white, with an ugly red-mauve-stained gash down the side of her right cheek. There was a drip attached to her good arm. Fran wished Nick was here to support her. She took a deep breath, steadied herself and went to the bedside of her beloved child. 'Tina, my darling daughter,' she whispered.

Tina responded by opening her heavy eyelids. 'Fran.'

Gently, Fran touched Tina's free hand, it was so cold and limp. Tears welled up in her eyes and she forced herself to speak. 'How are you feeling now?'

'My head hurts.' Her eyes flicked to her legs encased beneath a support tunnel. 'Julie, where is she?' she whispered.

'Julie is fine. She's with Rufus and his wife, Helga, and they are looking after her until I go home. So don't fret about your daughter, just you get well, my darling.'

'Joe, can I see Joe?'

A sob caught in Fran's throat. How could she answer? The nurse nearby intervened.

'Mrs Meredith,' said the nurse quietly, 'time to go.'

Outside the ward, the shock unbearable, she collapsed, sobbing into Nick's waiting arms.

'Come on, let me get you home,' he urged.

The next day, both Fran and Nick were present at the hospital when the doctor decided it was now safe to tell Tina of Joe's death.

'I knew,' Tina whispered. And then she wept. Fran held her hand as her daughter began her grieving for the man she loved, the daddy of her baby girl.

Caring for Julie, doing something useful, helped Fran not to dwell on the fragile figure of her daughter lying in the hospital bed. What did surprise her, was the co-operation of Helga, Rufus's wife. After caring for Julie on that fateful night, she sent hot meals down to High Bank with Rufus. Though appreciative of Helga's help, Fran was thankful when Nancy came home. They shared the hospital visiting and the caring of Julie.

Deirdre Baker, Isabel's friend, on hearing of the tragic death of Joe and of Tina's injuries, telephoned to offer her help. 'I can drive you to the hospital.'

'Thank you, that's very kind,' said Fran.

'No problem, dear. Michael must be devastated at the terrible news of Joe's death.'

'Michael?' In all the happenings, Fran hadn't given a thought to Michael. 'Michael doesn't know.' Just then Julie, who had been popped into Will's arms when the phone rang, let out a holler. 'Sorry, I must go.'

She went back into the kitchen and relieved Will of the precious bundle. 'You all right, love?' asked Will, seeing her strained face. 'Not bad news?'

'We haven't told Michael, Dad.' A heavy sigh escaped her trembling lips.

'He should know, our Michael.'

'Yes, he should.' But she made no move to say when.

Deirdre dropped Fran off at the hospital entrance saying, 'I'll wait in the reception area.'

Fran nodded her appreciation and hurried into the hospital. She prayed so hard for Tina to pull round, to recover from her accident and the terrible trauma of Joe's death. Beyond that, she couldn't comprehend her thoughts.

In the ward, there was an air of efficient quietness as the nursing staff attended to their patients. She stood for a moment, looking into the empty side ward and felt a surge of panic attack her. She couldn't see Tina. *Oh my God!* she thought, *Don't let her be . . .* Just as her legs were about to buckle, a nurse came up to her. 'Mrs Miller is in ward one.'

'Thank you,' Fran whispered, relief flooding through her mind and body.

At Tina's bedside, Fran stood, just looking down at her daughter sleeping, so still, so unnatural for a young woman. She drew up the hard, brown metal chair and sat down, reaching for Tina's translucent, motionless hand. It felt weightless in hers. 'Hello, my darling,' she whispered.

Tina's eyes opened and her face crumbled. 'I want to go home,' she whimpered.

'You will, my darling, just as soon as you are well enough. The doctor won't keep you in hospital any longer than necessary. Now, let me tell you all our news.' Fran tried to keep her voice light and positive. 'Helga, Rufus's wife, is, surprisingly, a very nice person. She's offered to look after Julie again. She's a good cook.' So she continued cheerfully chatting away, though careful not to mention the visit of Joe's sister, Maureen. She was arranging his funeral.

On Fran's next visit, Tina asked, 'Why can't I see Joe?' Fran's stomach knotted.

'Oh, my darling daughter, you remember . . .' Her voice trailed.

'I want to see him.' Tina said stubbornly, her eyes filling with tears.

It was then Fran realised Tina wanted to see Joe in the Chapel of Rest to say her goodbyes.

The hospital management were very understanding and made all the necessary arrangements for Tina. Fran offered to go with her, but, no, Tina wanted to be alone with Joe.

Fran visited Tina a few days later and, after telling her all the news from home and how Julie was settled into a routine, they lapsed into silence. The hum of the other visitors talking to patients drifted. Tina was now in the main ward as her condition, physically, was much improved. But her emotional state swung up and down. Suddenly, Tina said, 'Joe loved his bike, the freedom. Now, he's free to roam where he likes. I want him to have a wreath in shape of a motorbike. Can you order it for me, please, Fran?'

Fran reached out and hugged her daughter's good side, saying, 'Of course I will. I think it's a lovely tribute to Joe.' For the first time, Fran saw a glimmer of a smile pass across Tina's face.

Within a couple of days, Tina was well enough to leave hospital. It was obvious to Fran that Tina couldn't manage on her own, let alone with Julie. 'I'd like you to come and stay with me until . . .' She stopped, unsure what to say. Then she added, 'If that's what you want.'

'I want to go back to my own little flat, but not yet . . .' Her voice trailed off.

Later, alone, Tina mulled over in her mind what she had done and not told Fran. She had written to Michael, explaining their relationship. *I am your twin sister and our mother is Fran and you have a lovely niece, Julie.* What she couldn't write about was Joe's death. She needed to keep him close to her, for just a little longer.

Joe's funeral was a quiet, sad affair. The Reverend Fairweather officiated at the service. Maureen and her father laid on drinks and sandwiches at their local pub for Joe's work mates and friends. It was their way of trying to come to terms with the loss of a dear son and brother. Tina, in a wheelchair borrowed from the hospital, went with Fran, Nick, Will, Reverend Fairweather and Nancy back to High Bank.

On the way home, they collected Julie from Helga's. As Tina cuddled her daughter on her knees, she shed more tears. 'She's not forgotten me,' she repeated over and over again.

For quite some weeks, High Bank House was topsy-turvy with the baby teething and keeping everyone awake at night, but they managed. Will just took a longer nap in the afternoons and so did baby, and everyone else went to bed earlier.

Each day, Tina hobbled to pick up the post, willing a letter to come from Michael.

Chapter Thirty-Two

The taxi juddered to a halt and Fran said, 'We're home.' There was no answer. so she turned her head, her heart squeezing with love at the sight of her sleeping daughter and granddaughter. They had been to lay flowers on Maggie's grave and it had been a long journey, staying overnight at the Reverend Fairweather's home. 'Wake up, my darlings.' Tina yawned and Julie sleepily opened her eyes, looked at her grandmother and smiled.

Holding a wriggling Julie in her arms, while Tina paid the driver, Fran glanced up at the house. Just then, Nick opened the front door and came out to help with their baggage. She smelt his freshness, his maleness, prompting the tantalising thought of his naked body and hers intertwined. She caught Nick's eye and thought he might be thinking the same. But he wasn't. His eyes held a glazed look which she couldn't read.

In the quiet kitchen, Will was sitting in his usual chair, smoking his pipe. 'Hello, Dad.'

'Hello, love.' He glanced at her but didn't meet her eye.

Suddenly, the door from the hall burst open and he stood, framed in the doorway.

'Michael!' Instantly, Fran's face lit up with pure pleasure. But his did not.

'Hi, Mike,' said Tina, standing by her mother's side. She stared at her twin. 'What a surprise.'

Still, he didn't say anything or move, but his gaze, fixed on Fran, did not falter.

Fran broke the silence. Her heart racing, she asked, 'Michael, what's wrong?'

Michael came into the kitchen and stood before her, his eyes seeming to bore into her very soul. She shivered and her insides knotted.

Then, in a quavering voice, Michael said, 'Why didn't you tell me that you are my real mother and Tina is my twin sister?'

The colour left Fran's face and she felt shock waves rip through her body as she began to tremble. Tina gasped and Julie whimpered. Flashing through Fran's mind was a series of pictures, painfully agonising memories representing the times over the years when she had tried so desperately to reunite with her baby, her son. How could she reply in a simple sentence? All she longed to do was to take this handsome son of hers into her arms and hold him close. From far off she heard a thin voice, her own, saying, 'Michael, it's complicated.'

'Try me!' His voice was harsh. He came close and she felt the fire from his breath on her face. She reeled back, knocking against Tina, and Julie began to cry.

Nick stepped in between Michael and Fran. 'That's enough! Any explaining can wait until the morning.' He put his arm protectively about Fran's shoulders.

Without a word, Michael turned on his heels and stormed from the kitchen, banging the porch door on his way out.

Nick led Fran to a chair at the kitchen table. Even the relief of crying was denied her as she felt too numb with shock. Nick placed a glass of brandy in her hands. 'Drink this, darling.'

As the liquid slipped down her throat and the glass emptied, only then did her emotions release. She sobbed and sobbed. When, at last, her tears were spent, she said to Nick, 'All those longing years, the yearning, the hope for Michael to know he is my son, but I never dreamt it would be like this.' She sniffed, dabbing her eyes on a sodden handkerchief.

After a while, she looked round the kitchen and panicked. 'Where're Tina and the baby?'

'Tina's putting Julie to bed. I'll run you a bath and an early night will help you.'

'But, what about Michael?'

It was Will who answered her. 'I'll wait up for him.'

She'd forgotten about her father, sitting so quiet and still. 'Oh, Dad!' She felt the hot ache behind her eyes and the knotted turmoil gripped her again.

'Best talk to your son in the morning, lass.'

Michael avoided Fran. His time was spent with Tina and Julie. Fran was pleased he was bonding with his sister and niece. Outwardly, she approached the situation of Michael ignoring her philosophically, but inside she was bleeding. She felt as if her life's energy was draining away. If only she'd stood up to Agnes, been more assertive and demanded her son be returned to her. But Agnes was cunning and, knowing Fran's vulnerability, she attacked her conscience. She argued that the boy wasn't a parcel to be passed around, it would disrupt his schooling, wait until he's older. So she did. Of course, she realised later, too late, that children are adaptable. How now to explain this to a seventeen-year-old, a young man? It now seemed such a weak excuse.

Also, she had Tina and Julie to consider. Their happiness was important to her. Fran knew Tina had held up her plan to move back into her flat, to rebuild her life with Julie. Instead, Tina spent time with Mike, getting to know him as a brother. He loved his niece and she loved him. You could tell by the way Julie's baby laugh sang and the way Michael held her high in the air then swung her down like a swooping bird.

Coming in from the garden, Fran watched this play. Her whole body contracted with the pain of love. She felt a stranger, an outsider. Just then, Tina came into the kitchen from upstairs and was dressed for going out. 'We're meeting Shirley in town.' She smiled uneasily at Fran. 'We'll be back for tea.'

'Not dinner?' Fran couldn't keep the note of despair from her voice.

'No.' Tina turned away, unable to bear seeing the hurt in her mother's eyes. She took Julie from Mike's arms, saying, 'Come on, my little beauty, let's strap you in your pram.'

Fran moved forward. She murmured, 'Michael,' and she held out her hands to him, but he totally ignored her.

Tina came and kissed her cheek, and whispered, 'Give him time.'

'Bye, Grandad,' they both called.

'Do yer think Isabel might ring?' asked Will. Fran, lost in her misery, turned.

'Isabel?' Fran repeated, as if she'd never heard her sister's name before.

'Aye, you'd think she'd want to know our Michael's arrived safely.'

It suddenly dawned on Fran that Isabel might not know Michael was here and, if she did, why hadn't she been in touch?

'I'll ring Isabel now.' She glanced at the clock. It would be seven in the evening in Melbourne. It was John who answered and said Isabel was too upset to come to the telephone.

'Michael rang me when he'd arrived at the airport. I was going to give him a few days to settle before I contacted him. How are things?' John enquired.

'Not good.' Her voice faltered. 'Michael blames me as well as Isabel.'

'It was a shock to him. Give him time to adjust. He's a sensible young man. Though what the outcome will be, I cannot guess. It's his decision.' There was a sad note in John's voice.

Fran picked up on his thoughts. 'You want Michael to return to you?'

'Yes, I've arranged for him to study the wine trade, to get a career behind him. When that's complete, then he can make up his own mind about his future.'

Fran replaced the receiver. She was full of thought. Time, John had said, give Michael time. Maybe there was hope that Michael would accept her. Her spirits lifted a notch.

They didn't come home for tea. Tina rang from a call box, explaining, apologetically, that they'd met Nancy and they'd accepted her invitation for tea. 'I'm sorry, Fran, but I couldn't refuse without a scene. Mike was adamant and I didn't want to upset Nancy.'

'I understand, but I do need to talk to Michael. Try and persuade him to talk to me, please.'

'He's stubborn, but I'm trying.'

They came home late and Michael went up to his room. Fran slept fitfully that night.

She woke early the next morning and lay listening to the dawn chorus, thinking how wonderful it was. Then she remembered.

Michael. How could she begin to tell him the truth? With Tina, it had been easy. She had been looking for her birth mother and they hadn't expected too much of each other. Their love and bonding, after the initial hiccup, came naturally. But with Michael, it was different. He hadn't been looking for her. And yet, she had envisaged their reunion to be 'ever-after' happiness, not this painful ache in her heart. She could see it was too much for him.

Early morning the next day, she said to Nick, 'I'm going for a walk by the river.' Crossing the yard, she slipped through the gate slotted into the willow fencing Nick had erected. The air was tangy, fresh on her flushed skin, but guilt assailed her. The guilt she had accumulated over the years, for lacking the strength to tell Michael the truth. He must want to ask her questions and she would answer them with honesty. She was waiting for him to come to her and, if he didn't, she knew she would have to force the issue. But then she didn't want it to go wrong.

Seeking her haven of refuge of childhood days, she scrambled down the river bank and flung herself down on to the rough grass. She shaded her eyes and, from her position, she could see the curve of the river going upstream through the open plain of farm land. Moorhens darted in and out of the reeds on the opposite side of the river. Dragonflies, taking advantage of the warmth of the late summer's day, skimmed the waters. With the quietness and peace of the countryside around her, Fran closed her eyes, willing its peace to invade her body and mind, to help her make the right decision.

She lay for a while, feeling safe, wishing she could stay here for ever, both mentally and physically. But it wasn't possible, never an option. She could no longer hide from her responsibilities. Agnes was dead and Isabel was in Australia. Now, it was just her and Michael, and he had a right to know the whole truth. She'd give herself a few more minutes, and then she'd go back to the house and face Michael. So, wrapped up in her thoughts, she did not hear the rustle of grasses, the crunching of stalks or the sighing of breath.

'Fran.'

Startled, she looked up, seeing a figure towering over her. She shaded her eyes against the morning sun. 'Michael!' she exclaimed with surprise, her heart pounding.

He dropped down onto the bank beside her. Neither spoke, both staring ahead. Fran knew it was up to her to break the silence.

'How did you find out?' The question was clumsy and so was her voice, but it was the first thing that came into her head.

'Shirley wrote to me and then Tina.'

Fran felt her eyes smart. She had no idea that Tina had also written. She must have been so desperately unhappy. She swallowed hard, finding the words. 'I'm sorry you had to find out that way. I always hoped Isabel would tell you the truth.'

'Mother went hysterical.' His voice shook with emotion.

He still thought of Isabel as his mother. That hurt Fran. Then, what could she expected? Pulling up a blade of grass, she ran her fingers along its sharpness, drawing blood. Then words came out of her mouth which she didn't expect to hear. 'You've been happy with Isabel?'

She felt rather than saw his nod. 'She's been a good mother to you?'

She turned to look into face and saw the confusion in his eyes. 'I suppose.'

Tears pricked her eyes, but she mustn't cry. She couldn't bring herself to tell him about his conception, not yet – later.

Instead, she asked him, 'Michael, what do you want to know?'

He stretched out his long limbs and she knew he was trying to form some kind of question. 'Why didn't you look after me and Tina if you were our mother?'

She watched the reeds and rushes on the far bank sway rhythmically, but her voice was flat, her chest throbbing with pain as she began. 'I was sixteen when I gave birth to you and Tina, and afterwards I was very ill. Agnes, your grandmother, took charge and Isabel helped to look after you.' Her voice faltered and was barely audible. 'I never meant it to be a permanent arrangement. Obstacles were placed in my way. But that is no excuse. I should have asserted my rights as your mother. I should have made a home for you.' Her fingers sought the rough grass and she pulled again, inflicting pain.

'Is that why you gave me a hundred pounds – guilt money?' he shouted, callously.

She recoiled at his words, because they were true. 'I'm sorry,' was all she could say.

'Sorry,' he repeated, harshly, springing to his feet, once again towering over her. 'You think saying "sorry" will make everything right? You're sad!' He paced back and forth. 'Do you realise, when I went to Australia I was happy, with a future to look forward to. And now?' He flung up his arms in despair, his voice cracking. 'Now my best mate, Joe, is dead and I hear Tina is my twin sister and you are my real mother. What if Shirley and Tina hadn't written to me? Would you have left me in ignorance for ever? I'm seventeen. I'm not a child. You should have told me.' His face contorted as he desperately fought to hold back his tears.

Her heart overflowing with love for her son, she was instantly on her feet holding out her arms to him, wanting to comfort him.

But he held his arms up in horror. 'Don't touch me.'

She froze. He twisted away from her and lumbered up the bank, running along the path, away from her. She watched till he was out of sight. Then she slumped down and stared vacantly at the dark, swirling water. She feared her son was lost to her for ever.

She allowed herself only moments of self-pity and sat up sharp, saying out loud, 'Frances Meredith, you have no right to give up on your son. You show him how much you love him and care for him.' She stood up, brushed the grass off her skirt, and walked purposefully back towards the house.

Chapter Thirty-Three

A few days later, Fran arrived home from Mr Barleyfield's bookshop in Beverley, where she was helping him out temporarily, mostly when he went to book fairs and with cataloguing his new stock. She was surprised to find Tina in the kitchen perusing a cookery book. Julie was on the rug at Tina's feet, playing happily, cooing, with her arms and legs waving in all directions.

Tina looked up at Fran, saying, 'Thought I'd cook tonight, if it's alright with you?'

Fran shrugged, replying, absently, 'Yes.' Then, as if a switched had been flicked on, she felt a spark within her ignited. 'You're not going out?'

'No, thought we'd have a family night in. There's something I want to run past you.' Tina paused slightly. 'And something I need to tell you.' She lowered her eyes, studying a recipe.

Fran experienced a sinking feeling. Her blood ran icy cold and the light within her extinguished. What could it be? Surely not? Hastily, she glanced about, seeking any diversion.

Julie, tired of playing on her own, whimpered, so Fran dropped to her knees to play with her. To feel the infant's warmth and hear her laughter and gurgling lightened Fran's heart and she caught Julie's infectious laugh. It was into this scene that the three men came in from their walk.

Will, his legs aching with the unaccustomed exercise, made straight for the comfort of his arm chair. 'Hello, darling,' said Nick.

Fran looked up, acknowledging Nick, and glanced towards Michael, but he didn't meet her gaze. He went over to Tina, looking over her shoulder. 'What are you doing, Sis?'

'I'm deciding what to cook and thought we might have a try tonight.'

'I'm not much of a cook – billy tea and damper, that's my lot.'

'That doesn't sound appetising.'

Michael grinned. 'Not to be recommended.'

Fran listened to the banter between brother and sister, and she felt sad. Here she was, in the same room as both her children and yet she couldn't communicate properly with them. Since Michael's arrival, she felt that her relationship with Tina had deteriorated. It seemed forced, not natural and everything seemed unreal. Was Tina preparing to tell her that she would be going back with Michael to Australia? Fran's heart lurched at the thought. She couldn't bear to lose her daughter and granddaughter as well as her son. She was just about to blurt out her jumbled thoughts, and to hell with the consequences, when she caught Nick's eye. His look said it all. He had read her mind. She bit on her tongue.

Later in the afternoon, while brother and sister argued over what to cook for the evening meal, Fran took Julie out for a walk. She was thankful for the support of the pram.

At last, the evening came. A cold wind had whipped up,

coming east across the river, making it unsuitable for eating outside, as the siblings first planned. Fran, after a relaxing bath, came downstairs into the kitchen and glanced with admiration at the table. It was in a festive mood with yellow serviettes and place mats, and the centre piece was a vase of golden and bronze dahlias. Nick and Will were already seated at the table, and she sat next to Nick.

She watched a flush-faced Tina place a dish of sweet and sour chicken accompanied by stir-fry vegetables on the table, and Mike placed a bowl of steaming rice. 'It looks and smells delicious,' commented Fran.

Will eyed it suspiciously. 'Will I like it?'

'Sure thing, Grandad,' Michael enthused, as he poured out the beer.

They all tucked in and Will's face turned from uncertainty to mild appreciation. The conversation seemed to flow as freely as the beer. Only Fran found it difficult. She ate very little and perhaps drank too much. Every now and then she stole glances at Tina and Michael, looking for a clue as to what was going to be said.

Eventually, the meal was over and Tina produced a bottle. 'It's only bubbly.' She gave a mischievous giggle. 'But, I thought, why not?' Glasses were filled and Fran sat on the edge of her seat, her insides in turmoil. Tina cleared her throat. 'Two things I want to talk about, well, three actually. First, I want to thank everyone for their support after Joe's death, especially Fran.' Their eyes met and a lump rose in Fran's throat as she fought back the threatening tears. 'To Fran.' They all raised their glasses and drank a toast.

Tina was in her element, so full of confidence, helped by the bubbly. 'Secondly, Julie's christening. That was Joe's wish.'

Her eyes misted, but she continued, 'I'd like her to be baptised at Saint Peter's in Stillingham.' She glanced at Fran, her gaze lingering. 'I'll need your help.' Fran nodded, not trusting herself to speak. 'Thanks. I'd liked my friend Reverend Fairweather to conduct the service. For godparents, Mike's going to be one, I'm going to ask Joe's sister, Maureen, and I'd like you to be one too, Fran.'

Astonished, Fran replied, 'Me?'

'Yes, you.'

'I'd be delighted.' And she was, richly so.

'Reverend Fairweather is ever so kind. He's going to host the christening tea in the vicarage. He said his housekeeper would arrange everything. He's a wonderful friend to me,' Tina exclaimed, her voice full of pride. 'Now, for my third thing. I've got Mike to thank for this.'

Fran felt her body burn up. She looked at Tina, but the heat blurred her vision and she couldn't see her daughter's face. *Oh my God, don't let me faint.* She held on tightly to the seat of the chair. This was what she was dreading. Tina was going to Australia. *I'm to lose my daughter as well as my son.* The room rolled and buzzed. From a great distance came Tina's voice.

'Next year, I'm going to enrol at college on an interior design course.'

Fran slumped from her chair and was caught by Nick just in time to prevent her from hitting her head on the corner of the table.

She recovered after a sipping a glass of cold water. 'The heat,' she murmured, making a mental note to see the doctor. She must keep strong for her daughter. 'I'm sorry, Tina, for interrupting your wonderful news.'

For a while, they sat round the table, discussing the christening plans and then they retired to bed, and Fran slept well in the knowledge that her daughter was staying close by.

One morning, a couple of days later, when only Fran and Michael were in the kitchen, Michael suddenly asked, 'What should I buy Julie for a christening gift?'

Fran was taken aback because their previous conversation had been limited to monosyllables: yes, no, please, thank you and such like. She quickly recovered her equilibrium and answered, 'How about a keepsake to commemorate the occasion? There are jewellers in town that will have a good selection of gifts.' She smiled at her son, her heart lifting.

He didn't return her smile. He just said, 'Thanks. I'll give it a try.' Then he was gone.

Fran would have suggested that she went with him, but . . . So she busied herself with the mundane task of ironing, though it did nothing to alleviate her frustration or the deep ache within her. She wanted to talk to him about whether he'd decided to return to Australia to continue with his studies in the wine industry. She knew he'd spoken with John on the telephone and told Tina what was discussed. Fran felt very sad. From Michael's point of view, she could see how he had felt let down by her, his natural mother. She could have prevented it, but she didn't, and now she was paying the penalty. How on earth did she think that she could just walk into his life and be accepted by him? It was a devastating situation for her but, for Michael, it must be much harder. How to make things right? Over and over in her mind, the problem twisted and turned, but she couldn't come up with a suitable answer. What she did know was that she loved Michael and his happiness was paramount to her, and, if that meant him going back to Australia, so be it. Her heart ached at the thought that she might not see him again.

Whatever happened, she must be grateful and comforted for having Tina and Julie close by.

Chapter Thirty-Four

On a golden-bronze autumn day in October, they gathered round the font in Saint Peter's church, the bright sunlight of the afternoon illuminating the happy faces of the baptism party: Joe's sister, Maureen, and father, and Nancy and Cyril, Will next to Michael, and Tina by his side. Fran held close the sleeping Julie, drawing warmth from the child's body and comfort from Nick's arm around her waist. The Reverend Fairweather beamed upon them all.

Suddenly, Fran turned, instinctively feeling Michael looking at her. She reached out to him and placed his sister's child into his outstretched arms. Joy filled his face and, for the first time since he had returned, he looked Fran fully in the face and smiled. His eyes, warm and tender, held hers for a few seconds, enough to give her hope. Fran knew then, but wasn't sure when, the past could be resolved and they would have a future as mother and son.

Nick tightened his arm around her waist and she glanced up at him, her heart filled with love. Soon his arm wouldn't go so far around her waist as it expanded. She placed her hand on the gentle swell of her stomach and marvelled at the tiny life growing within her.

That evening in bed, she whispered to Nick, 'I've a secret to tell you.'

Nick, who was almost asleep, opened one eye and looked at her, murmuring, 'I don't want to know what you've bought me for my birthday.'

'It's something more precious than that.' Now she held his full attention.

Taking hold of one of his hands she placed it on the gentle curve of her naked belly. 'What can you feel?' she whispered, her eyes shining with love.

His eyes widened and he stuttered, 'Something fluttering.' He lifted up his hand, looked at it then replaced. 'There again,' he cried with excitement.

'It's our precious baby.' Her voice broke with the emotion of pure happiness.

Nick gathered her into her arms, his voice husky with love and wonderment. 'My darling, it will be all right.'

'I know,' she cried. 'I'm so happy. I never thought I would become pregnant again. I've seen the doctor and he said I'm fine and healthy. You are pleased?' She lifted up her joy filled face.

'Completely.' He kissed her passionately and they clung to each other.

She thought he was asleep until he spoke. 'You do know I'm an old-fashioned man?' He startled her by leaping from the bed and kneeling by its side. Before she had a chance to speak, he said, 'Fran, will you marry me?'

Overwhelmed, she was stunned for a few seconds, then, with a voice quivering with fervour, she replied, 'Oh, Nick, my darling, yes I will.' She slid from the bed and into his outstretched arms.

Back in bed they talked, sleep impossible. 'When shall we marry?' she asked.

'As soon as possible. Before the old year is out.'

'As quickly as that?'

'Yes, my darling, I don't want to lose you.' She cuddled closer to him.

The next morning, while Fran was feeling overjoyed at being pregnant and the forthcoming wedding, she wondered how Tina and Michael would take the news. What would Michael say?

'Are yer going to stand there all day with that pot? I'm waiting for me cuppa,' Will grunted.

Fran mentally shook herself and began pouring the tea. Since Michael was here, Will had taken to sitting at the table for his breakfast. Nick put a plateful of toast on the table. Michael yawned and stretched. Tina was busy feeding Julie. Suddenly, Fran couldn't hold back any longer. Her whole body was tight and rigid with tension. The clanging of her cup as it hit the edge of the saucer caused them all to look at her. She caught Nick's eye and he nodded.

She cleared her throat. 'We, Nick and I, have something to tell you all. Well, two things.'

No one spoke, they just stared. She floundered. Nick was by her side, taking hold of her hand.

His voice was quiet and strong. 'Fran and I are expecting a baby.'

No one spoke. Tina broke the silence. 'Blimey, I'm gonna have a brother or sister.' She jumped up and flung her arms about Fran and Nick, kissing them both.

Will exclaimed, 'Another grandbairn. Just wait until I tell, Larry. I've beaten him now.'

Michael said nothing.

'You said two things,' said a happy Tina.

Nick smiled at her. 'Yes, Fran and I are to be married.'

Tina screwed up her face in concentration, then blurted, 'Will you be my dad?'

Nick laughed. 'Stepdad.'

Fran looked at Michael. He didn't speak. She took a deep breath, quelling her racing heartbeat, and then she spoke to him. 'Michael, we wanted to tell you all together, as a family. There are to be no more misunderstandings, no secrets. What do you think about our news?'

As she spoke, his colour drained away. Her instinct told her to take him into her arms, to comfort him. But, her hands seemed incapable of moving and remained by her side.

His voice was a whisper and she had to strain to hear him. 'I can't get my head round it. Sorry.' He lumbered up from the table, the screech of his chair grating the stifled air of the room. Then he fled. But not before Fran witnessed the tears in his eyes.

She made to go after him, but Nick caught hold of her arm. 'Not now, love.'

It was later that afternoon and Michael had been missing all day. Tina, taking Julie with her, had set off to find her brother. Nick was busy working with Rufus and Will had taken a taxi to see his friend Larry to tell him about his expected grandchild. Fran, in an attempt to clear the turmoil raging within her, went for a walk. She breathed in the smell of the sharp, autumnal air, felt the play of the wind round her cheeks. For the umpteenth time, she wondered where Michael was and what was he doing or thinking.

She slipped through the gate onto the riverbank and stood

looking towards Beverley. The glorious flaming colours of red, orange and yellow of the sun setting over the Minster towers dazzled her for a few seconds. A magnificent sight. But even that couldn't blot out thoughts of Michael or of the mistakes she had made with his life and her life. If only . . .

'Fran.'

At the sound of his voice her head swam, her heartbeat pounded and her whole body trembled. Slowly, she half turned to look at this tall, handsome young man to whom she had given birth. But would he ever be her true son? 'Michael,' she acknowledged, her emotion rising higher.

He came to her side. 'Can you forgive me for being such a pain?' His wide blue eyes looked earnestly into hers.

She caught her breath and instinctively reached out and touched his arm, and, for the first time, he didn't recoil from her. Finding strength, she said, 'Of course I can. I'm truly sorry for all the hurt I've caused you. It must have been a terrible shock for you to find out that I am your birth mother. You've had so much to take in such a short time.'

'Sure, but I'm not a kid. Tina's coping and she's had a tougher life than me.'

Thinking of when she'd held him as a baby in her arms, Fran said, 'I have a most precious photograph of you, taken when you were only a few days old and one of Tina too. I'll show them to you back at the house.'

He gazed at her. 'So, you are really my mother?'

'Yes.' Her voice was clear and firm, though her body trembled.

'When I've done studying, I'm coming back to see you. There's something else,' he blurted.

Alarm must have registered on her face because he laughed. 'It's nothing bad, it's just that Grandad wants to come back with me for a visit, but he doesn't want to upset you.'

'Dad wants to go with you. That's wonderful news.'

'You don't mind?'

'Of course not. It will do Dad the world of good.' She couldn't bring herself to mention him seeing Isabel, not wanting to speak her name and break the spell.

'Michael,' she held out her arms and he came to her, and she hugged him lovingly, breathing in his wonderful scent. Tears of joy ran down her face as she, his birth mother, held her son close.

'Cooee,' a voice called.

Michael said, as they drew apart, 'That'll be Nancy. She's come to baby-sit. Tina and I, we've booked a table at the new Chinese restaurant for a celebration meal. It's for you and Nick.' He finished, almost breathless. He cast an anxious look at Fran who hadn't spoken a word. 'Is it okay?'

She found her voice, though it was little more than a whisper. 'You've done this for me and Nick?' She clasped her hands together as if in prayer. 'Oh, Michael!' Her heart overflowed with love. 'Thank you.' She wanted to say more, but words jumbled up inside of her and she didn't want them to come out all wrong. The wind suddenly whipped along the bank and she shivered.

'It's cold, come on,' Michael said. And mother and son linked arms.

Inside the kitchen, the glow of the fire greeted Fran and Michael, but the warmth and love radiating from the people within was increased a thousand times with pure happiness.

Will was bouncing a gleeful Julie on his knee. Tina, her face shining with pleasure, flung her arms around Fran and Michael, hugging them. 'It's wonderful! We are a real family now.'

'Sure thing, Sis,' Michael agreed.

That evening the celebration was swinging as corks popped and the waiters poured champagne into tall fluted glasses. Nick caught Fran's eye and winked at her. Her hand slid into his and she felt his quiet strength, his love. She looked across at Tina and Michael, seated on either side of Will, and smiled at them and they all returned her smile. She remembered part of a quote from her school days: *and my cup runneth over.*

Everyone held a glass. Nick cleared his throat. 'First, I want to give my own toast to Fran. I fell in love with her the first time I met her on the train to Beverley. When she kicked me.'

'Nick!' she gasped. 'You never said anything.'

Fran and Nick were married by special licence at the registry office. Nancy and Helga catered for the buffet held at High Bank House and Tina made Fran's bouquet of creamy apricot roses to match her dress of apricot silk. Everyone else had buttonholes of deeper apricot. The wedding was a lovely, family occasion, something Fran had never dreamt of – to marry the man she loved and having her son and her daughter by her side to make her happiness complete.

A week later, Will and Michael were packed and ready for the trip to Australia. Fran stood in the kitchen with the men in her life. She felt sad at Michael's leaving and, hugging him close, she whispered, 'Take care. I love you.' Tears trickled down her cheeks.

Michael gently brushed them away. 'I'll be back. And I'll write to you just as soon as I can.'

She hugged her father. 'Enjoy yourself, Dad. Love you.' Then they were gone.

Tina was happy and settled back in her flat. Small it might be, but it was her and Julie's home. She still missed Joe. He would always be her first love and Julie's daddy. She was beginning to enjoy life again. She was going to the pictures with Wendy, a girl she met at the college enrolment day. Wendy had asked Tina to go with her to the Young Farmers' New Year's Eve dance as a guest of her two older brothers and she was thrilled to be going. Nancy was happy to have Julie to stay for the night.

'The last day of 1959,' Nick said, as the old year was fading fast. Fran and Nick were having a celebration meal with Rufus and Helga at their home, Helga having revised her opinion that Nick posed a threat to their safety.

'I'll drink to that,' said Rufus, and they all raised their glasses.

By eleven-thirty, Helga was yawning and looking very tired.

Fran nudged Nick and said, 'Helga, Rufus, would you mind if we went now? We've had a lovely evening, but we thought we'd see the new year in at home.'

They said their thanks and good wishes and, as Fran and Nick walked down the lane hand-in-hand, they stopped to gaze up at the clear night sky of burnished blue. 'It's so beautiful and clear after the rain,' Fran sighed, her eyes brilliant with happiness, mirroring the millions of tiny stars twinkling above.

Nick's answer was to take her in his arms and kiss her passionately. 'I'm a lucky fellow,' he whispered.

'And I'm the luckiest girl.' Fran replied, her heart singing with joy. On reaching High Bank House, they went through the yard and onto the riverbank. From here, they could see the lights of the town and, as clocks struck the hour of midnight, church bells pealed and river craft sounded their hooters, welcoming in the new year of 1960.

'Happy New Year.' Nick stood behind Fran. His arms were wrapped around her body, his hands on the swell of her belly, when the baby within her kicked. And it kicked again.

'A footballer or boxer,' said Nick.

'A dancer,' said Fran.

Boy or girl, it didn't matter. She already had a son and daughter, Nick's stepchildren.

'Our very own baby,' Nick whispered, turning her round to him, his lips seeking hers. The stars twinkled down on the lovers locked in a passionate embrace.

After a while, they wandered round the side of the house, through the sleeping garden, arms entwined around each other. The scent of the late hardy rose, sheltered by the lea of the house, filled the magical night air. Fran breathed in its soft fragrance and sighed with contentment. 'So happy,' she murmured.

Hand in hand, Fran and Nick entered by the front door of High Bank House. As it swung open, they stood for a moment, then, stepping over the threshold, they let the old house embrace them. It welcomed their love, their creative energy, the new life to be born and their future.

Acknowledgements

I wish to thank my dear friend, Dorothy Hailstone, for her invaluable support and encouragement during the writing of this book.

SYLVIA BROADY was born in Hull and has lived in the area all her life, although she loves to travel the world. It wasn't until she started to frequent her local library, after World War II, that her relationship with literature truly began and her memories of the war influence her writing, as does her home town. She has had a varied career in childcare, the NHS and the East Yorkshire Council Library Services, but is now a full-time writer.

sylviabroady.blogspot.com
@SylviaBroady

To discover more great books and to
place an order visit our website at
allisonandbusby.com

Don't forget to sign up to our free newsletter at
allisonandbusby.com/newsletter
for latest releases, events and exclusive offers

Allison & Busby Books
@AllisonandBusby

You can also call us on
020 3950 7834
for orders, queries
and reading recommendations